"I want t̲ ... think you ... ̲ ̲ ̲ ̲ said.

"It's against club rules for me to make a date with you, but that's all that has kept me from trying to ask you out."

For heaven's sake, there are other ways, Jackie thought, but to him she said, "I appreciate your discretion, sir."

"I don't know how to take that," he said, surprising her with his directness, "and please stop calling me sir. Are you saying you're not interested?"

Jackie stared into his eyes, darker now than usual and with a fire blazing in them that she had no trouble identifying as passionate attraction.

"Is that the only conclusion you can come up with?" she asked, determined to keep him guessing.

"I wasn't trying to be subtle or discreet. I merely stated a fact. And I'd be a lot closer to you this minute if club rules didn't forbid that, as well...."

GWYNNE FORSTER

is a national bestselling author of twenty-three romance novels and novellas. She has also written four novels and a novella of general fiction. She has worked as a journalist, a university professor and as a senior officer for the United Nations. She holds a master's degree in sociology, and a master's degree in economics/demography.

Gwynne sings in her church choir, loves to entertain at dinner parties, is a gourmet cook and an avid gardener. She enjoys jazz, opera, classical music and the blues. She also likes to visit museums and art galleries. She lives in New York with her husband.

her
secret
life

GWYNNE
FORSTER

KIMANI

KIMANI PRESS™

ISBN-13: 978-1-58314-771-9
ISBN-10:   1-58314-771-3

HER SECRET LIFE

Copyright © 2006 by Gwendolyn Johnson-Acsadi

www.kimanipress.com

Printed in U.S.A.

Dear Reader,

Thank you for reading *Her Secret Life*.

Once I began to bring Jacqueline Parks—the heroine of this title—to life, she became one of my favorite female characters. I empathized with her, having at various times led a double life; I've been a teacher/student/babysitter, student/disc jockey and grad student/waitress/vocalist. Remembering the different faces I've worn and the demeanors that I've adopted, I thought it might be fun to create a character whose double identity was at once necessary and a threat to her well-being.

I had to find a man who matched her in intelligence, accomplishments and concern for others, and I think Warren Holcomb fits the bill. I like most his humanitarianism, which is expressed primarily in his Harlem Clubs. In this story, Warren's clubs get youngsters off the street and expose them to a life beyond boxing and basketball.

If you'd like to learn about other titles by me, please visit my Web site at www.gwynneforster.com.

Sincerely yours,

Gwynne Forster

Chapter 1

Jacqueline Ann Parkton closed her laptop computer, put it into her desk drawer and locked it. She had one hour and twenty minutes in which to go home, change and get to her evening job on time. For the past three years, Jacqueline had worked two jobs in order to maintain her standard of living while providing the best possible care first for her mother, when her father's resources had become depleted, and then for her father.

She stepped out of the building on Fifth Avenue and West 30th Street in Manhattan, which housed *African American Woman* magazine, took a taxi to her apartment on West End Avenue, and began the metamorphosis that she underwent every evening that she worked. Jacqueline Ann Parkton led a double life, and she was plagued by a constant fear that someone in one of her two worlds would appear in her other world and recognize her.

In less than two hours, she transformed herself from the conservative and sedate senior editor and crime reporter for *AAW* (*African American Woman* magazine) to a sexy bombshell who served drinks at the most prestigious private men's club in New York City.

On that cold November day, Jacqueline Ann Parkton, known as Jackie Parks at Allegory, Inc., the men's club in which she worked, adjusted her micro-mini pleated pink skirt, tied the strings of her tiny pink paisley apron and gazed down at the three-inch, pencil-slim heels of the sandals on her feet. "These things are a blueprint for curvature of the spine," she said aloud and began brushing out the wig that nearly reached her hips. She put the brush on her dressing table and looked around at the sand-colored walls, the royal-blue and beige Kiernan carpet, the antique gold-framed mirror and her chair with the same antique gold finish. At least she had a comfortable and attractive dressing room.

When the bartender rang her bell, Jackie glanced at the mirror for a last inspection and went to work. With her right hand, she balanced a large silver tray filled with vodka martinis and gin comets against her shoulder and headed for the private lounge where Warren Holcomb entertained half a dozen business moguls.

As she approached the lounge, the unmistakable feel of a hand on her buttocks nearly caused her to spill the drinks. Normally, she showed the powerful men her perfect white teeth or winked when they became familiar and pretended not to mind, but that one had stepped over the line. He'd touched her. She had no tolerance for that order of brazenness and, by reflex, her left hand raised immediately as if in defense. However, her presence of mind returned just as fast, and she lowered it. *Don't forget girl. You need this job.*

"Keep your hands to yourself, mister. No man paws me."

"Do you know who I am?" It came out as a growl.

"Who you are makes a difference to me only when you stay in your place and keep your hands to yourself."

She walked on, but she made a mental note to watch him. As far as she was concerned, he stood out in that group of men with a street quality that belied his status and position.

Ignoring the man's face-saving remarks, she entered the private lounge and walked over to Warren Holcomb, a man with a commanding presence, but whose demeanor otherwise bespoke kindness, or was it sensuality? Maybe it was both.

"Good evening, sir. Would you like me to serve now?" She thought his smile should be patented, and that his large, almost obsidian eyes should be hidden. Every time she looked at him, carnal thoughts filled her head.

"Please. And thank you for bringing my order right away."

"My pleasure, sir," she replied and meant it. She pretended not to see Warren Holcomb discretely cataloging her feminine assets, but tiny, pinprick-like jolts of heat shot through her when his gaze landed on her breasts and settled there. She'd have given anything if she could rub them. Thank God, he didn't pick that moment to shift his gaze to her face. She couldn't even take a long, deep breath without giving herself away. A few minutes in the man's presence would discombobulate her if she were less resolved.

"Anything else, sir?"

He didn't seem to have heard her; a newcomer who sat nearby had his attention. That man, whom another guest had referred to as Mac, seemed out of place in Allegory, Inc., especially among Warren Holcomb's guests. Jackie looked for a reason to linger. She wanted to observe the man closely.

"Did you say that was all, sir?" she asked, stalling for time.

"Well, perhaps you could bring us some hot hors d'oeuvres."

She went to a phone about five feet from where he sat and phoned in the order, watching Mac as she did so. He was a misfit, and as a reporter, such characters always arrested her attention. Whenever she was in the club, her antenna didn't stop working, for she had much to lose by working as a cocktail waitress in that high-profile, rich-man's club, and she was always on the lookout for anything unsavory.

Where is my head? she asked herself when she was serving the hors d'oeuvres, suddenly aware that she moved at a much slower pace than usual. She justified it by telling herself that to move slowly and graciously rather than to gallop like a horse was more feminine.

Besides, it wouldn't hurt to know what Mac was saying to one of the other guests. Never good at fooling herself, Jackie was smart enough to know that Warren was her main reason both for lingering there and for wanting to seem more ladylike than she appeared in the skimpy and revealing uniform.

Whenever she looked at him, or when he looked at her, she got a warm feminine feeling all over, and she couldn't remember when last a man could lay claim to causing that.

"Anything else, sir?" she asked him, her right hand on the doorknob as she prepared to leave the private lounge.

"No. These are delicious. Thank you."

"You are welcome, sir."

She felt a small amount of pride as she noticed his failed attempt to appear businesslike. His furtive glances set her blood to racing, and what a pity that was. She had told herself time and again that she didn't want an involvement with any man who frequented the club, and she believed she meant it, but Warren Holcomb was the epitome of temptation. Whenever she met him in the club corridors or saw him standing talking with someone, she thought of him as a young bull. Trim and powerful, the man's six-foot four-inch physique made most of the club members suffer by comparison. It wasn't his race but his bearing that distinguished him, and if he realized what a standout he was, he didn't show it.

The following morning, she telephoned a former classmate, a law enforcement officer in Washington,

D.C. "Hi, Clayton. This is Jacqueline. What can you get me on a guy named Mac with this description?" She described Mac.

"Right on, girl. Have it for you in a couple of hours. Why don't you give up magazine editing and stick with crime reporting? You're good at it, and I'll bet it pays more."

Let him think whatever he liked. "Because I like to eat, and *AAW* pays me a regular salary."

"Marry me. You'll be as poor as Job's turkey, but when you're in bed every night, you'll be as happy as a little pig in hog heaven. How about it?"

Laughter flowed out of her as it always did minutes after she began speaking with him. "You're a certified nut, but at least you're a first-class one."

"Thanks for nothing. Call me at one this afternoon."

"Will do. Thanks, friend."

By one-fifteen, she knew that Mac had been indicted twice for acting as a pimp for a Washington, D.C. madam, but had no convictions. She wondered whether Warren Holcomb knew Mac's record. If he did, why would he associate with such a person?

At five-thirty each evening that she worked, Jackie Parks removed her eyeglasses, inserted prescription contact lenses that changed her irises from dark brown to dark hazel, donned a black wig that had hair that hung almost to her hips, put on a heavy coat of makeup, dressed and headed. for the club. On this particular evening, to shorten the distance to her dressing room, she entered the club through a side door rather than through its imposing Fifth Avenue entrance, intending to take an elevator that she rarely used.

She was about to enter the elevator when Warren Holcomb charged out of it and sent her sprawling. Stunned, she lay on the floor, gazing up at him.

"Damn!" he said. "Have I hurt you? Are you all right?" Even as the words left his mouth, he hovered above her, reaching for her. And as if her five-foot, nine-inch frame didn't weigh one hundred and forty-five pounds, he lifted her as he would a small child, cradling her in his arms.

"I'm...I'm okay. J-Just a little shaken up."

He didn't release her, but held her and stroked her back. "I'm so sorry. You're the last person I'd want to hurt." Jackie knew she should get out of the man's arms, but her whole body tingled. Alive. Warmer and getting hotter. He had an aura of power, but to her, he communicated warmth and gentleness. Mastery. She wanted to put her head on his shoulder and rest it there. Her mind told her she was insane, but her body wanted to be close to him forever. Coming to her senses, she stepped back from him, found a spot beyond his shoulder and focused on it.

"Sure you're okay?" he insisted. His voice, mellifluous, low and urgent sent tremors through her.

"I'm fine."

The first to reclaim her wits, she tried to smile, but failed. She bent to pick up her pocketbook but, simultaneously, he attempted to retrieve it, and their heads collided.

"Ooh," she said and, immediately, his arms went around her as if to soothe her.

"Looks as if I'm trying to kill you, but believe me, I'm not." It seemed to her as if he hugged her; at least, she'd swear that he held her closer. He gazed down at her, his eyes ablaze, less with concern than with desire.

"I know that. Accidents will happen." He was dragging it out, playing it for all it was worth, she knew, but she didn't feel like calling him on it.

"Am I forgiven?"

"Of course." Oh, the glorious feel of his hands on her, strong and masculine! Possessive, as if they had a right to her body. Man. All man. Lord! She had to straighten out her head. After a minute, she managed to step out of his arms.

"Where on earth were you going at that rate of speed?" she asked him. At his height and with his solid build, she was lucky to be conscious.

At her question, a troubled, almost frightened expression settled over his face. "Shoot, the parking meter. It would be my luck that the traffic cops would have my car towed."

She frowned. "The parking meter? You mean you don't have a chauffeu?"

"No. Why would I need one? I know how to drive."

"B-But every man here has a chauffeur. I thought… never mind what I thought." Hmm. So Mr. Holcomb was one big-shot who didn't have an inflated estimation of himself. He'd just gone up several notches in her opinion.

* * *

Warren Holcomb had begun life at the bottom of the heap, so to speak, and remained there for almost half of his life. However, by his wits and ambition, he became, by age forty, sole owner of luxury hotels in Washington, D.C., Nairobi, Kenya and Honolulu. He was currently planning to build one on Adam Clayton Powell Jr. Boulevard in Harlem. He'd accepted membership in Allegory, Inc. to show that success and manners meant more than skin color, and he was always happy to inform anyone interested that he hadn't applied for membership, but had been invited to join. So far, he wasn't sorry that he was a member.

"I told the traffic cop that that Lincoln belonged to a brother, one of the very best," the doorman said to Warren when he rushed down to check on his car. "She said you shouldn't park it so close to Fifth Avenue, but she didn't ticket you."

"Thanks," he said to the doorman, greatly relieved. "I'll do as much for you sometime." He handed the doorman a twenty dollar bill. "I'm not trying to pay you, but I am truly grateful for your help."

"Yes, sir, and I do appreciate it."

He walked back into the club, took a seat at the bar and ordered coffee and two aspirin. He didn't have a headache. He needed to settle his libido, and a pain killer usually did the trick. Jackie didn't know it, but when he'd had her in his arms and she'd looked up at him with lips parted and glistening, he'd come close to an erection. He couldn't remember when he'd last reacted in that way to a woman he hadn't kissed or fondled. It was his good fortune that she hadn't seemed eager to move out of his arms. If he was lucky, it meant she was attracted to him. He cocked an ear when he heard her name.

"Man, that woman could melt snow in a blizzard just by showing up," one man said.

"Yeah. I'll bet she's got a forty-inch top, and that's just about the sweetest little ass I ever saw in my life. How tall would you say Jackie is, Ben?" the second man asked the bartender.

Warren drained his cup and stood, disgusted. He hated to hear men speak that way about women, and it doubly irritated him that Jackie was the object of their lewd expressions of admiration.

Wanting to put an end to it, he answered for Ben. "She's about five-nine, and you guys sound as if you're still living in Hell's Kitchen."

The offender stood and looked up at Warren. "Just because she's black doesn't mean you own her. She's a hot piece. And I never lived in Hell's Kitchen."

"Aw, knock it off," Warren said. "You're CEO of a big company, and it ought to show someplace other than in your wallet."

"Come on, guys," a fourth man said. "Jackie's the reason I come here every evening. After I look at my horse-face secretary all day, I need to see that chestnut-brown beauty with those long legs that go on forever, that neat little waist and…" He looked at Warren. "Not to worry, buddy, I'm not touching the rest."

Warren decided to call it a night. Hearing other men

talk about Jackie in that way stuck in his craw and made him think of shortening the distance between their ears. He didn't see himself attached to a cocktail waitress whose skirts barely covered her flawless hips, but that woman had something special, and he had a mind to investigate it.

He left the club, got into his Lincoln Town Car and headed for his home in Brooklyn Heights. As he drove, it occurred to him that the reason why the men had such loose tongues around Jackie was because they considered her a sexy bombshell who didn't have a brain. He'd bet she would surprise them.

Warren couldn't know the accuracy of his assessment. With a superior memory, Jackie knew more about some of the club members than they would guess or wish. At home, after a long and tiring day, she sat before the mirror of her dressing table, massaging her temples and relaxing, ruminating about the day's happenings before preparing for bed.

Those rich men think a cocktail waitress is so empty-headed that they can discuss their business and personal secrets in her presence, and she's too stupid to pick up on it. Well, this one isn't. I'm not interested in disabusing them of their ignorance; they may one day become victims of their prejudices, and I hope I'm around to see it.

She fought the rising anger that welled up in her as she recalled how careless some of those men were with their manners and their talk, because they thought she didn't deserve better. Not all of them. Holcomb respected her, and so did Ben, the bartender, and most of the older men.

Holcomb, how she wished they'd met in different circumstances. She had just completed that thought when the telephone rang. "Hello," she said into the receiver.

"Hi," her older sister, Vanna, said. "You've been on my mind lately. How's Papa?"

"Pretty good. I'm going to see him tonight. How're the children?"

"What can I say? Raising three kids by myself isn't what I thought I'd be doing when I had 'em, but they're precious, the little darlings."

They talked for a while, and when Vanna said goodnight and hung up, Jackie looked at her watch. If she hurried and pretended that Charlie Rose and Tavis Smiley didn't exist, didn't turn on the television, merely said her prayers and went to bed, perhaps she wouldn't be so sleepy when she awoke the next morning.

As she did every morning at eight o'clock, Monday through Friday and an occasional Saturday, Jacqueline left her home for her office unrecognizable to the members of Allegory, Inc. On that morning, dressed in a conservative business suit and wearing medium-heel shoes, her shoulder-length hair in a braided chignon and her skin devoid of makeup, a smile settled on Jacqueline's face when Jeremy, the guard, rushed to meet her as she entered the building that housed *African American Woman* magazine.

"'Morning, Dr. Parkton," he said, tipped his hat

and, as usual, took her briefcase and walked with her to the elevator.

"Good morning, Jeremy. You spoil me."

"Yes, ma'am, and I'm gon' do that every chance I get. You the nicest person that comes in here. Have a good day."

"Thank you, Jeremy. You, too."

"'Morning, Dr. Parkton," the secretaries and clerks called out as she walked through the section. Jacqueline smiled as she greeted them, aware that each of them treated her as if she were special, different from the other editors who were her subordinates. She hung her Do Not Disturb sign on the door of her office, sat down and checked her mail.

"That man is boneheaded," she said aloud and, for the second time, returned a short story to an Edmond Lassiter as unacceptable. "Please don't send this to me again. It's more suitable for a men's magazine," she wrote across the top of the page. Jacqueline hated to reject a manuscript for she empathized with writers, but what else could she do with that one?

Warren parked the Town Car in his garage and went to the deli two blocks away on Montague Street to buy his dinner. He hated eating alone in restaurants, and he disliked the idea of making a date with a woman when he only wanted company while he ate. Dressing up, going across the city, or even farther, to get the woman, making reservations at a fancy place and talking intelligently when he was so tired he felt like falling into the food? Give him the deli or the Chinese take-out window any day.

While he waited for his shrimp salad, rolls and cheesecake, his mind settled on Jackie Parks. How would she look if she wore less eye makeup and rouge? She had a body to die for and, at times, it seemed as if he would die wanting it. He didn't allow himself to get hooked on the idea of having a particular woman with whom he didn't have a relationship. But he wanted Jackie Parks.

"Here you are, sir," the Korean lady said, handing him the bag that contained his supper. "Have nice day."

He thanked her and left. What was he going to do about Jackie? Was she the one? He wanted eventually to have children, and he couldn't imagine that hourglass figure swollen with a pregnancy.

The following afternoon, Saturday, found him where he spent most of his afternoons, at Harlem Clubs, Inc., his financial and personal investment in keeping children off the streets of Harlem and en route to a productive life.

"Come here, Charlie," he said to a potential troublemaker. "Sit down. Would you like to fence in the Olympics two years from now?"

The boy's shrug expressed a careless lack of concern. "Yeah."

"Well, you are not going to."

Charlie jumped up from his perch on the edge of the windowsill. "What? What do you mean? I'm the best here."

Warren stared hard at the boy, having discerned that only challenge motivated him. "But your attitude is the worst, and I'm sick of dealing with it. Furthermore, I am not going to hire a coach for you any longer if you don't work hard and practice. Got that?" Immediately, Charles shed his arrogance, grabbed a foil and began to practice.

On a sunny weekend, approximately ten days later, Jackie was Dr. Jacqueline Ann Parkton at Hampton University giving a sorority-sponsored lecture on the deleterious effects of teen pregnancy and crime in contemporary society. She noted that her audience included several men and a number of older women. In response to her question, half of the young women present were sexually active, and yet less than one fifth of those had had an orgasm.

When she asked why they had sex if they didn't enjoy it, one student asked, "How do you say no if you want to be popular?"

She replied. "It's spelled, n-o. Why buy a cow if you can get free milk whenever you want it and when you can have fun checking out different cows?" She had planned to discuss the hazards of drug use, but time went quickly as the students bombarded her with questions about sex, sexuality, virginity and male attitudes. At the end of her talk, the students crowded around her, asking questions, and a man fought his way through the group and introduced himself as Edmond Lassiter.

"I've wanted to meet you, Ms. Parkton, and when I read in the Norfolk, Virginia *New Journal & Guide* that you'd be here today, I wasn't about to miss you. You are a very impressive speaker."

He could spread butter on her as much as he liked, but she was not going to publish his chauvinistic short story. "Oh, yes. I remember returning your story a couple of days ago, and for the second time, too."

His smile was that of a man accustomed to getting a lot of mileage merely by changing the contours of his face. "Let's not discuss anything so unpleasant just now. I came a long way to meet you." He looked at his watch. "It's a quarter after one, and I'm starving. Would you do me the honor of having lunch with me?" She began to gather her papers. "Please. I came a long way to see you."

Suffolk, Virginia, where he lived, was practically across the street from Hampton, but she didn't remind him of that. She pretended to focus on the papers in her hand, her casual attitude belying her appreciation for his masculine attributes. He was a good-looking man and very much aware of his appeal.

"All right, but only if you promise me I'll never see that short story again."

His right hand went to the left side of his chest and, as if he'd taken lessons from Morgan Freeman or Jack Nicholson, his smile radiated. "You wound me, but what can I do? I promise."

As he ate, he chewed his food slowly, deliberately, causing her to imagine him savoring the delights of a woman he adored. He might have attracted her interest if he hadn't kept inserting bits of propaganda for his short story into the conversation. She refused to respond.

"How do you manage to write that provocative column along with all the other things an editor has to do?"

She was tempted to tell him that he was too free with the compliments. What she said was, "I try not to waste time…like going over your manuscript twice."

He put a serious expression on his face. "I know you said you didn't like it, but I wanted to give you a chance to change your mind."

"You did, and now it's set in stone, Mr. Lassiter." She looked straight at him, and when he quickly diverted his gaze, she realized that he was attracted to her and preferred not to be.

"Send me something equally well written that doesn't focus on women's body parts and I'll consider publishing it."

It amused her that he had the grace to blush. "I think it's a good story, but…" He threw up his hands as if in resignation and then let his face dissolve into an engaging grin. Looking at his dazzling smile, her thoughts went back to Jeff Southwall, the man whose mesmerizing masculinity had trapped her into making the biggest mistake of her life.

Before she realized she would say them, the words, "You're wasting your time," slipped out of her mouth.

But as if he hadn't heard her, he said, "Thanks for having lunch with me. When I asked you, I thought you'd refuse." He walked with her to the car she'd rented and opened the driver's door. "You haven't seen or heard the last of me. I don't give up easily." He extended his hand for a shake and added, "Be seeing you at one place or another."

"I told you not to waste your time, and I meant it."

However, she doubted he heard her for, without answering, he turned and walked off, whistling as he went.

She let the engine warm up for a few minutes before heading to the airport. The man's hands were those of a working man, calloused and hard, but he had the manners and demeanor of an educated person. She couldn't reconcile the two traits. There was something about Edmond Lassiter that didn't add up—something besides his terrible story.

Then she thought of Warren Holcomb, a warm and tender, yet equally masculine man. Captivating. The man she wanted with mounting urgency each time she was in his presence. There was no comparison. Edmond Lassiter was not even in the running. Granted, she'd been taken aback by his earthiness and blatant sexuality but, even before they separated, she'd become used to him and his sly way of seduction. She released the brake and put Hampton University behind her.

A she drove, she envisaged a life with a strong, warm and gentle man, a man like Warren Holcomb. One who made her forget everything and everyone but him. "It isn't going to happen," she said aloud. "If he hasn't made a move yet, he never will."

Jacqueline went from LaGuardia Airport directly to Riverdale to see her father. "You look wonderful," she told him as they embraced. Her father always made her feel as if she was the apple of his eye, although she knew he loved her sister, Vanna, as much as he loved her. "How are you feeling, Papa?"

"I feel a lot better, so you can move me out of this

mansion. It must cost a fortune, and I know you can't afford it." She didn't tell him that she had an evening job that enabled her to afford comfort for them both.

"I learned it from you, Papa. I'm only taking care of you the way you took care of Mama, except that I haven't mortgaged my pension to do so. Stop worrying."

"It's time you gave me a grandchild," he said when she rose to leave. "Find a good man" rang in her ears as she kissed him goodbye.

When she arrived at work the following evening, her first call for service was to Warren Holcomb, who sat alone in one of the private lounges.

"Good evening, sir. What may I get for you?"

His right eyebrow shot up, and she reminded herself to be cautious about her language. He had detected her proper use of the word "may" instead of "can," which a less-educated person might have used.

"Coffee."

"Uh…anything else?"

"No. Look, I don't really want any coffee. I want to apologize to you for having knocked the wind out of you the other night. It was careless of me, and I've stewed over it ever since. Are you certain that I didn't hurt you?"

She tried to smile in order to put him at ease, for she knew he didn't really want to apologize again for that accident, that he was using it as an excuse to talk with her. Still, she appreciated his subtlety. "You didn't hurt me, and you certainly would never—" she emphasized the word *never* "—do so intentionally."

Leaning forward, he braced his hands on his knees and seemed to study her. "You're right. I wouldn't." Although silent for a moment, he gazed steadily at her until her nerves scrambled themselves throughout her body and her blood began a headlong rush to her lower region. But she refused to blink. It was his move.

Finally, he sat back in his chair, and although his gaze softened, his eyes nevertheless gleamed. "I want to see more of you, and I think you know that. It's against club rules for me to make a date with you, and that's all that keeps me from trying."

For heaven's sake, there are other ways, she thought, but to him, she said, "I appreciate your being discrete, sir."

"I don't know how to take that," he said, surprising her with his directness, "and please stop calling me sir. Are you saying you're not interested?"

She stared into his eyes, darker now than usual and with a fire blazing in them that she had no trouble naming. "Is that the only interpretation you can give it?" she asked. She was determined to keep him guessing.

"I wasn't trying to be subtle or discrete. I merely stated a fact. And I'd be a lot closer to you this minute if club rules didn't forbid that as well."

"You're a lot bolder than I thought. I'd better get back to my station."

"I'll take that coffee strong."

"How many?" she asked and hated herself for letting him know that he'd rattled her.

But he didn't capitalize on her slipup. "I have no

guests this evening. I didn't sit in the main lounge, because I wanted to speak with you."

"I'll be back in a few minutes with your coffee." As she left the lounge, she threw him a look over her shoulder. Just because he knew she melted when he picked her up off the floor and held her was no reason for him to get a big head. More than one man would affirm that she was the queen of denial. If he was as smart as he seemed he would realize that she hadn't said she wasn't interested, but she'd merely avoided answering his question.

Carrying a silver tray that contained a pot of coffee and an elegant coffee service, Jackie paused as she approached the private lounge. The small, illuminated yellow bulb indicated that the lounge was occupied. Did Holcomb realize that, with that light blinking, only she, the waitress, would enter that lounge or even knock on the door? The lump in her throat seemed to grow by the second. She opened the door, put the tray on the service table nearby, poured a cup of coffee and took it to him.

He examined the porcelain cup with what seemed like relish. "Thank you. I like it with milk instead of cream, and no sugar," he said as he reached for it.

"I know how you like it."

Both of his eyebrows shot up. "Mind my asking if you know how each of the forty-seven members of this club likes his coffee?"

"I don't mind at all."

A smile lit up his face, and the twinkle that always mesmerized her began to dance in his eyes. "Well, do you?"

"Definitely not."

He put the cup and saucer on the table beside him and leaned toward her. "Are you playing with me?" An expression of disbelief roamed over his face.

She didn't try to suppress the mirth that welled up in her and grinned when she said, "No more than you're playing with me. You knew the answer before you asked the question."

His smile broadened, displaying a left dimple. "Well, I don't know the answer to this. How can I manage to spend some time with you without violating club rules?"

She let her gaze sweep over him. "If you figured out how to achieve such success that Allegory *invited* you to join before you were forty, you can figure out how to see me without breaking the rules. Since I'm not a whiz kid, and I'd rather not get fired, don't expect any help from me."

He crossed his knees, appeared to get more comfortable, and sipped his coffee. "Just the way I like it. Do you want me to figure out a way?"

On the verge of becoming exasperated—he had the privacy he needed; why didn't he use it—she put her right hand on her right hip and stared at him. "Mr. Holcomb, nothing in this life is certain but taxes and death. From the moment babies begin trying to walk, they learn that they have to take a chance."

As if he'd missed the point, intentionally or not, he asked, "Have you had any experience with babies?"

A moron would know that a straight answer to that question would give him more information than he was entitled to, so if he wanted to know, he would have to ask a direct question. "Only during the first year of my life," she retorted.

She watched, fascinated, as he closed his eyes, rested his head against the back of the overstuffed chair and let the laughter roll out of him. When he stopped laughing, he said, "I can't wait to get you all to myself."

She didn't answer, but she hoped that managing that trick wouldn't take him too long.

Chapter 2

I don't know what possessed me to agree to speak to that sorority on this particular day, Jacqueline said to herself as she rolled out of bed at four-thirty in the morning. *I'm beat. Lord, I should have spent the night in Charlotte.*

But she hadn't. She was in New York, and she'd better get moving if she wanted to get that seven o'clock flight.

By the time the propeller plane landed in Charlotte, she was certain that her insides had been rearranged. In the terminal, she bought a bottle of cold water and drank it to settle her stomach. Then, she picked up a rental car and headed for Johnson C. Smith University. Whenever Jacqueline visited a university—and she did that often—she invariably felt old, compared to the vibrant, youthful students around her.

Jacqueline had accomplished a lot in the ten years

after getting her undergraduate degree in English. She'd earned a doctorate in criminology and had become the senior editor of a very prestigious magazine, but she was also lonely. Her life was devoid of the intimacy she craved, and she saw little likelihood of a change in her single status. What man would be willing to share the burden of her father's expensive illness or to settle for a woman whose father's well-being came before everything else? Would a successful, polished man like Warren Holcomb allow himself to care for a cocktail waitress? And would he still be interested if he discovered who she really was?

She turned into the university's campus, asked for instructions to the library, drove there, found a parking space and walked a few paces to the James B. Duke Library. She had to banish her passion for Warren Holcomb—and there was nothing else to call it—for she was playing with fire.

"Welcome, Dr. Parkton," a pretty girl of about eighteen said when Jacqueline stepped into the lecture hall, where about seventy-five students and, she surmised from their apparent ages, teachers as well, awaited her. "I'm your escort for the day. The students are all excited, and I've already collected lots of questions for you."

And so it went on many of Jacqueline's weekends. The money she made from her lectures went into a special account from which she would pay for her father's surgery in the event that he agreed to have it. She didn't allow herself to consider the consequences if he refused. Lunch with the class that sponsored her appearance there followed the lecture and questioning period. She enjoyed the exchange with the eager students, but she was glad to leave.

I'm old enough to be their mother, she said to herself of the freshmen as she drove to the airport, *and I definitely did not enjoy being addressed as ma'am.*

She walked into her apartment at eight-thirty that night, had a glass of milk and two pieces of toast for supper, stripped and fell into bed. She couldn't wait for Monday. Monday evening, in fact. Surely, if Warren— she thought of him as Warren, not as Mr. Holcomb— put his mind to it, he ought to be able to figure out a way to spend time with her in forty-eight hours.

Warren spent most of his weekend thinking about Jackie Parks and pondering schemes to be alone with her outside the club without violating Allegory's rules. Expulsion from the club would mortify him and practically assure that, for years to come, Allegory wouldn't have another African American member. Membership in it had enabled him to obtain generous donations to Harlem Clubs, Inc., funds that he used for scholarships and for professional tutoring for the children who frequented the clubs.

He could get Jackie's address and wait for her at her home one night after she left work, but that strategy involved asking the club accountant for information about Jackie. He couldn't do that. He could follow her, but that was unseemly. And what if she lived with a man? From his one conversation with her, he didn't think so, but who could tell?

I'll ask her where she lives. That's not the same as making a date. I'd call her at home, but she's not in the phone directory. Damn, but this woman is in my blood!

He was never at a loss for something constructive to do, but Harlem Clubs didn't open on Sunday. The only person in New York City who he wanted to see was unavailable to him and he was at loose ends. He put on his jogging suit and a pair of running shoes and went for a run down to the promenade, but instead of returning home at once, he sat on the bench overlooking the East River and lower Manhattan. A chilly, but otherwise perfect day, he thought, as the early afternoon sun warmed his face. All around him leaves floated lazily to earth and a tugboat hooted hoarsely for wider access with its burdensome tanker. The couples who strolled along the promenade holding hands, hugging and staring into each other's eyes increased his sense of loneliness.

"I wonder what she's doing and who she's with?" he mused as visions of her long, silky legs and her large round eyes filled his mind's eye. "Something about her doesn't add up. Women who exploit their sexuality have never interested me, but with that skirt barely covering her...Oh, what the hell!" He got up and jogged on home and wondered if he could bear to wait until Monday evening.

After fighting the covers all night, he arose early Monday morning, not because he was invigorated—

enervated was more like it—but because he wanted to hasten the beginning of the day. He didn't wait until he got to the club to reserve a private lounge as he usually did. Instead he telephoned his reservation as soon as the club opened at noon.

She had to stop, Jacqueline thought to herself after she changed clothes for the third time that Monday afternoon. If she didn't hurry, she'd be late for work, and that sleaze Duff Hornsby would have an excuse to get her alone under the pretext of reprimanding her. Green wasn't her best color, and suppose she ran into Warren before she changed into her uniform. *Oh what the heck! If I'm late, I'm late*. She took off the green dress and put on a red woolen sheath, added a strand of pearls and a spritz of Opium perfume, put on her coat and headed to work.

She walked into Allegory at precisely six-thirty and let herself relax. She was on time and Hornsby, the club's president, wouldn't have an excuse to harass her. She changed into her uniform and the stiletto-heel sandals she was required to wear and went to the storage room to get some linen cocktail napkins.

"What on earth!" She gasped and backed out of the storage room, closing the door on the half-naked couple she'd just interrupted. Was that Carl Spaeder's wife? And if it was, why didn't they save their lovemaking for their bedroom at home? And why didn't they close the door? *Have I been missing something about this ritzy place?* she asked herself. *Is Warren Holcomb the only man here who obeys club rules?*

The light flashed on her intercom, indicating a call to the Reagan Suite. Wondering who had summoned her, she opened the door, and when she saw Duff Hornsby, she didn't move two feet from it.

"Yes, Mr. Hornsby. How may I help you?"

A smile crawled over his face. "For starters, you can move closer. Over here."

"I can hear whatever you say standing right here. I have another call. What do you want?"

"I want you."

"Mr. Hornsby, I've worked here for going on three years, and you're the first member of this club to break club rules and harass me. I suppose you know that my contract provides for redress in such an event."

"Oh, come now. You can't prove a thing. Besides, I'll make it worth your while."

"That's impossible. Not if you owned every ounce of gold in Fort Knox. And don't be too sure that I can't prove you got out of line." She let the door slam behind her, aware that eventually Duff Hornsby's shenanigans could force her to leave Allegory.

She went back to her station and saw the light flashing for the lounge that Warren frequently used. She got a glass of ice water, a pot of coffee and a coffee service, arranged them on a silver tray and entered the lounge.

"I've been ringing you for the past ten minutes," he said. "I was afraid that you didn't come to work today. How are you?"

Thank God for the serving table beside the door, for it seemed that her arms and legs turned to rubber and she quickly set the tray on the table. "I'm...fine. I hope you had a...an enjoyable weekend."

"I had a lonely weekend, and it lasted forever."

What was she to say to that? Her weekend hadn't been a rousing celebration, either. "I'm sorry to hear that, sir. I brought you some coffee."

Even from the distance, she couldn't miss the warmth of his gaze. "Thanks for your thoughtfulness. It's just what I want. I'd ask for a vodka comet, but I don't want it badly enough to drink it alone."

"I'm sorry, sir." She poured the coffee, put about two tablespoons of milk in it, placed it on the cocktail table in front of him. Shock reverberated through her system when his hand covered hers, and, unable to do otherwise, she stared into his eyes. Eyes bright with warmth, affection and, yes, riveting desire.

"Would you p-please g-give me b-back my h-hand?"

"Don't ever call me 'sir' again, Jackie. My name is Warren, and that's what I want you to call me."

She looked down at him, and at his restive and agitated demeanor. *If I don't get out of here, we're both going to explode.*

"I'd better go. If you want something else, just ring." She didn't wait for his reply, but walked out as quickly as she could and closed the door.

She returned to her station, saw that Ben had called her and, instead of calling him, she went to the bar. "What is it, Ben?" she asked trying to sound normal.

"Hornsby's in the main lounge, and he wants these drinks."

"Ben, what am I going to do about that man? He keeps hitting on me, and I can't stand him. He's so sure that nobody will believe he'd harass a cocktail waitress. But Ben, he actually propositioned me."

"I'd believe it. The guy's gray suit on the outside and pure trash on the inside. Don't let that jerk upset you. I'll send Jack in with this." She thanked him and, on her way back to her station, glanced toward the main lounge and saw Hornsby huddled with Mac. Birds of a feather, she said to herself as she got ready to deliver another order.

Warren Halcomb had been aware of Jackie's reaction to his touch, and knowing that he made her tremble had excited him. But at that moment, he'd had more self-control than she, for if he had stood and put his arms around her, she wouldn't have moved until his tongue was deep inside her mouth.

Long after Jackie had left, Warren sat alone in the private lounge, leaning against the back of the leather chair musing about her. She wanted him as badly as he wanted her, or at least he thought so, but he couldn't be sure. Maybe she had merely been frightened that he would take advantage of her. He'd certainly had the opportunity, for no one would enter a private suite other than a waiter or waitress called there to give service. But she was safe with him, she should know that by now.

What a mess!

He got up and went to the bar hoping for a glimpse of her. He found Ben squinting his eyes over a tattered copy of Tolstoy's *War and Peace*. Ben looked up, saw Warren and lay the book, open and facedown, on the counter.

"Can I get you something?" he asked Warren.

He wasn't going to pour out his intimate thoughts to any man, including Ben, whom he'd taken into his confidence on many occasions. "I was considering a vodka comet, but I think I'll just head home."

"We're having stuffed crown of roast pork and drawn lobster for dinner tonight. You can't get a better choice. Makes you wanna eat two dinners. If you don't have an engagement..." Ben didn't say more. They had a strange friendship, but Ben never allowed himself to get familiar with Warren. Too bad, Warren thought. In different circumstances, they could have been as close as brothers.

He rarely ate at the club more than the required four nights each month, and Ben knew it. "Thanks, buddy," he said, ignoring Ben's concession to rank. "Two of my favorites, but I can't stay tonight. Thanks for letting me know." Ben nodded, poured some vodka and aquavit over shaved ice, drained it into two glasses, added a few drops of lime juice and handed one glass to Warren.

"I know you don't drink by yourself, so I'll toss this one back with you if you like."

Warren smiled. "I would indeed like it, Ben, and I appreciate the gesture. First time I decide to drink alone, it'll be the last time I taste alcohol."

"Can't say that I blame you. It's a habit that can quickly get out of hand." The light flashed for service in one of the lounges, Ben turned to the business at hand. "You have a good evening," he said to Warren over his shoulder. Warren had noticed that Ben never put anything or anyone ahead of work, and that probably explained why the man had succeeded at Allegory, Inc. In addition to his salary, the members tipped him twenty percent of the cost of every drink ordered, and he received a two-thousand-dollar bonus at Christmas. All of which allowed him to live comfortably in an attractive home in upscale Ardsley, New York, and send his two daughters to Princeton University.

"See you tomorrow," Warren said, and with no reason to linger, he left without seeing Jackie again.

At eight-thirty on Thanksgiving Eve, Jackie started to the bar for an order and stopped. "Oh my goodness!" she said and groped toward the wall as darkness engulfed her surroundings. A few minutes later, she heard the guard's voice over the loudspeaker. "New York's in a total blackout. You can't use the elevators, so take the stairs. I'll have a light in the stairwell in a couple of minutes." As she felt her way toward her dressing room, she heard a clicking sound and breathed deeply in relief when a faint light appeared.

"There you are." She'd never been so happy as when she heard Warren's voice, because she couldn't see who held the light and had considered the possibility that she might have to deal with Duff Hornsby in the darkness.

"You don't know how glad I am that it's you and not—" She caught herself and didn't finish the remark.

"May I drive you home?" he asked her. "Subways

won't be running, and buses will be scarce. Unless you want to spend the night here?"

She didn't want to be at Duff Hornsby's mercy. "If it isn't too much of an inconvenience for you, I would appreciate a lift, but I live up on West End Avenue, and that's a distance from here."

"It will be my pleasure. I wouldn't be comfortable knowing that you couldn't get home. Get your things, and we can leave."

He handed her the flashlight, and she changed into her regular shoes, got her handbag, put on her coat and rejoined him. She knew he would wait while she changed into her street dress, but she didn't want to risk Hornsby's seeing Warren standing beside her dressing room and making an issue of it.

"This may take a while," he told her a short time later as they fastened their seat belts. "Without streetlights or traffic lights, I'll have to drive slowly."

"Are you sure you want to take me home?"

"I've never been more certain of anything. Just be patient, and we'll get there safely. I've spent a lot of time figuring out a way to see you away from the club, and Providence has given me a hand. I'm sorry so many people are inconvenienced by this blackout, and the day before Thanksgiving at that, but I'm glad for this opportunity to be with you."

I've never been tongue-tied in my life, she thought, but... Why am I so nervous? He's just a man, for goodness' sake. The sound that was supposed to be her voice surprised her with its calm and intelligence when she said, "I thought you'd decided that you could find better things to do with your time than to spend it thinking of ways for us to be together."

"You didn't think any such thing. If you did, when you were in the lounge with me tonight, you found out how wrong you were." He stopped at the corner to allow pedestrians to pass. "It wouldn't hurt you to give a guy some encouragement."

"How much more do you want than what you got tonight?"

"Now, I really have to be careful," he said.

"I'm sure you're always careful," she said.

"Careful and thorough. I leave nothing to chance. Whatever I do is done well." She didn't miss the underlying meaning, either. He found a parking space a few doors from the building in which she lived.

"It took less time than I expected," he said as they entered the building. "Which way is the staircase?"

When she stopped walking, he said, "You don't think I'm going to let you walk up those stairs in the dark by yourself, do you? What floor do you live on?"

In the dimly lighted lobby, she looked at him and spoke softly. "The twenty-first." She gave silent thanks that the doorman was busy and hadn't addressed her as Dr. Parkton.

To her amazement, he grinned and took her hand. "Then we'd better get started."

He lit their way with his flashlight, and they said few words, saving their breath and energy for the tiresome climb.

"Thank God," she said when they reached the twenty-first floor. He walked with her to her apartment door, and she said, "Come in and rest for a few minutes."

"Sure you don't mind?"

"If I minded, I would have thanked you and said good-night."

She found half a dozen pillar candles, put them on a tray, lighted them and placed the tray on the coffee table in her living room. "Have a seat. I'll be back in a minute." *I am definitely not going to sit with him in this romantic setting with nothing on but this skimpy waitress uniform.*

She put on a pair of flared black silk pants and a flattering dusty rose sweater that hung loosely around her hips. "I can offer you ginger ale, orange juice or cranberry juice. What would you like?"

"Cranberry juice. Is there a reason why you aren't offering me an alcoholic drink?"

"I'd be glad to if I had any in the house."

"So you don't drink."

"I drink wine in restaurants and here, too, when I have dinner guests."

"I see. This is a very elegant apartment. I like your taste. It's cozy and very…subdued. You like warm colors, and I suspect they're a reflection of your temperment. Am I right?"

"I've never thought about it. Am I a warm person? I like people, and I don't sort them as if I were grading food for sale in gourmet shops, supermarkets and mom and pop stores in El Barrio. I try to treat all people the same."

"Do you have siblings, Jackie?"

"I have an older sister. She's a divorced single mom of three. She isn't having an easy life. My mother died three months ago, and my father has taken it very badly. We all did."

He leaned forward. "I'm so sorry. I know how difficult it is to cope with the loss of a parent. Were you happy as a child?"

"Oh, yes. My parents were wonderful people. They loved each other deeply, and they adored my sister and me. And we could feel it. We weren't wealthy, but we didn't want for anything, and our home was rich in love and in the little day-to-day kindnesses and thoughtfulness that made a happy home life."

He spoke softly, soothingly, and she realized that she loved his voice. "Where is your father now?" he asked.

"He's in a private clinic in Riverdale. He needs an operation, but he hasn't consented to it. If he doesn't, I don't know what I'll do. He's been a wonderful father, and I'd do anything for him."

"How old are you, Jackie?"

Only a confident man would ask a woman that question with no preliminaries and no sugar-coating. "I'm thirty-three. I don't know anything about you, except that Allegory invited you to join. You can't imagine what a buzz that created at the club. It had never happened before. By the way, since you're sitting here in my home, I assume you are not married."

He sat forward and looked directly into her eyes as if he wanted her to know that he spoke the truth. "No,

I definitely am not and have never been." He draped his right ankle across his knee and leaned back. "The invitation to join the club is about the only thing that came easily for me. I worked like a dog for everything else. I was born in Durham, North Carolina, grew up there and finished high school there in the top ten percentile of U.S. high school graduates that year. That got me a scholarship to MIT, and after I graduated, I went to work in Silicone Valley developing computer hardware and software. The boom became a big bust, and I thought I'd have to sell shoelaces, but after about four months, I got a job with Pearson Triangle, an Internet facilitator. Being out of a job for four months was a great teacher, and I made it a point to become financially savvy. Pretty soon, the field became overcrowded, so I sold my shares in Pearson and bought a hotel in Honolulu. I made it stand out by targeting honeymooners, offering live classical jazz nightly and screening the latest movies right inside the hotel. I subsequently built similar ones in Nairobi and in Washington, D.C. where every patron gets a free tour of historic Washington."

"What's the name of the one in Washington?"

He told her and added, "My next hotel will be on Adam Clayton Powell Jr. Boulevard."

"And your success has moved you to help change the lives of African American children where you live."

"I live in Brooklyn Heights, but I built Harlem Clubs, Inc., for children five to eighteen years old, and I volunteer there for a few hours most days and every

Saturday that I'm in New York. I want to do everything I can to eliminate crime among our children."

Now Jackie leaned forward, for what she heard told her that they dreamed the same dream and worked toward the same goal. If only she could tell him about herself, who she really was and why Jackie Parks even existed. But she couldn't risk it. He was a man who played by the rules, and she didn't know whether his loyalty would be with her or with the club. She went into the kitchen and brought him a glass of cranberry juice.

He accepted the juice and drank a few swallows. "This environment really becomes you. You have created such a peaceful, gentle setting."

Suddenly, she wished he would ask what she did during the day, for she wouldn't be able to lie to him. She longed to reveal herself to him, to meet him on equal terms.

He looked at his watch and seemed shocked. "Would you believe it's a quarter to one in the morning? I had no idea, Jackie, and I apologize for staying so late."

She followed him to the door. "Don't," she said. "I've enjoyed every minute that you've been here." When his eyes blazed with the fire of a man looking at the woman he wants, chills shot through her, and she got a feeling that she stood at a precipice.

He stepped closer and gazed down at her. "Don't tell me that or anything else unless you're sure you mean it. Do you?"

She couldn't make herself speak, so she nodded. His hand stroked her left arm, and the fire of it shot straight to her loins. She knew better than to lower her gaze, for he already had the upper hand.

"You and your job at the club don't match," he said as he stared into her eyes, "but one of these days you'll explain it to me. I don't give up easily, Jackie. You've been in my blood, and now, you're in my head as well. What am I to you?"

She sucked in her breath and, without thinking, covered his hand on her arm with hers. Her gaze dropped to his lips and, at last his fingers pressed into her flesh as he wrapped her in his arms.

"Open up to me. Let me feel myself inside of you," he said, groaning as if in pain. His breath, warm and sweet, washed over her face, and she felt herself trembling in his arms as his hot mouth singed hers, and his tongue pressed for entry. She opened her mouth, took him in, and desire gripped her as he claimed her with his stroking, dueling tongue and pressed her body to his. She sucked his tongue into her mouth. More. Deeper. She needed, wanted all of him. She thought she'd go crazy if he didn't get all the way into her. Heat permeated her vagina, and when her nipples tightened against his chest, he held her closer and groan after groan poured out of him. She rubbed from side to side against his chest to ease the pain in her nipples. Oh, how she wanted to feel his mouth on them. Her head told her to stop it, but her body begged for the feel of him deep inside of her. Crazy for more of him, after years of emptiness and deprivation, her hips betrayed her, and when she realized that she had undulated against him, she forced herself to step away.

"I didn't mean for it to go that far," she whispered.

"Say my name, Jackie. I've never heard you say my name."

She looked into his eyes and breathed the word. "Warren. Oh, Warren."

He brought her back to him and folded her in his arms with a gentle caress. "I wish we could go even further…but at least, I know that you care for me."

"You don't understand," she whispered. "You brought something out of me that I didn't know was there, and I…I don't know whether I'm happy about it."

"There are things about you that I don't understand, but your reaction to me tonight is not one of them. We're attracted to each other, and there's nothing wrong with that. You're concerned because you would have preferred to control your feelings, but your passionate response has made me want you that much more." He released her and took out a pad and pen. "What's your phone number? I'll call you in the morning around nine. Okay?"

She gave him her number, and he wrote it down. "Get home safely."

A wide grin roamed over his face. "Don't think for a minute that I'm leaving here without another kiss. You've got a lot to make up for."

She opened her arms, but his kiss was quick. "You are one sweet woman. Good night."

As Warren loped down the stairs, somehow he didn't notice the distance. He stopped at the eleventh floor not because he was tired, but because he was so overcome with excitement that he felt light-headed. Jackie's response to him had exceeded his wildest fantasies about her. He'd been at the point of erection—something he used to be able to control—when she stepped away from him and called a halt to the sweetest and most honest loving be could remember.

He leaned against the wall and breathed deeply. What would she do if she decided to make love with him? What would she be like? Shudders raced through him when he thought of the way she moved against him. "Get yourself together, man," he said aloud. "You've got a long way to go with the mysterious Jackie Parks. You need to take it slowly."

Nevertheless, when he awoke Thanksgiving morning, he could hardly wait until eight o'clock, which he considered a reasonable hour to telephone a person. He'd said he would call her at nine, but an hour didn't make a big difference, did it?

"Good morning, Jackie," he said when she answered. "I know it's early, but I've been waiting for a decent time to call you."

"This isn't a decent time."

He flushed with unexpected heat. "You're still in bed? I…" He caught himself. He wished he was in that bed with her, but it was a little too soon to tell her that. Warren suspected that Jackie had some lines that he'd better not cross. He sensed that she was holding back. So instead, he said, "I'd lie if I said I was sorry. I couldn't wait to talk with you. Think you can wake up sufficiently to talk with me?"

"Sure. I just have to get a drink of water or something. Catch me when I'm half-asleep, and I'll promise you Fort Knox."

He stared at the phone. Who was this woman? Nearly asleep, she spoke in a voice that was as refined as if she were wide-awake and measuring every word.

"I'm back. What time is it?"

"Eight o'clock. Do you always sleep late?" he asked with a chuckle. "Well, I guess you do, since you work at night."

"No, I don't," she said, "but I woke up around seven, and I just didn't want to get up. Besides, I'd been having such a wonderful, restful sleep that I—" She stopped as if she'd said too much.

"That you what?" he asked her.

"I'm not going to tell you."

"Then I'll take it that you dreamed about me."

"Worse things have happened."

He couldn't help laughing. "You're wide-awake now, and I can hear that you have your wits about you. Can we have lunch? I'd like to go home later today to have dinner with my folks, but I also want to share Thanksgiving Day with you. Will you be hungry at noon?"

"I'd love to have lunch with you, but I want to have lunch with my father today since I can't have dinner with him. They serve dinner around five-thirty at the clinic and, as you know, I have to be at work at six-thirty."

The temptation to ask her to skip work loomed large, but he didn't know her financial circumstances and, in any case, he valued dependability in an employee. "Then, can we have lunch tomorrow and spend the afternoon together? I'd like you to visit my Harlem Clubs."

"What time?"

Nothing coy or coquettish, and he liked that in a woman. "May I come for you at twelve-thirty?"

"I'll be ready. What time did the electricity come on last night?"

"It was on when I awoke at a quarter of seven. I'll be eternally grateful for that blackout."

"Come now, Warren. You would have figured out a way for us to spend time together. I can't believe you wouldn't have."

"After discounting half a dozen ideas and being frustrated because you're not in the phone directory, I had decided to give you my phone number and suggest you use it. Fortunately, I was saved by the inefficiency of Consolidated Edison."

Her laughter, soft and sensuous, rolled over him, warming him like a sweet promise on an early spring evening. "That's a stretch," she said. "I can't imagine there's anything you set yourself to do that would get the better of you."

"You know how to make a man feel good. Did you mean that?"

"Of course I meant it, otherwise, why would I say it? Hang up so I can get my act together. I want to buy some flowers and a box of chocolate for my dad, and it takes a while to get to Riverdale. See you tomorrow."

"A really sweet woman would give me a kiss."

She made the sound of a kiss. "Somebody's been spoiling you."

"How I wish! I haven't stood still long enough to enjoy that, but I'm definitely going to change my ways. Until tomorrow."

Tomorrow wouldn't come fast enough for him. He told himself not to speculate about her, but to ask her anything that he wanted to know. Yet, he'd had enough experience to realize that an answer didn't necessarily reveal the truth. He'd always thought that neither her manners nor her speech were what one would expect of a woman serving drinks in a gentlemen-only club. And as far as he could see—and he was a careful observer—she didn't have a relationship with any man in that club.

She had impressed him as being modest when she changed out of that skimpy uniform, obviously unwilling to entertain him in her home while wearing it. A more worldly woman would not have done that. *More points in her favor. But if I'm wrong, God help me. She's in me, and she has been for months.*

He went to the kitchen, put some frozen Belgian waffles into the toaster and four strips of bacon in the microwave and reheated coffee. "I'm not going to give up on her," he said to himself. "I've got a gut feeling that whatever she is underneath is what I want."

He didn't care to eat lunch alone, so he dressed and went to the Holy Apostles Soup Kitchen on Ninth Avenue and helped serve food to the more than a thousand homeless and poor, who came there for a free Thanksgiving Day meal.

* * *

Sitting on the edge of her bed, Jacqueline placed the receiver in its cradle and braced her hands on her knees. Hadn't she vowed not to get involved with any man at Allegory, regardless of his status as a member or an employee? Yet, in all of her thirty-three years, she had never felt the passion for a man that she felt for Warren Holcomb, nor had she responded to one as she did to him. She got up and headed to the kitchen. Maybe a cup of coffee would help her clear her head. If he preferred the type of woman she appeared to be in her micro-mini waitress uniform and spiked-heel sandals, he wasn't for her, nor she for him.

When I went to work at Allegory, I was only trying to be a dutiful daughter. Lord, please help me out of this mess. I believe he's a good man, and I...I want him. What am I going to do? His type of man doesn't fall in love with the woman he thinks I am.

If she continued to worry about her relationship with Warren Holcomb, she'd soon be a basket case, so she called her sister. "Happy Thanksgiving, Vanna. What are you and the children doing today?"

"We're having a picnic with a neighbor down the street. She has a girl and a boy the age of my oldest two, and they get on well together. I called Daddy a few minutes ago, and he really was upbeat. He even told me one of his jokes. When you see him today, give him a hug for me."

"I will. I plan to see him at lunchtime. He's always liveliest at midday. By dinnertime, he's usually tired. I'll call tomorrow and let you know how he's doing."

"All right, Jacqueline. The Lord will bless you. I know that taking care of our father is a sacrifice on your part. If I could do more, I would, but I haven't received a child support payment in three years. The court can't locate Arnold to serve the papers, and my teacher's salary hardly enables me to pay the mortgage on this house. The moral of my story is be careful who you marry. Love and passion don't necessarily last."

"I'm not thinking marriage these days, Vanna, but sometimes I wish I was."

"Your day will come. Whoever he turns out to be, I hope he'll be worthy of you. Have a wonderful day, sis. Bye."

She hung up and told herself not to think about Vanna's situation. As inexperienced as she was with men, she knew enough to shy away from men like Vanna's ex-husband. The man was all charm and no substance, but neither she nor their parents had been able to make Vanna see it. Shaking off her gloomy thoughts, she dressed, walked over to Broadway to buy flowers and chocolates for her father, picked up her rental car and headed for Riverdale.

She found her father sitting in a chair beside his bed, and his face glowed with delight when she walked in. "How are you feeling, Daddy?" She put the roses in a vase and handed him the chocolates.

"Pretty good. Thanks for the candy. You know I love chocolate." He nodded toward the flowers. "I love flowers, too, and your mother always had them in the house. They say I can go to the dining room, and we can eat lunch in there." She went to the nurses' station, got a wheelchair, helped her father into it and wheeled him to the dining room. Tables for two and four were covered with white tablecloths, vases of flowers and attractive place settings. She moved a chair from one of the small tables, settled her father there and sat opposite him.

"Isn't this nice?" he said. "You know, they want me to have that operation, but why should I at my age? Seems pretty silly to me."

She stared him in the face, careful not to glare at him, for she knew he would regard that as sass, a thing he didn't allow. "What about Vanna and me, Daddy? We've lost our mother. Are you suggesting that we don't need our father? Besides, you're only sixty-four." He didn't answer, and she didn't press the issue. She hoped he would think on her words.

After a very good turkey dinner, she took him to the lounge where they played rummy—a game she'd almost forgotten because she hadn't played it since she left home to go to college—and his concentration on it was as much of a present as she could have wanted.

She left her father at four o'clock and drove to Manhattan, returned the rental car and went home and dressed for work. She was scheduled to begin her shift at six-thirty. As she approached Allegory's front door, she remembered that Warren would not be there that night. She was so disappointed at the thought of not seeing him that she sat in her dressing room taking deep breaths to calm her emotions for ten minutes before heading for the bar.

Chapter 3

Warren left the soup kitchen at twenty minutes past one, hailed a taxi and made it to LaGuardia airport at five after two. He breathed a sigh of relief when the plane took off at three o'clock as scheduled. He wasn't in a habit of disappointing his mother, and certainly not on Thanksgiving Day. He put his key into the lock of her front door at five o'clock and walked into the waiting arms of his nieces and nephew. He hugged them and went to find his mother, a stately woman of considerable accomplishment and of whom he was extremely proud. He walked into the kitchen, opened his arms to her and enjoyed her embrace, the love that he knew he could always count on, for no matter where he was or what he did, he was her son, and she loved him.

"Where's Dot?" He loved his only sister and hated not seeing her when he went home.

"She went to buy some charcoal. The children want to toast marshmallows after dinner tonight. How long can you stay?"

"I just came for dinner. I need to be back in New York by midnight."

She raised an eyebrow. "I won't ask what you'll do at midnight that you can't do tomorrow morning, but you know your business."

"I have an early appointment, and I want to be sure that I make it on time."

She smiled and patted his shoulder. "That makes sense. Hold the pan while I turn this bird."

He did as she asked, but his thoughts were elsewhere. What would she think of Jackie? If he didn't tell her that Jackie was a cocktail waitress, she wouldn't guess it. *I can't have a woman whose occupation I dislike. Oh hell! I'm not making sense.* He sat on the high stool beside the kitchen window and watched his mother make biscuits as he'd done since childhood.

"Have you found a nice girl yet, son?" He expected that question at least once during his visit, because she never failed to ask it. What could he say? He'd found one that he wanted desperately, but he wouldn't say she would be his life's choice.

"You always ask me that, Mom," he said, hoping to put her on the defensive. "I don't meet many women like you and Dot, but I'm open to being swept off my feet."

She rubbed the flour off her hands and wiped them on a paper towel. "In other words, you've met someone, and you're keeping her close to your chest."

He nearly fell off the stool. If she was clairvoyant, she'd never mentioned it to him. "You're right. I'm in the process of figuring out what to do about her, and when I know, I'll be glad to tell you. But for now, there's nothing to tell. Is Rob coming in today?"

"No. Your brother-in-law flew out last night, and he'll fly to Russia before he comes home. Then he'll have two days off. People think a pilot leads a glamorous life, but every time I see Rob, he's just tired."

Warren looked out of the window, saw his sister building a fire with the charcoal bricks she'd just bought, and got up. "I see Dot's back and building a fire in the barbecue pit. I'm going out to help her.

He greeted his sister with a hug, helped her build the fire and strolled around the property that he'd given to their parents. As he gazed at the beautiful house, terrace, gardens and swimming pool, he was more proud of that gift to his parents than of anything he'd ever attained. But his father was gone now, and his mother was there alone, except when Dot and Rob brought her grandchildren to see her.

He went back into the house. "Mom, did you ever consider marrying again?"

She seemed startled. "Good Lord, no. Whatever made you think such a thing?"

"It's not so far-fetched. You need someone to share this with. It isn't good to be alone so much."

She pulled a chair from the table and sat near him. "Are you in love with this woman you've met?"

There it was, a mother's uncanny intuition. "I don't think so, but it could develop into that. I'd rather not talk about her, because I don't want to influence myself one way or the other."

She sat there silently looking at him for a few minutes. He was used to that. Finally, she said, "I'll pray that it works out in the way that's best for you."

"Thanks." He leaned back against the wall and closed his eyes. "She's…she's so sweet. She's so unbelievably sweet." When he opened his eyes, a smile glowed on his mother's face.

"I'm happy for you, son. When you think it's appropriate, bring her to see me."

"If I get to that stage, I certainly will."

He helped his mother and his sister put the dinner on the table, and at six-thirty, they all sat down to a traditional Thanksgiving dinner of the type he'd known all of his life: corn chowder, roast turkey with cornbread dressing, cranberry relish, mustard greens, candied sweet potatoes and apple pie à la mode. His father hadn't liked pumpkin pie, so his mother never served it.

At the end of the meal, he helped take the dishes to the dishwasher, clean the kitchen and straighten the dining room. "I'll bet you don't know another executive who's willing to scrape dishes and clean up after a meal like this one," Dot said to him. "As long as you stay this close to earth, brother, you'll be a happy man, and the woman who gets you will be blessed."

"Thanks," he said to his older sibling, "but don't tell me that. I'm acting the way I was raised. Well, I gotta split if I'm going to make that plane." He hugged his sister and her children and went to find his mother.

"Thanks for a great dinner, Mom. I'll call you when I get home."

She walked with him to the door and wrapped him in her arms. "Get home safely, and don't forget to pray."

"I won't," he said.

An hour and a half later, he fastened his seat belt, said a word of prayer, leaned back and trusted God and the pilot of the Delta Airlines flight to bring the plane to New York City.

He walked into his apartment at five minutes after eleven, phoned his mother and began checking his calls. Three calls from the manager of his Honolulu hotel. She had fired the head of housekeeping and wanted to know if it was appropriate to hire a man for the job. He dialed her number. "Ms. Frazier, this is Warren Holcomb. As you know, we run an equal-opportunity business. If the man is your best-qualified candidate, and if he has a suitable personality and temperament, hire him."

"The maids want a woman."

"I'm sure you know how to tell them that you do your job as you see fit. You have my support. Good luck with it." He hung up and waited for half past twelve when he could call Jackie.

Jackie kicked off her sandals, stepped out of the mini-skirt and low-cut blouse, jumped into her dress, zipped it up, slipped into her shoes and coat, grabbed her handbag and raced out of Allegory. If he called, she didn't want to miss it, because he might not call back. She hailed a taxi, got in and breathed a sigh of relief that she hadn't encountered Hornsby on her way out. He'd have used any pretense to delay her departure. She'd been home less than ten minutes when the phone rang. She ran to answer it and stood beside it with her left hand holding her chest as she tried to calm herself.

"Hello."

"Hello. This is Warren." The air seeped out of her. "Are you there?"

"Uh…yes. Did you go see your folks?"

"I did indeed, and I got home a little after eleven. Do you realize how long an hour can be?"

"What do you mean?"

"I had almost that long to wait until I could call you. You got home quickly."

She didn't tell him that she almost broke her neck doing it. "I took a taxi. How was your family?"

"I had dinner at my mother's home with her, my sister and her three children. I always enjoy being with my family. How is your father?"

"Surprisingly energetic. We ate in the dining room, although I pushed him there in a wheelchair. That was the first time I'd seen him out of that bed in months. If only he would agree to the operation, he'd get well."

"I'm glad he's better. How old is he?"

"Sixty-four."

"Hmm. That's young these days. If you'd like me to

talk with him, let me know. I'm told that I can be persuasive when I put myself to it."

She couldn't believe what she was hearing. Warren Holcomb couldn't know that if she took him to meet her father, her dad would assume that the two of them had a commitment. "Thank you. I've had this burden practically alone for so long that I forget to ask for help. Besides, I wouldn't want him to get the wrong impression."

"Like what?" In her mind's eye, she could see both of his eyebrows shoot up.

"Like thinking there's more to our relationship than actually exists."

"Not to worry, I can fence with the best of them, although I admit I've never crossed swords with a woman's father. I'd like to help if you think I can, Jackie."

"I have a feeling I'm going to admire you," she said, and wished she hadn't. "I wonder when I became loose-tongued," she went on, before he could respond.

"I wouldn't call it that. You spoke truthfully, because you don't know me well enough to admire me. In fact, we don't know each other, and I intend to change that if you'll let me."

"Come now, Warren. You wouldn't normally look to a cocktail waitress for a meaningful relationship."

"That wasn't well put, Jackie. I am not prejudiced against any group, and it's a good thing, or I'd have missed what I think is going on with us. Would you have turned your nose up at me twenty or so years ago when I waited tables at Seafood Forever, in Boston? Or would you have tried to find out who I really was?"

She heard what he didn't say, and her heart nearly exploded with the joy that she felt. "Thank you for the vote of confidence. You won't regret it."

He was silent for a few seconds. Then he said, "I don't think I will. You agreed to go out with me tomorrow. Remember?"

"I remember, and I'll be downstairs at twelve-thirty." Fortunately, her office had closed for the holiday weekend, or she'd have been hard pressed to give him a reason why she wasn't free at midday, when he thought she only worked nights.

"Why downstairs?"

She didn't intend for them to create a spontaneous combustion every time they were together, and he might as well know it. "It's easier to prevent a fire than it is to put it out once it gets started."

"Good Lord, you're frank. It's refreshing, though. I'd better let you get to bed, but I don't want to. I could talk with you indefinitely."

"I enjoy talking with you, too, but you're right…I'd better get to sleep or I'll be yawning all through lunch. Good night, Warren. Sleep well."

"Not even a tiny kiss?"

She made the sound of a kiss and said, "That was a tiny one."

She heard his kiss just before he said, "Good night, sweetheart."

She hung up, but she couldn't move. Her life was changing with the speed of a down-hill roller coaster, and it could be her ruin, but she didn't want to change course. Every one of her senses told her that Warren Holcomb would introduce her to a whole new way of feeling and a new appreciation of life. And then what? Would he leave her adrift, to become another walking, breathing tragedy?

She mused over it as she prepared for bed. "Heaven help me, but I have to take the chance."

He saw her at once, seated in the lobby facing the front door with her knees crossed and her left foot swinging, as comfortable as if she had been in her own domain. She rose with the grace of Aphrodite emerging from the Aegean Sea and walked to meet him.

He took both of her hands. "You're the essence of grace," were the words he said, but his mind was engaged with one question. Should he kiss her there in the lobby of the building in which she lived? She settled the matter by reaching up and kissing him on his right cheek.

"I appreciate punctuality," she said, "because I hate to wait. Where are we going?"

"There're lots of nice restaurants up in Harlem, but I thought we'd eat before we got there. I'm in the mood for Italian. What would you prefer?"

"I love Italian food, and I hope one of these days to go to Italy and eat my fill of it."

"Then Italian it will be." *If I ever get the opportunity and we're still together, I'll show her Florence, Italy.*

As they entered the restaurant, he noticed that two women leaving it wore shoes with heels three or four inches high and sharp pointed toes. He glanced at

Jackie's boots and relaxed when he saw that their heels didn't exceed an inch and a half in height and that the toes of her boots were rounded.

"You're not a slave to fashion, are you?" he said after they ordered.

She raised both eyebrows. "Me? Not! I wear what suits my lifestyle. Half the things in my closet are six or seven years old. I hate shopping, and I don't make bills that I can't pay at the end of the month."

He leaned back, eager to hear more. "Girl after my own heart. Carrying charges have bankrupted many an honest person." He decided to take a chance. "Something tells me you don't like your waitress uniform."

Her change in demeanor told him that he might have pushed the wrong button, and she seemed defensive when she said, "Do I look like the type of woman who would choose to wear that skimpy outfit?"

"No. That's why I asked the question."

The waiter brought their food—spaghetti with white clam sauce and tiny clams for her with a chef's green salad, and veal marsala with an arugula and mushroom salad for him.

She could tell that he didn't want to linger over the meal, that he wanted to move on to their destination. "I hope we'll have more leisurely meals together, but right now, I can't wait to show you my baby," he said.

"This is your building." It was less a question than a statement expressed in awe. "This is a community center. I had no idea I was coming to a place like this," she said as they walked through the building. "It's huge and ultramodern."

"I try not to do anything halfway, Jackie. We use this facility for daily tutoring, sports, theatre, dance and music education, and each activity is carried on in a room built for that purpose. We have programs for children ages five to nine and ten to eighteen."

"This is...wonderful."

"My aim is to keep as many of our children as possible off the street and out of crime. This is home for a lot of them. I've been blessed to have the money, and I'm glad I found something useful to do with it."

"You must be proud of this," she said, but her thoughts were on the similarities of their interests and the things they had in common. If she could only share with him the part of her life of which he knew nothing. She longed to write a human interest story on the man and Harlem Clubs, Inc. for *African American Woman*, but she couldn't do that without exposing herself. She made up her mind right then to find another night job that would enable her to care properly for her father.

"Have I lost you?" he asked her

She didn't answer directly. "In my mind's eye, I can see every room here filled with children, happy children eager to take advantage of a rare opportunity."

"Most are like that, but quite a few are sullen or have big egos or are unhappy because they can't keep up. Not many are troublemakers, because I don't tolerate it, and they know it."

He stopped to inspect a computer that a teenaged girl

was building. "She's very bright," he said as they moved away from the busy teen, "but she has a bad home environment and spends as much time here as possible."

"Mr. Holcomb, what's wrong with this formula?" a boy asked him.

She noticed that he placed an arm around the boy's shoulder as he looked at the problem. "You forgot the *t*. Rate of growth takes place over time. Remember?"

The boy grinned. "Yes, sir. I forget it every time. I'm going to make up my own formula."

"Great," Warren said, "as long as you remember the *t*." He patted the boy's shoulder and walked on. "He likes attention, so he always pretends he doesn't know something. He knows it all right." He unlocked a door. This is my office. I'm thinking of closing the one downtown and making this one my headquarters. If Bill Clinton's office is around the corner, why can't I have mine here?"

She peeped in and saw the luxurious accommodations that one would expect of a successful executive. "Elegant," she said.

The touch of his hand at the curve of her back sent shivers up and down her spine. "Come on in."

She stepped into his office and turned to face him. "Jackie." His whisper of her name had the sound of reverence. "Jackie, let me hold you. Just let me feel you in my arms." He didn't touch her until she raised her arms to his shoulders, and then he laid claim, gripping her to him. What was happening to her? She wanted his hands all over her, but he only stroked her back as one would soothe a baby. She wanted to scream her frustration.

"Warren...I—"

"Shh. This isn't the place for me to show you what I'm feeling right now."

Get it together, girl, she told herself. *Later...when he takes you home.* She moved away from him with all the grace she could muster, and as if he hadn't said a word, she spoke calmly the first repeatable thing that came to her mind. "If your theater group puts on a play, I'd like to see it."

When he didn't answer, she glanced up at him, and saw his perplexed stare. "Was I too abrupt?" he asked her, ignoring her meaningless remark. "I didn't mean to unsettle you, but I know the consequences if I went any further with you. You're a new experience for me, Jackie. I've always been able to control my feelings for a woman, if need be, but I can't do that with you." His right hand caressed her cheek. "I risk burning up every time you touch me, and your kiss...well, I don't even want to think about that right now. Come on. I want to show you the sports and gymnastics halls and the swimming pool."

Was she such an open book with this man that she allowed him to know that she wanted more than he gave? *He's a new experience for me, too, and I'd better learn how to deal with him.*

He completed the tour and spoke to a man who walked out of the computer room as they approached it. "I noticed that one of the computers is missing, Ron. Order four new ones and keep the computer room locked unless you or one of the volunteers is in the room. Keep a record of who supervises that room and at what times."

"Right, Warren. I'll get on it Monday morning."

"Forgive me. Ms. Parks, this is Ron Hackett, the club's manager."

Ron's quick appraisal was not lost on Warren. Nevertheless, Ron spoke graciously. "I'm glad to meet you Ms. Parks." She acknowledged the introduction, careful to make it as impersonal as possible.

When they walked outside, darkness surrounded them. "I didn't realize we'd been there so long," she said. "What wonderful opportunities you've given those children. I feel privileged to be with you." And she did. She had liked him, indeed she cared for him, but now, she deeply admired him, and she had a sense of humility that, with his numerous options, he chose to spend his time with her.

"When I think of my own good fortune, Jackie, that isn't so much."

"Thanks for bringing me here, Warren. You've shown me a side of you that I wouldn't have imagined." She glanced at her watch. "I'd better get home and change so I can get to work by six."

He appeared crestfallen. "Yes. Somehow, I forgot about that. In the back of my mind was the idea that you and I were going to have dinner and a leisurely evening together." He shrugged. "So be it. I'll drive you home." He found a parking space a few doors from the building in which she lived. "May I see you to your apartment?"

If she said no, she would miss his kiss, and if she said

yes, she risked her doorman greeting her as Dr. Parkton. *I'm damned if I do and damned if I don't.* If members of Allegory, Inc. knew that she was a reporter and unit manager for a national magazine, overhearing their conversations, witnessing business deals and the like, she would be fired summarily and probably sued for false representation. As he stared into her eyes, his gaze—hot and hungry—riveted her, and her breath shortened almost to a pant. Without another word, he got out of the car, walked around it, opened the door and held out his hand to her. She took it, and his fingers closed around hers, settling the matter.

When they entered the lobby, she managed not to look in the direction of the uniformed man who always greeted her with such reverence. In the elevator, she wouldn't look at Warren, until he squeezed her hand. "Look at me, Jackie. You can't escape what is happening to us. If you go to Japan or Australia, you'll still feel it." Suddenly, a smile lit his countenance. "At least we didn't have to walk up this time."

She still couldn't find words. Maybe he could sound lighthearted, but she knew what was happening to her, and it frightened her that this man could so captivate her. As they stepped off the elevator, his arm slid around her.

"Warren, this is…moving too fast."

He didn't answer, but when she put her key into the lock, his hand covered hers. He turned the key, opened the door and waited. She walked in, heard the door close behind her, and then she was in his arms. Oh, the sweet feeling of his body tight against hers and of his heat firing her from head to foot. She looked up, and his mouth claimed her, stunning her with the tremors that it sent through her body. His tongue swept the seam of her lips and she opened to him and sucked his tongue deeply inside of her, as her arms gripped his shoulders. He let the wall take his weight, pulled her close and, with a hand at the back of her head, his other one gripping her buttocks and his tongue swirling and dipping in her mouth, he possessed her as no man ever had.

Heat settled in her groin and she tightened her hips in search of relief, but she needed more, much more, all of him. Her nipple hardened and, frenzied, she grabbed the hand that held her head, placed it inside her coat and caressed her breast with it.

He groaned as he rubbed the tortured areola. "I want my mouth on you."

"Yes. Yes," she moaned.

In a second, her coat and jacket fell to the floor, and she felt his hand on her naked flesh moments before he bent and sucked her nipples into his moist, warm mouth. "Oh," she moaned and, in spite of herself, she undulated against him. *Tell him to stop,* her mind told her. *Break it off before it goes too far,* her common sense dictated, but she held his hips with one hand and pressed his head to her with her other one. Suddenly, his erection bulged against her belly, and she broke his kiss and leaned her head against his shoulder, unable to move or speak.

"There's nothing to be ashamed about," he said, when he couldn't get her to look at him. "I know you didn't mean for it to go so far, and I certainly didn't mean for—"

"It's all right," she managed to say. "Considering what was going on, I don't see how you could have avoided it. I…uh…I'd better get ready for work."

"I'd take you, but if I do, someone will certainly see you get out of the car. I hate this secrecy, Jackie. I don't like the idea of having to hide my behavior from anybody."

She looked at him then. "I have no choice right now, Warren. It's an honest living, and I need the job."

"I know. Go on and get ready. I'll wait here. I can at least see that you get a taxi."

She didn't want that, but to have refused would have raised his suspicions. She dressed conservatively, as she usually did, and took comfort in the fact that the doorman would be on his break when she left the building. She decided not to apply the heavy makeup that she wore as a waitress, and put her makeup kit in her handbag. Maybe he wouldn't notice the difference.

But he did. As soon as she joined him in her living room, he said "You're so much more beautiful without the makeup you wear at work. Why do you wear it?"

Her shrug was intended to suggest that the makeup was of no consequence. "My job description calls for a glamorous, sexy woman, and specifies that I wear that ridiculous uniform and high-heeled sandals."

He stared at her with raised eyebrows. "Well, I'll be damned. I wonder what idiot wrote that. It must have been Hornsby."

"Whoever he was, I don't thank him."

He drove over to Broadway at 66th Street, double parked and hailed a taxi. "I'll see you later," he told her.

"I'll have some guests tonight, so when you get a call from me, remember that I won't be alone." He kissed her quickly, gave the address to the driver along with a twenty-dollar bill and said to her, "He's been paid and tipped. Bye for now."

She made it through the night in what she could best describe as a fog, thankful that she made no blunders and got her work done with a semblance of efficiency. But she couldn't remember ever having been in such a daze. In every minute, she could feel him and taste him. And when she went into the private lounge to answer his call, she was practically tongue-tied.

"I'd like a round of vodka comets and a selection of hot hors d'oeuvres, please," he said when she failed to ask what he wanted.

"Yes, of course, sir," she replied, and left the lounge as quickly as she could without inquiring as to whether he would like anything else.

Twelve o'clock came slowly, but at last she could change into her street clothes and go home. She stepped out onto 63rd, walked toward Fifth Avenue to get a taxi and stopped for the light. Warren's Town Car eased to the curb where she stood. "I'll be on 64th just east of Fifth," he told her, and drove off before she could answer. She walked to the next block and got into his car.

"I couldn't let you hang out here trying to get a taxi after the difficult time you had tonight," he said. "It wasn't easy for me, either. I hated having you wait on all those people, and I knew you were battling your emotions. Hearing you address me as 'sir' made me feel sick."

"Maybe one of us will leave Allegory. Out of sight, out of mind."

He slowed to a quick stop, turned onto Broadway and parked beside a fire hydrant. "Are you telling me that I don't mean any more to you than fuel for your libido? Is that what you're saying?"

"I neither said that nor implied it. I meant that if we don't see each other—"

He interrupted her. "That is precisely what I thought you meant. So if you don't see me, you won't think about me or have any feelings for me? Is that it?" His voice was steady, but she heard the pain in it.

Her hand covered his, for she needed desperately to make him understand. "I meant that perhaps with time you would forget about me, because I'll never be convinced that you would want a serious relationship with a cocktail waitress. I was not speaking about myself."

"If you think your job puts you at a disadvantage, change places with the cook or the bartender, and get it into your head that it's you I want, not the waitress. You. Don't you think I see beyond that persona you've cultivated for Allegory? I saw it the night of the blackout when you were unwilling to entertain me in your home while you wore that waitress uniform. That told me more about you than anything you can say."

"I'm sorry if I misrepresented you, Warren. Each time we're together, I get in deeper with you and, for the first time in my life I don't control what's happening to me."

He pulled away from the curb and continued the drive to her address. "Haven't you ever been in love?"

"I was once in deep *like*, you could say. When it was over, I realized that I had been blessed to escape."

"Did you live with him?"

"No, and when he said it was that or nothing, I walked. Later he wanted to make up, but I wasn't willing to chance linking my life with his. I got over it."

"That guy wasn't smart. May I see you to your apartment?"

"I'm not ready to be more intimate with you than I've already been, Warren, and considering what happened between us earlier this evening, we know what to expect if you go home with me. It's too early for that."

"You're saying that you want me?"

She raised both eyebrows. "If you don't know the answer, we're in trouble."

His laughter, joyous and robust, wrapped around her, and he enclosed her in a loving embrace. "All right. I'll walk you to the front door. If you insist on keeping a distance between us at the club, you set the rules, and I'll try to abide by them. Now, kiss me?"

Her arms went around him, and she parted her lips for his kiss, but the explosion that she expected didn't come. His lips pressed lightly on her cheeks, eyes, nose and neck. Then he sucked the tip of her bottom lip into his mouth. Frustrated and anxious for more, she held his face in her hands and would have instigated a hot exchange, but she glanced at his face and saw the contentment, the glow of peace and joy that enveloped his visage, and a tenderness washed over her. She kissed his cheeks, his eyes and his forehead.

"You're a darling, darling man."

He gazed down at her. "Do you think you could care for me? Really care, I mean."

"You're already very special to me."

"That's not what I wanted to hear, but I'll settle for it. For now." He walked with her to the door. "Good night, sweetheart."

Half an hour later, Warren parked in his garage, entered his house through the kitchen door, barely glancing at the chrome appointments and the yellow brick walls. He'd painted the brick walls yellow on a whim and each day found it more and more distasteful. He left it that way because he used the kitchen mainly for making coffee, heating waffles in the toaster and frying bacon in the microwave oven. He got an apple out of the refrigerator, washed it, turned out the light and headed up the stairs to his bedroom.

After flipping on the radio and tuning it to an easy-listening station, he undressed and went to the shower. Something about Jackie did not add up. She wore a pound of makeup at work and what he now realized was a wig that gave the appearance of hair down her back. But she was not brassy, vulgar or overly familiar with the men at the club. Further, she spoke like an English professor, her manners were those of a woman tutored by Emily Post and she had beautiful taste in clothes and in her apartment furnishings. Sweet, gentle and passionate, the more he saw of her, the deeper his feelings for her and the more he wanted her. From the outset, he had been taken by her gentleness and her soft femininity. She was definitely an enigma, yet he was certain that she was not a phony person.

"I'll have to take a chance. If I can teach her to love me, I can't lose."

He had wanted to ask her if she could love him, but thought better of it. She cared for him; a woman couldn't respond to a man as Jackie had responded to him unless she had deep feelings for him. He knew the difference between that and pure sex drive. Besides, she shied away from every other member of that club and had done so for the two and a half years he'd been there. Ben told him that Hornsby hit on her, and that she avoided the man. That was music to his ears. Hornsby was rich among the rich, and if she resisted him, money was not Jackie's goal.

Perhaps if they went away together for a weekend… Would she trust him enough to put herself in his hands for two or three days? He wouldn't know unless he asked her.

Jacqueline stepped off the number five bus at 29th Street and walked back up Fifth Avenue, her steps light and springy, feeling as if she'd never been more alive. She turned the corner and headed to the building that housed *African American Woman* magazine.

"Good morning, Jeremy," she sang. "Isn't it a beautiful morning?"

"Yes ma'am, Dr. Parkton. A little chilly, but we have to be thankful that we're alive to see the day." As usual, he took her briefcase, walked with her to the elevator and pushed the up arrow.

"Thank you, Jeremy," she said. "You're one of the people who makes coming to work a pleasure."

He blessed her with a brilliant smile. "Thank you, ma'am. You're everybody's favorite around here." She knew that by "everybody" he referred to the nonprofessional staff.

As she walked from the elevator to her office, she greeted each of the secretaries and clerks by name and stopped at the messenger station. "Good morning, Felix. I heard that your wife isn't well. How is she?"

"It was something she ate. The doctor said it was salmonella. She's back home now. Thanks for asking."

"If you need any help, let me know."

"Yes, ma'am. Thanks."

She laid out a section of the February edition of the magazine, checked with the advertising officer and human interest columnist and went to lunch. Her afternoon passed slowly, as she counted the time until she would see Warren. In the midst of writing a sentence, she would lean back in her chair, close her eyes and drift back to the previous afternoon when they had come so close to making love, and to last night when he had cherished her as if she were precious to him.

"Snap out of it, girl," she told herself. Oh, what she wouldn't give if she could bring Warren Holcomb into the life of Dr. Jacqueline Parkton. Then, she could go after him with every bit of the arsenal at a woman's disposal. But she had to bide her time. If he really loved her, she would tell him everything and stand a chance of his not walking away from her because of her deception.

Four-thirty arrived at last, and she packed her brief-case, told her secretary good-night and hurried to the elevator. Still floating on air, as a woman does when she's falling in love, Jacqueline was unprepared for the shock she received when she stepped out of the building.

"Hello, Jacqueline."

She whirled around, stunned at the sight of Edmond Lassiter three feet away and his face the picture of in-nocence. "What are you doing here?"

"I had to see you. I…believe me, Jacqueline, I fell for you completely and unequivocally. I just can't forget you. Give me a chance. Get to know me."

She didn't want to believe him, but her woman's in-tuition told her that he told her the truth, so she spoke gently to him.

"I'm sorry about this, Mr. Lassiter. A relationship between you and me is not possible. There's already someone in my life."

He looked her in the eye. "That doesn't surprise me, because you're beautiful, clever and so nice. But I can't give up, and I won't."

"You'll be wasting your time, so stop now before you get in any deeper."

"I can't get in any deeper. I'm in love with you." Abruptly, he walked away, and she stood and watched him get into his car and ignite the engine.

"Oh, no you don't," she said aloud as recognition of his next move dawned on her. "You're not going to follow me home." She went back into the building, left by a side door, walked through an alley to 64th Street and over to Madison Avenue, from where she took a taxi and went home. She sympathized with any person who nursed an unrequited love, but she couldn't allow Lassiter's feelings to interfere with her life. If he persisted, as much as she would dislike doing it, she would have no choice but to get a restraining order against him.

Chapter 4

The following evening, Jackie answered a call to Hornsby in a private lounge and when she saw that Mac was his guest, she couldn't have been happier for the man's presence. "Yes, sir. How may I help you?"

"A double scotch mist for each of us and some cold snacks. Later on, I might want some coffee."

She understood that when he called for the coffee, he would be alone, and he could bet she wouldn't be the one who brought it. "Yes, sir."

She took the order to Hornsby and went back to the bar. "Ben, if Hornsby wants anything else tonight, send Jack in there. I need this job, but I'll leave it if I have to, and Hornsby will be the reason."

"You don't have to leave, Jackie. I've got his number.

He's not as clean as he looks. Just let me know if he tries anything."

"But he's the club's president."

"That's no big deal. Every man here has to serve two years in that post, and they get the job according to seniority. You and I aren't the only ones who know that Hornsby spends most of his time wallowing in a pigsty."

She thanked Ben and went back to her station, a tiny office next to her dressing room. She had to keep an account of each service to the members and, at the end of the month, the accountant added her bills. If her total was five thousand dollars, she received one thousand in tips, plus her salary. She used her earnings at the club to pay for her father's care at the clinic. Her tips and end-of-year bonuses went toward payment for the surgery that he needed.

She needed her job at Allegory as much as she cherished her position at the magazine. But maintaining two such opposite and conflicting identities, two personas, had begun to wear on her. Being the target of Hornsby's lust made her dread coming to work at the club. Were it not for Warren's presence there, she would hate every minute of it. She knew that some of the members considered her a hot number—as if a miniskirt and stiletto heels could make a woman appealing—all except Hornsby kept their opinions away from her as required by club rules. And if her colleagues at *African American Woman* were to see her in this miniskirt… She shivered at the thought of being exposed and then fired from the job she loved.

It's a small price to pay for my father's health, she

told herself. *Until I found this job, I was frantic about how I would manage.*

Her call light flashed and, instead of answering it, she phoned Ben. "Who's call is it?" she asked him.

"Holcomb. I'll see what he wants and have it ready when you get here," he said. She thanked him, peeped in the mirror, took a few deep breaths, tidied her little apron and went to the bar.

"He's in the Kennedy room," Ben said and handed her the tray.

With her heart in her mouth and her knees trembling, she knocked on the door and waited. "Come in."

To her surprise, he stood when she entered, walked to meet her, took the tray from her and placed it on the serving table. "I waited all evening for this moment. Let me hold you. That's all. I just need you close to me."

She stood as she was, looking at him as if in a dream world. "What is it? What's the matter?" he asked her.

Recovering her aplomb, she held out her arms to him and knew again the heaven of his caress. Then she stepped away from him. "I asked what's the matter, Jackie?"

She touched his bottom lip with her right index finger. "I still have another hour to work. You may be satisfied with holding me for a minute or two, but that will only whet my appetite," she answered.

His frown slowly dissolved into the smile that she loved. "It wouldn't be enough for me either, and I'd get you into one of our famous clinches. You're right. We'd better keep in between the lines. May I take you home this evening?"

She thought for a minute. "It's not smart, Warren. We risk you losing your membership here. Wait for me on 64th Street east of Fifth."

"I will." He grasped her hand and attempted to smile, but the smile didn't reach his eyes. "I guess the best solution is for me to leave here by ten-thirty, so I won't be tempted to get the better of fate." He plowed his fingers through his hair, punishing his scalp. "I do not want you out there after midnight looking for a taxi."

"I'll be all right, hon. Honest."

"What did you call me?"

"Nothing. I said—look, I'd better get back to my station." But she couldn't move, for his arms were around her and his tongue was dancing at the seam of her lips begging for entrance. She took him in and loved him shamelessly, trembling as desire gripped her.

"I'll pick you up right where we met last night." She turned and left with the picture of his stormy eyes forever sealed in the mirror of her mind. Eyes that said I want you, and you will not escape me. She wondered what her eyes said to him.

When she opened the door to leave Allegory that night, she saw Hornsby's custom-built Cadillac—he was the only club member who drove a Cadillac—parked in front of the building, and she knew he was waiting for her. She whirled around, went to the bar and said to Ben, "Hornsby's parked in front of the door, and I know he plans to harass me. Would you please walk out with me."

He seemed uncertain, though only for a second. "Be

glad to. There's no club rule that says we can't leave here together."

She walked out with Ben and when they reached the corner, he said, "Let's stand here for a few minutes and see what he does." They stood facing each other as if talking, and eventually Hornsby's Cadillac turned onto Fifth Avenue and headed south.

"Thanks, Ben. I owe you one."

"No problem, Jackie."

She walked rapidly toward 64th Street praying that Hornsby hadn't circled the block. Then she remembered that 64th was a one-way going east. Warren stood outside of the car at the passenger door and opened it as she neared him.

"Hi," she said. "Where was Hornsby when you left the building?"

"I didn't see him. What kept you so long?"

She took a deep breath and decided to talk, because both of them had better watch Duff Hornsby. "Hornsby was parked directly in front of the door, and the motor was running, so I walked back inside and asked Ben to walk out with me."

"Did you think Duff would bother you?"

"Why else would I ask Ben to walk out with me? Ben knows the kind of man Hornsby is."

"I see. And you've confided in him. Has Hornsby propositioned you?"

"I don't think you want to continue this line of questioning, Warren."

"So he has. If he touches you, I want to know it."

"I can't promise to tell you, Warren, because I don't want to be responsible for what I know will happen. I keep Ben posted on what goes on, and I no longer answer Hornsby's calls. Ben gives them to Jack. Since Hornsby's the only man there who bothers me, there isn't really anything to get freaked out about. I can handle him. If necessary, my judo should come in handy."

"Judo?"

"Right. It's a great way to keep in shape."

"Your shape doesn't need judo or anything else. It's natural, and it's perfect." Suddenly, laughter rumbled in his chest. "I'd like to be a fly on the wall if you ever flatten him." He stopped laughing. "Did you know Hornsby's married? The man is a philandering jerk and he'd better keep it between the lines, because he's less popular than he thinks."

He turned onto West End Avenue and parked in front of her apartment building. "I'll walk you to the door. When we get there, tell me whether I can see you to your apartment."

She didn't move. "Warren, I want you to walk with me to my apartment, and I want to kiss you good-night, but I'm not ready for anything more. Can you handle that?"

She watched him closely for signs of annoyance. What she saw was a broad smile that lit his face. He leaned over and kissed her on the mouth. "Of course I can handle it. I was afraid you'd send me off without so much as a kiss."

At her apartment door, she handed him her key, he opened the door and walked in and took her into his arms. He folded her into the warmth of his body, hugging her tightly, and then he gazed down into her face. She rimmed her lips with the tip of her tongue, parted them and he plunged into her. Immediately, demon desire raced through her, sending her blood to her loins and a throbbing heat to her vagina. As if he knew the signs, knew when passion held her in its grip uninhibited, he broke the kiss, held her to him and stroked her back.

"We're going to have to do something about this, sweetheart, and soon. You test me to my limit."

She kissed his neck and the side of his mouth, but neither confirmed nor denied his statement. They would make love one day. She wasn't stupid enough not to see that he was the most beautiful thing that ever happened to her.

He gazed, unsmiling, into her eyes as if to impress upon her the truth and importance of his words. "Don't you have an answer to that? Baby, am I hanging out here all by myself? I'm in deep here. You won't tell me you care for me, even though you behave as if you do. I know how you respond when I touch you, but I need more than that."

The back of her hand caressed his cheek. Up and down she stroked, almost absentmindedly. "If you only knew! There's never been anyone like you. Not for me. Never. The first time you had me in your arms, I realized that I didn't know myself. Do I care for you?" She whispered the question. "Oh, yes."

He closed his eyes, raised his face toward the ceiling and took a deep breath. Then, his arms tightened around her, and the feel of his lips brushing over hers electrified her. However, he didn't communicate passion, but tenderness, and she knew that what she felt for Warren Holcomb exceeded caring. How had she allowed herself to fall for a man who didn't know who she was?

His smile seemed to her something of a struggle, a fight between what he felt and what he wanted her to see. "I'd better get out of here," he said. And as if he remembered something important, his long, lean fingers rubbed his chin. "When Allegory's board meets two weeks from now, I'll try to get some changes introduced. The club can afford to send you and Lee Ann, the second cook, home in a taxi. She's already had several unpleasant incidents on her way home. You're at risk, too. Considering the club's annual budget, that wouldn't amount to peanuts, and I'll know you're home safe when I'm not at the club. That ought to take care of Hornsby's tricks, too."

She kissed his cheek. "Scat."

"I hate to leave you. Woman, you move me." He teased her with a quick kiss on her mouth, but opened the door and left.

I've fallen for her, and I have this awful feeling that I don't know who she is. Yet, my mind tells me that whatever else she is can't be bad, so I have to stay with this and let it run its course.

He drove into his garage and, as usual, entered his house through the kitchen. He walked up the stairs thinking that the home of which he was so proud suddenly seemed so empty. In his bedroom, he looked at the king-size sleigh bed that was now so uninviting and walked over to the window that gave him a view of lower Manhattan and of the East River that separated him from it. Winter wind rippled the river, and its ghostly dance in the moonlight gave him the feeling that no one but he existed. The wind whistled around the window, and on the street he could see the trees, bare and silent, bend with the will of the mighty force.

"What a night to be alone!"

Warren went into his den, flipped on the television and read the notice of a winter storm warning. "Serves me right," he said with a half laugh. "I don't even have bread in the house. I'd better get up early and head for the supermarket."

By seven-thirty the next morning, he had filled his shopping cart with grocery essentials along with batteries, bulbs and candles. He trudged home into the wind and through at least a foot of snow, and he had a feeling that Jackie might be in trouble. He hadn't seen a market near the building in which she lived. After musing over it, he consoled himself with the thought that, if she needed help, he could take the subway. He waited until nine o'clock before calling her.

"Hello."

"Hello, sweetheart. Have you looked outside?"

"Hi, hon. Huh? Warren?"

"I woke you up again, and I'm not sorry, because I love hearing your sleepy voice. Look out of your window."

"Okay. What do you want me to see?"

"What do I… Are you awake?"

"Just about—"

"Move over." That should get her attention.

"All ri… *Move Over?* Where *are* you?"

"Me? I'm home."

"You tricked me. Hi."

"We've got a foot of snow out there, and maybe more. How are you fixed for groceries?"

"Gee. I guess I'm pretty bare except for coffee, some eggs and a few onions. I didn't go to the market last weekend."

"Tell me what you need, and I'll bring it over."

"But I thought you said you live in Brooklyn. You can't drive through that much snow." Her voice had strengthened, and he assumed that she was sitting up or she was out of the bed.

"I'll take the subway. What do you need? Apart from me, that is."

"Do you mind if I check and call you back?"

Hmm. So she didn't pick up on his quip. "Fine, but try not to wait too long. The snow is really coming down out there."

"I won't, and you're sweet to offer. Bye for now."

Jacqueline jumped out of bed, opened the blinds and gazed out at the falling snow, white and thick for as far as she could see, and that wasn't any distance to speak of. She couldn't see the street, but she didn't doubt Warren's assessment. One more reason why she was glad she didn't own a car. She threw on a robe, stuck her feet into a pair of mules and went to the kitchen.

Grits, oatmeal, seven eggs, four onions, three potatoes and half a head of romaine lettuce. She knew she had nearly a full can of Columbia coffee somewhere. She found it in the back of the refrigerator.

Now what? She didn't want Warren to travel such a distance in that weather to bring her the few things she needed, but if she didn't let him do it, she knew he would be upset with her. She looked at her watch. *I'd better call him.*

"Hi," she said when he answered. "Warren, I don't want you to brave this weather in order to bring me just a couple of things. I appreciate your thoughtfulness and your kindness, but it's not necessary."

She listened to the silence that came to her through the wire. "Are you still there?"

"Of course, I'm still here. Did you think you said something that would make me hang up?"

"Warren, please don't be annoyed. I know you offered because you care about me, but I'm refusing for the same reason."

"The subway station is a block and a half from where I live and a block and a quarter from where you live. What do you need? Dammit, if I can't make love to you, at least I can take care of you."

She laughed. She couldn't help it. "You mean if you make love with me, you won't have to take care of me? Does that make sense?"

"That's not what I said. I'm coming over, so you'd better tell me what you need."

She gave him a short list and added, "Since you

insist. By the time you get here you'll be starved, so bring the kind of pizza you like." She thought for a second. "And Warren, you're so…so sweet. Thanks." She built a fire in the fireplace that was the centerpiece of her living room, opened a bag of chestnuts and placed them beside the fireplace where she would later roast them. She also turned on her music system and selected a Mozart concerto to play quietly in the background.

I wish I had the ingredients of a real meal. Nothing's more romantic than the feeling that you're snowbound with a man you…. Oops! I'm not going there, she said to herself. After a shower, she dressed in a pair of brown suede pants and a cowl-neck burnt-orange cashmere sweater.

Her gaze fell on a copy of *African American Woman,* and she collected all that she could find, put them in a bedroom closet, closed the door and looked around for any other things that would implicate her as Dr. Jacqueline Ann Parkton. She phoned the front door station, learned that the morning doorman hadn't been able to get to work and relaxed. The handyman was at the door, and he didn't speak English. But one day, her charade would catch up with her, and she hoped the cost wouldn't be too high.

Her doorbell rang. Good heavens, she hadn't combed out her hair. She raced to the bedroom, grabbed a comb and corrected the error. Halfway to the door, she looked down at her pink mules, kicked them off and threw them in the bedroom. Better not to have on any shoes than to greet him in those.

"Hi," she said.

He leaned down and kissed her. "Hi. Why are you out of breath?"

She looked up at him from beneath lowered eyelids, "'Cause I ran to open the door."

His whistle split the air. "Take it easy. A man's nerves will stand only so much. Where can I put this?"

"Right here on the floor, so I can hang up your coat. Didn't you wear anything on your head?" He pulled a hunter's cap out of his coat pocket and showed it to her. She walked with him to the kitchen, and he put two large shopping bags on the counter. "Here's lunch. You said bring the kind of pizza I liked, but I didn't feel like pizza. I brought veal parmigiana with buttered noodles and spinach, pecan cookies and beer instead."

"Wonderful. I'll warm it up. Let's roast some chestnuts while we're waiting. Uh, did you say beer?" She tried not to frown, but didn't manage it.

"Yeah. This is the perfect day for it. And a real fireplace? Let's put the food on a tray and eat in front of the fire. I've always loved doing that."

While the food warmed, and the roasting chestnuts perfumed the apartment, they put the groceries away, and she couldn't help thinking how much Warren Holcomb suited her temperament. Everything about him pleased her.

He sat beside her on a big hassock in front of the fire, and she cracked the nuts and fed them to him. "Be careful, Jackie. I spoil easily."

She peeled one for herself. "Not a chance," she told

him. "If you made it here through the snow to spoil me, I can at least make you feel at home."

She went to the kitchen, prepared the trays, and he took them from her and carried them to the living room. "Do you like the music?" she asked him.

"Absolutely! So you like Mozart," he said as they sat down to eat.

"He's my favorite composer."

He reached for her hand and held it as he said grace. "Mine, too, though I also like other composers and other kinds of music."

"Me, too," she said, then added, "This food is delicious."

"Next weekend you have four or five days off, don't you?" he asked her. "I want us to spend as much as possible of that time together."

"Alright, but my sister Vanna is coming to visit with me. We don't see each other often, and it will give us a chance to visit our father together."

"I'll be good. I won't say a word about how you drive me nuts when you kiss me. Honest." He crossed his heart.

"Okay, but there's one thing. I don't want Vanna to know I work as a cocktail waitress. She's so straitlaced, if you get what I mean."

"I won't say a word about that, either. I'll tell her we met at church."

"For goodness' sake, don't say that. She'll expect the three of us to go to church together Sunday morning."

"Fine with me. I was raised in church."

"Do you still go?" she asked him.

"Once in a while. Do you?"

She couldn't wipe the grin from her face. "Once in a while."

He got up, put another log on the fire and then looked out of the living room window. "This snow hasn't slacked up one bit. What will you do if I get snowed in here with you?"

"I'll cook you a nice dinner, put you to sleep in here on the sofa and give you a nice healthful breakfast tomorrow morning."

His face bore the expression of a mischievous puppy who'd been caught chewing the carpet. "You wound me. Don't I deserve better than the couch?"

"Let's pray that it stops snowing soon, and I won't have to answer that."

His face molded itself into a frown. "So you'd make me sleep on the couch?" he said and suddenly smiled. "Do you walk in your sleep?"

"Not to my knowledge, but my psyche hasn't been subjected to that kind of temptation, so who knows?"

"Hmm. So if I turned on the heat before telling you good night, I might luck out?"

She didn't respond but took the dishes to the kitchen, glanced over her shoulder and saw that he'd followed her. "I don't believe in letting a woman tire herself out doing things for me, and especially not you." He rinsed the dishes, put them in the dishwasher and disposed of the bags in which he'd brought the groceries. "This has been wonderful, Jackie. I like you in this environment. Give me a kiss. I want to get home before dark."

She told herself to be circumspect with the kiss, but the second his arms went around her and his tongue entered her mouth, she felt the pulsations in her vagina and moved into him, moaning her need for relief.

He gripped her in a fierce hug. "When you feel that you're ready to consummate what we feel for each other, will you give me a sign?"

"Yes."

"I'll call you when I get home. Don't attempt to go to work tonight. You won't be expected to brave this weather and those streets in order to get there. Anyhow, don't risk it." His kiss, hard and brief, sent tremors through her. "We'll talk later."

Jacqueline stood at the living room window hoping for a glimpse of him as he trudged through the snow, but she could only imagine that his was the figure she saw from her window on the twenty-first floor. She put another log on the fire, sat on the hassock and gazed at the dancing flames.

Would she give him a sign? He had never pressured her or made her feel as if she led him to expect more than she gave, although she hadn't once used much self-control when they kissed. He had probably figured out that she was more conservative than her waitress outfit suggested, but she wouldn't blame him if he decided that she had misled him. Unfortunately, she couldn't ask Vanna for advice, because she didn't want her to know that she had to work a second job in order to give their

father the best care. If Vanna didn't have financial
problems, she could have called on her sister for help.
She wouldn't have needed the waitress job.

"Am I going to meet your sister?" Warren asked Jackie
during one of their conversations the following week.

"Vanna's planning to spend as much time as she can
with Dad, and I should be with her, Warren. I want you
to meet her, so would you settle for taking us to dinner
Sunday night?"

"If that's all I can get, I'll take it. Make a note that
I'll call for the two of you at about six o'clock Sunday
evening, and we'll grab a cocktail and then eat at a nice
restaurant. If I only get one chance, I'm damned well
going to impress her."

She didn't laugh, because she knew he was serious.
"Thank you, Warren. Will you spend Christmas with
your mother and sister?"

"I expect I will. My nieces and nephew make Christmas very special. The problem is, I don't like the idea
of not spending it with you. I would invite you to go with
me, but that would mean you couldn't be with your
father at Christmas, and I'm sure he'd feel abandoned.
I don't think I can organize Christmas the way I managed
Thanksgiving, because there's so much more going on."

"I know. Maybe if I spend Christmas Eve with Papa
and… No, that won't work. He'll still be alone Christmas Day."

"When is your sister coming?"

"She'll get in shortly after noon Friday."

"If you need a chauffeur while she's here, I'm at your disposal. I imagine taxis between New York and Riverdale can be very expensive. I'll see you tomorrow night, love. Good night."

He knew she wouldn't ask him for help no matter how badly she needed it, so the next morning, he called her. "Wake up, sleepyhead," he said when she answered his call that Friday morning.

"Hi. I've been awake for at least half an hour. How are you this morning?"

"Fine." And that was true, for hearing her voice the first thing in the morning was fuel for his engine. "Do you have a driver's license?" She assured him that she did. "Then, I'll leave my car and car keys with your doorman this morning, and you may keep it until your sister leaves."

"You're kidding. You'd do that?"

"Of course. On the other hand, with parking such a problem, it would be better if I gave you the car and a driver. What time do you want him to be at your place?"

"Warren, I don't know what to say."

"Just tell me what time. His name is Allen. Here's his cell phone number—555-1969. I want you to call him whenever you need him, even if you're only going four blocks. When you have definite travel plans, give them to him. He works at Harlem Clubs, and he is very reliable. He's a close friend."

"How will you manage without your car?"

"Easily. If I need one, I'll get a rental or, I'll either take a taxi or public transportation. I wasn't born in a Lincoln Town Car."

"But Warren—"

"I want you to enjoy your sister's visit. There are no strings attached to this, Jackie."

"I know that. Subterfuge is not your style." He could see that he'd stunned her when she stammered," I… uh…I-I appreciate this more than you can imagine. I'll need to leave here at about eleven-fifteen."

"He'll be there." After telling her goodbye, he phoned Allen, gave him instructions and added, "I could hire a professional chauffeur, but I can't afford any slipups. Jackie Parks is important to me, Allen, and I know I can entrust her to you."

"You know I'll do my best, Warren."

He went to the kitchen, made coffee, toasted a bagel, buttered it and sat down to eat, but immediately his cell phone rang, and the number for his Washington, D.C. office flashed on the window. He put the bagel down.

"Holcomb."

"This is Patricia Ames. I think we ought to change booking agencies, Mr. Holcomb."

"What's the problem?" He listened while his hotel manager outlined her grievances against Kira, the agency that booked events held at the hotel. "I agree that we need a change, and I'll be down there this afternoon."

He phoned Jackie. "I've just learned that I have a problem at my Washington, D.C. hotel, so I'll be leaving for Washington in a few minutes. Wish me luck?"

"Indeed, I do. You'll be in my thoughts every minute. When are you coming back?"

A smile crawled over his face. Did she know that her question implied possessiveness? He liked it, for it told him that she knew—consciously or not—that she had a right to question him. "Tonight, if I get everything straightened out. What time may I call you?"

"After nine. We should be back from the clinic by then. Take good care of yourself."

"Does that matter to you?"

"Surely you know that you matter to me, Warren."

"All right. Give your sister my regards. I'll call you, but if you have a problem, you know my cell phone number. Call you tonight."

He hung up, picked up the cold bagel and lukewarm coffee and then pushed them aside. He was falling in love with Jackie Parks.

"You look great in that red," Vanna told Jacqueline of the short, sequined spaghetti-strap dinner dress. If that doesn't knock his eyes out, he hasn't got any."

"You look good in that antique gold, too, and it amazes me that you can have such a perfect figure after giving birth to three children."

"I eat my veggies. Besides, I get plenty of exercise. Three kids will run you ragged. Now let's see. You're Jackie Parks, and I'm to keep my mouth shut about your work. He sure is trusting, if he never asked you about it. Still, if a man put that custom Town Car at my disposal, and he didn't want to pick me to pieces, I wouldn't press my luck. What about the doorman?"

"I gave him a big tip."

Vanna shrugged. "You'd better be careful. More than one person can tip."

"Mr. Holcomb to see you, Ms. Parks," the doorman said, when Jackie answered the buzzer.

She wasn't a nervous person, so why was she wringing her hands and wearing out the carpet? She sat down, but got up immediately, headed for the door and stopped. What was wrong with her?

"I wish you could see yourself," Vanna said. "My Lord, he must be the Duke of Padooka." She laughed until Jackie slapped her on her back.

"It wasn't that funny."

The doorbell rang, and, as if minutes earlier she hadn't had a fit of nerves, she strolled casually to open it. "Hi."

"Hmm. All this for me. You are lovely."

"And you look wonderful," she said, taking in his navy blue suit, white shirt and red-and-blue striped tie. "Come meet Vanna."

"Don't I get a kiss?"

"Believe me I'd love to do that, but this lipstick will probably come off."

"Really? Well, when I bring you home, it won't matter," he said with a wicked twinkle in his eyes.

She took his hand and walked into the living room where Vanna sat in a big over-stuffed chair, relaxed, with her knees crossed and her right foot swinging. "Vanna, this is Warren Holcomb."

Vanna stood. "I don't know what I was expecting, but it wasn't this. I'm happy to meet you, Warren, and thank you so much for making life easy while I'm here."

He stared at her. "Are you suggesting that I'm a disappointment? I was expecting a matronly mother of three, and what do I get but a siren who looks like a college sophomore."

Vanna raised an eyebrow. "I hope you're referring to my age, honey, because some of those sophomores are all butt, bust and pimples with empty spaces between their ears."

His head snapped around and he stared at Jackie as if to say, what do I do now? Jackie didn't bother to suppress a grin. "You're on your own."

"I, uh…think we'd better get started," he said, helped them into their coats and held out his hand for the key. He locked the door, gave the key to Jackie and, with an arm around each of them made his way to the elevator. "How'd you get on with Allen?" he asked.

"When a man is intelligent, good-looking, neat, has good manners and clean fingernails and doesn't say 'ain't,' what woman wouldn't get along with him?" Vanna said. "Allen is a pleasure to be around."

"I'm glad to hear it," Warren said. "I've always had high regard for him. By the way, Vanna, how did Allen get along with *you?*"

As if she didn't know he was needling her, she said, "Evidently fine. He wants to see me again, but after I told him I live in Florida, I think he changed his mind."

Warren seemed to have warmed up to the idea. "Not Allen. If Allen wants to see you again, trust me, he'll manage it. I've known him since I was eight. He's got the tenacity of a bull."

"Really? I hope to see some evidence of it."

"Don't worry. I expect you will." They reached the car and, although Allen got out, Warren opened the front door. "Vanna, suppose you sit up here with Allen, and Jackie and I will sit in the back."

"Perfect," Vanna said, "provided it's all right with Allen."

"I couldn't be happier," he said, as he leaned across her and fastened her seat belt.

At 50th Street on Madison Avenue, Allen parked, gave the car keys to the doorman of the New York Palace Hotel and extended his hand to Vanna, who slid out of the car and into his open arms.

"Oops," she said. "Thanks for breaking my fall."

Jackie accepted the hand that Warren extended to her, got out of the car and whispered, "I had forgotten that my sister has the makings of a femme fatale."

His arm went around her as they walked into the famed Palace Bar. "I don't think Allen is complaining."

Inside, the men looked around for a booth or a table. "Do you see what I see?" Vanna asked Jackie. "In that dark gray suit and yellow tie, Allen Lewis is a number ten, one sweet looking brother. That man's working on my insides."

"Then work on his," Jackie said from the corner of her mouth as Warren signaled a waiter and walked back to them.

"What time are you leaving on Tuesday?" Allen asked Vanna, when they were seated.

He leaned back, comfortable with himself and his surroundings.

This man is no chauffeur, and Warren doesn't treat him as if he is, Jackie said to herself, but she couldn't ask what he did, because he could then ask her the same.

"I'm getting a four o'clock plane," Vanna said, replying to Allen's question.

"We can leave the car here and walk to the restaurant," Warren said, once they'd finished their cocktails. "We're dining at the Four Seasons."

They walked up to 57th Street and over to Park Avenue laughing and joking as if it were spring rather than a cold thirty degrees, and Jackie wondered at Allen's arm around Vanna's waist and the rapport that they seemed to have had all their lives.

"Something tells me you have a magic wand, Vanna," Warren said during dinner. "I've never known Allen to have as much fun as he seems to be having tonight."

"Just promise me you won't ask him to work on weekends," she said, "then maybe he can visit me once in a while."

"He's a workaholic, but I suspect that's about to be history." He looked at Jackie. "I'll bet Vanna doesn't keep a man guessing."

Jackie sipped her Pinot Grigio. "Do you know someone who does? Besides, with three or four hundred miles separating them, a person has to make hay while the sun's shining. From where I sit, Allen's no slouch." A sheepish smile floated over his face, and she wanted to hug him, to hold him in her body and love him. As he raised his glass to his lips, he looked directly at her, and when he nearly spilled the wine, she knew that her feelings lay naked on her face.

Allen's voice ended the sensual moment. "Jackie, I'm not here," Allen quipped. "So would you please let me know what they say about me?"

After they finished one of the best meals she remembered eating, she was surprised when Warren opened the front passenger door for her, allowing Allen and Vanna to take the backseat. "Let's give them a break," he whispered as he assisted her into the car. It did not surprise her when Allen accompanied them to Jackie's apartment, holding Vanna's hand as they walked.

Warren held out his hand for the key, opened the door and the four of them walked in. He continued with her to the living room. "If I get smeared with lipstick, I don't care. It's been days since I had you in my arms."

She brushed his cheek with the back of her hand. "Excuse me a minute." In the powder room, she removed the lipstick and rinsed her mouth. "Now where were we?" she asked him when she returned.

"You were making me wait." His arms went around her, and for a second, he stared down into her face. "I'm almost out of my mind wanting you." She pulled his tongue into her mouth as his hands roamed over her bare shoulders and back, igniting her flesh, possessing her as surely as if he had been buried inside of her. She tried to grip his buttocks, but his heavy winter coat foiled her effort, and in her frustration, she moved against him. But at once, he stepped back, his face alight with a tender expression. "Our time will come, sweetheart, but we don't want to teach them bad habits."

They stood gazing into each other's eyes and holding each other as tightly as their clothing permitted. She heard Vanna walk into the living room, but her mind was not on her sister.

"You're precious to me," he said and then flicked his tongue across the seam of her lips. She opened to him, sucked his tongue into her mouth, giving him what he wanted and receiving what she needed. "I'll call you in the morning, sweetheart." He released her and, still holding Jackie tight in his arms, he spoke to Vanna, letting both women know that he knew she had joined them.

"Where's Allen?"

"He's waiting for you in the car."

"I hope you gave him a proper good-night."

She winked at him. "Opportunity knocks but once. Thank you for introducing us and for your kindness to me, Warren. You're a gracious man, and I'm glad my sister knows you."

He hugged her. "Be careful with Allen. He has more fine traits than any man I know, but if you're not absolutely straight with him, he'll walk in a second." He wrapped Jackie in his arms, kissed her and left.

Vanna sat down, kicked off her shoes and flung her arms wide. "Honey, Allen is a man and a half. Thank God I'm staying with you and not in a hotel, or he'd have been inside of me right now. I don't think I should do that with him so soon. He's old-fashioned. Girl, in my whole life, I've never been heated up that fast and that thoroughly. He's taking me to dinner tomorrow night and taking me to the airport in his car. He said he's returning Warren's car to him tonight."

She leaned forward, seemingly more subdued. "Now I can tell you. As soon as I saw him standing with you in the airport, I was a goner, and I knew I had his eye, but I didn't want to embarrass you, so I tried to keep it between the lines. We both did. I'm going for it, Jackie, and you straighten things out with Warren. He loves you, so you let him know who you are. Don't wait till it's too late."

If she only knew, Jackie thought.

Chapter 5

Duff Hornsby was becoming reckless in his efforts to get Jackie into bed, and she avoided him as much as she could.

"My advice, get a small recorder and turn it on whenever you're around him," Ben said. "The only problem with that is that if you used it as evidence, no other club member would trust you. Look, if you have to go into his private lounge, just keep one hand on the doorknob."

She couldn't do that and serve drinks at the same time, but she didn't remind Ben of that fact. The next evening, she nearly dropped a tray of drinks when she met Warren as she entered the main lounge.

"When did you get back?" she asked him, not bothering to cover her irritation at seeing him unexpectedly when she thought he was in Hawaii.

"Ten minutes ago. I came here straight from the airport."

Moderately chastised, she managed a smile. "What room are you in?"

"I'm in the Reagan lounge. I asked for the Lincoln, but Hornsby's there, so watch your step."

She tossed her head and nearly sloshed the drinks. "It is my creed to watch my step with *every* member of this club."

Both of his eyebrows shot up, and then he narrowed his eyes. She waited for his response, but he only stared at her for a few seconds and walked past her. When he didn't call for service that night, she concluded that her comment had angered him. Too bad; he could have called her on her cellular phone and let her know he was in town instead of nearly causing her to make a fool of herself.

At midnight, she changed into her street clothes and hurried out of her dressing room. Hornsby attempted to waylay her, but she brushed past him, deliberately stepping on his foot. She stepped out of the side door, and a strong hand grasped her hand.

"Wh—Warren!"

He didn't utter a sound but, walking as swiftly as his long legs would carry him, he led her to his car, opened the door, put her into the car and sped down Fifth Avenue.

"Are you kidnapping me?" He turned onto 47th Street and drove over to Tenth Avenue without speaking to her. "I asked, are you kidnapping me?" she repeated, feeling as if she would explode.

"Definitely not," he said, as he turned onto 59th Street, eased the car to the curb and stopped beside a fire hydrant. "You can get out anytime you like, but before you do, I want to know why you smart-mouthed me when I warned you about Hornsby. So you watch your step with every member of Allegory including me, do you?"

"I didn't say *you*."

"Oh, yes you did, because you emphasized *every* member."

"And why shouldn't I? You spent three days out of the town and how many times did you call me? Once. And then, you don't care if you surprise me at work, almost making me drop that tray, when I thought you were still in Hawaii. What were you doing, trying to see how I behave when you're not around?"

"So my angelic sweetheart has a sharp tongue. What else don't I know about you?"

She turned fully to face him. "You don't answer my questions, so I won't answer yours. For all I know, you've got a harem in Hawaii."

"A *what?*"

She didn't want to fight with him; she wanted his arms around her, wanted to feel his strength and warm herself in his heat. She knew she was wrong, but she refused to give in. "You heard me. And you stop bullying me."

"Bullying you? I'm not doing any such thing. What's wrong with you?" He threw up his hands as if in defeat. "Oh hell, baby. Come here to me."

He brought her to him fiercely, his grip strong. It was

what she wanted and needed, and her arms went around him as his mouth came down hard and possessively on hers. She parted her lips and took him in. Heat spiraled through her, and she tried to get closer to him. Desire pulsed through her body and, unconsciously, she crossed her knees in an attempt to create the friction that she needed for relief. He pulled his tongue out of her mouth and kissed her eyes, ears, her cheeks, the tip of her nose and the side of her neck and, as if he, too, could not stand the frustration he flung himself back against the seat and stretched out his arms.

"Will you go away with me this weekend? We can't go on like this."

"I need to be with you, Warren, but my dad isn't getting any better, and I can't leave him without a visitor for an entire weekend. The nurses tell me that he's despondent."

He put the car in Drive and continued toward West End Avenue. "Thank you for telling me you need me. I'll see what I can work out. I'm not going to your door with you tonight, because I know that if I get that far, I'll go farther, and I need a helluva lot more than a couple of hours with you. Do you understand that?"

She nodded. Maybe Vanna would want to come up to see Allen for a weekend, but... No, she couldn't depend on that. Vanna would have to find someone to take care of the children. Sometimes life was really rough. "I'll try to think of something, too." She leaned over and kissed his mouth. "Sorry I was mean, but I felt neglected, and that's a new feeling for me."

"I left my cell phone recharger at home, and a pay

phone is difficult to find these days. Calling from my office was out of the question, because that secretary is not discrete, and she puts the phone on intercom so she doesn't have to lift the receiver. That, plus the time difference, made it difficult to call you. I'm sorry. Kiss me?"

She kissed him again gently and without passion. He then got out of the car and walked with her to the front door of the building. "I'll call you when I get home."

She didn't feel much like going into that apartment alone, but what choice did she have. After preparing for bed, she sat down at her computer and began listing the content of the March issue of *African American Woman*. She usually did it according to sections and gave the lists to the layout editor. But she realized that she was doing the listing, the writing assignments and the layout sketch.

"I must be losing it. Rosie will pout for a month if I continue doing the layout. It's after one o'clock. Why am I sitting up here working when I have to get up at seven-thirty?"

The telephone rang, and then she knew why as she raced to answer it. "Hello."

"You're still up." It wasn't a question.

She nearly told him what she'd been doing, but quickly recovered her wits. "I knew you were going to call me, so I waited up for it."

"Can you save the weekend for us? I know you have to visit your father, but maybe you and I can spend a few hours together in the afternoons before you go to work."

She couldn't afford it financially, but they needed

time together. "Maybe I'll take next Monday night off. It's a slow night anyway."

"If you're thinking about us, wait until I make some plans. Weekend after this one coming is your four-day break."

"We could eat a hot dog or something during a Saturday or Sunday matinee, or maybe see a morning movie. I've never done that," she said.

"Why don't we eat breakfast and maybe lunch, and I'll drive you up to see your father. I won't visit him, though, because he'll want to know my intentions or something like that, and what I feel right now is definitely not honorable."

She couldn't help laughing, and she let it roll out of her. After some minutes, she sobered up. "Why Mr. Holcomb, You wound me. What would your father say to that?"

"If he were still here, he'd probably say I deserve a medal. Just kidding, but knowing my mother, he'd probably have grounds for sympathizing with me."

"You poor baby. I promise to make it up to you."

"You swear it?"

"I wouldn't think you'd need that kind of affirmation. You ought to be certain of it."

"All I'm certain of right now is that I'm on my way out of my skin as surely as a crustacean sheds its shell, and sweetheart, I definitely plan to give you a chance to make amends. A lot of amends."

"Oh, dear. I think I'd better turn in."

"Chicken. Till tomorrow. Good night, love."

"Good night, darling." It was the first time she'd

called him darling, and it slid out of her as easily as melting ice cream off a cone. *I'd better be careful,* she thought. *He cares a lot, but when he finds out that I haven't been honest with him, he may walk.* She put the papers in her briefcase, turned out the desk light and got into bed, but hours later, sleep still eluded her. "I'm head over heels," she said out loud, and a tear rolled down the side of her face to her pillow.

She didn't consider revealing her other life to him, for the longer she knew him and the better she understood him, she knew that, at best, he would be torn between his feelings for her and the oath he took when joining the club. At the worst, he would feel obligated to tell Allegory's board of trustees that its cocktail waitress was a reporter, perhaps even a spy.

He couldn't remember ever having watched a movie or any part of one before noon, but life since Jackie had been a series of new experiences. Shortly after one, they left the theater holding hands and chatting about *The Philadelphia Story* and leisure-class decadence in the early part of the twentieth century.

"Do you think all those rich women wore mink-trimmed robes and matching mules at home, used long, ivory cigarette holders and played lawn tennis in the afternoon?" she asked him.

"Good question. Funny thing is the movies almost never showed them reading a book. Those people must have been bored and boring. Let's stop in here and get a sandwich or something."

He hadn't planned to wait while she visited her father, but he couldn't make himself leave her there to find transportation home. He found a parking space, decided not to wait in the car and went inside the clinic to sit in the waiting room. A quick appraisal told him that Jackie was spending a lot of money on her father's care.

"I'm not going to find out how much she makes monthly, he told himself. *It wouldn't be ethical, but her father's care must be costing her at least ten grand a month.* After half an hour, he went back to his car; he'd as soon she didn't know he'd been in that clinic.

She walked out of the facility, looked around—he suspected for a taxi—and he got out of his car and hurried to her. "How is he?"

A smile swept over her face, feeble and fleeting. "You waited for me. I won't pretend that you shouldn't have, because I…I appreciate it. He's fair. I wish he'd stop pretending that he's as good as ever. It breaks my heart."

He fastened her seat belt, leaned over and kissed her. "I'm glad I waited, because I can see you're in the dumps."

"I'll pull out of it."

She did seem perkier at work that evening and the next one, but on Monday evening, she didn't come to work, and she hadn't answered her cell phone or her home phone all day. Finally, when he called her at home around eight-thirty that evening, she answered.

"Jackie, I've been trying to reach you all day. Are you all right, and how is your father?"

"I'm not all right. The doctor said my father won't live another three months if he doesn't have that operation."

"Do you have the funds you need?"

"Yes. I've been saving for it for the last eighteen months. It's not the money. Oh, Warren, how can he do this? He won't listen to me, and he won't listen to Vanna. I don't know what to do. He refuses to have the angioplasty operation."

He heard the tears in her voice. "I'll be there in half an hour."

A sense of helplessness pervaded him, and it was a feeling with which he hadn't had much experience. He couldn't go to that clinic and shake the old man, as much as he'd like to. How could he help her? He didn't know Vanna's circumstances. Did he dare call her and suggest that she come to give Jackie support? He parked in a public garage on Broadway, three blocks from the building in which Jackie lived and walked the remainder of the way. When he got there, he didn't wait to get the doorman's attention but went straight to the elevator.

"Who is it?" she asked, and he didn't like the sound that greeted him.

"Warren."

The door opened, he picked her up, kicked the door shut, carried her to the living room and sat down with her in his lap. "Don't cry, sweetheart. I'm here for you. If you need anything that I have, it's yours. Just please don't cry." He held her close and rocked her. "Honey, don't. I can't stand it."

He picked her up, found his way to the kitchen and sat her on the counter. The first cabinet door that he opened yielded a glass, and he ran the cold water and gave her a drink. He looked into her reddened eyes, and the hopelessness in them gave him a sinking feeling. That man would hear from him. Courage was to be admired, but not a selfishness emanating from a fear of surgery.

"What is your father's name?"

"Clyde Parkton. Why?"

"No reason, other than to get you to focus on something. Put your head on my shoulder." She did, and held on to him with her right arm across his chest. "Too bad I don't sing," he said, "or I'd croon you to sleep." A smile flickered across her face, and she snuggled closer to him.

"Are you glad I'm here?"

"Yes. You'll never know *how* glad."

"I think Allen has fallen head over heals in love with Vanna. Her name slips into practically every sentence he utters. Apparently, she reciprocates. Looks as if he's way ahead of me."

"She fell for him on sight."

He rubbed his chin and wondered if Allen knew that. "Too bad that wasn't my luck."

"Quit complaining. You've had luck enough."

He hugged her closer, enjoying her softness and the way she gave herself completely over to his care. "Careful, Jackie. I never want to be guilty of taking advantage of a woman when she's vulnerable. Right now, you're like a little kitten, and I... You're so soft and sweet and lovable." He was about to set her away from him, putting a distance between himself and the temptation that fueled his already flaming desire, when she reached up and grasped his nape inviting him to kiss her.

"Sweetheart, I'm already simmering and have been for days. We don't want to pour gasoline on this fire."

"Kiss me," she whispered.

"You don't know what you're asking."

"Yes, I do. Warren, I need you."

Shudders shot through him as he gazed into her trusting eyes. "I want so much for us," he murmured, and as her fingers found their way into his shirt and stroked his naked chest, her lips moved toward his slowly like a marksman sighting his target. His blood pooled in his loins and his grip on her tightened.

"Are you sure? I've wanted you so long and so badly that I…"

Her hand crawled over his chest almost but not quite touching his flat nipple. And then, he was hard and hurting.

"Baby!" His mouth came down on hers, and he plunged his tongue between her parted lips. The way she sucked him into her, greedily as if she were starving for him, as if she couldn't get enough of him. He sampled every crevice of her mouth, her low and sexy moans exciting him, driving him on. He thought he would die from the pure sweetness of it. Her hand was on his, moving it, and he let her direct it to that precious globe, soft and perfect for his big hand.

"Kiss me," she said. "Right there. I want to feel your mouth on me."

Something broke loose in him. He yanked her sweater over her head, unfastened and pulled off her bra, and when he closed his lips over her nipple, she jumped as if he'd startled her, and cried out.

"Tell me you like it."

"Yes. Yes." Her hand caressed his head, and when he moved to the other nipple, she crossed her knees and tried to rub her thighs together. He suckled one nipple while he pinched and rubbed the other one, but as hot as he was he couldn't do that much longer. He stopped and gazed down at her.

"I want you, Jackie." He tore the words out of himself, punishing his scalp with the pads of his fingers as he did so. "I'm on fire for you, and I need to know that you want me, that you want us to make love."

"Take me down there to my bedroom," she whispered.

Shivering with anticipation, he stood, holding her as if he feared he might drop her and headed to the place where he would know her at last. He threw back the bed-spread and blanket, exposing satiny sheets, but he didn't let his mind dwell on that. When she unzipped her skirt and stepped out of it, he gasped at the feminine beauty his eyes beheld, and struggled to breathe as she pulled down the garter belt and stockings, leaving only a tiny red bikini to shield her treasure from his eyes. As his gaze seared her, she covered her breasts with her arms.

"No. No. Let me see you. You're so beautiful, I want to memorize every inch of you."

She opened her arms and, within a minute he'd stripped himself and stood looking down at her, his breath coming in short pants. Still gazing at her, he rested one knee on the edge of the bed and, half drunk with desire, she rolled closer, tested his flat belly with the palm of her hand and let her hand slide down until it rested on the bulge that filled his briefs. He jerked and grabbed her wrist, but she stroked him with her other hand, and when his moans filled the room she stripped away his underwear, grasped his buttocks and kissed the tip of his penis.

"Yes," he shouted when she took him between her lips and loved him. "No more," he cried out. "No more," and jerked away from her.

He crawled into the bed and wrapped her in his arms. "Did I do something wrong?" she asked.

"No. It was…so…so sweet and loving that I could hardly bear it." He loomed over her, so big and so masculine. His lips made her throat, cheeks and ears tingle, and when she thought she would never get his tongue, he said, "Kiss me," and she parted her lips and sucked his tongue into her mouth. His fingers teased her breasts until she began to rock beneath him.

"Why are you making me wait?' she asked him in a voice that she didn't recognize as her own.

"We have all night, love, so let's not rush it. It'll sweep us up by its own power."

She didn't know what he meant, but she trusted him. He stopped kissing her and his lips brushed her throat, her chest and she thought she'd go mad waiting for his warm mouth on her nipple.

"What do you want? Tell me what you want."

"I…I want you to…to kiss my breast."

He pulled the nipple into his mouth and sucked it, feasting on it as if he were starved. She reached down and tried to take him into her body, but he moved beyond her reach. With a hand on each one of her breasts, he slid down her body, kissing her belly, and then the feel on his lips skimming the insides of her thighs sent spirals of heat charging through her. He spread her legs, lifted her hips and kissed her, twirling his tongue until she screamed, nearly out of her mind from the sweet torture of his kissing and sucking.

"Get in me," she begged, as heat flushed the bottom of her feet and her thighs began a quivering motion. "I need you inside of me," she moaned.

"All right, sweetheart." He moved up, put an arm beneath her shoulder and a hand under her hip and said, "Take me in."

She brought his penis to her vagina, and he pressed for entry. When she bit her lip, he said. "This isn't your first time, is it?"

How she wished that it was! "No, but it's been a long, long time, and…and it wasn't successful."

He clasped her face in his hands and kissed her. "It will be this time." He put his right hand between them, found her vagina and let his talented fingers work their magic. Within minutes she was writhing beneath him. An awesome feeling, intense and electrifying, like the blaze of the sun going down, plowed through her. But he was going to give her more, and she wanted it, all of him.

"Please. I don't care if it hurts. I want to feel you inside of me. I want you to love me."

"I do love you, baby. Relax now." He pressed again, and she grabbed his buttocks and thrust herself up to him, taking him in. Her eyes widened, and then she looked up at him and smiled. He began to move, slowly at first and when she started to adopt his rhythm, he accelerated the pace. Then, he was all she knew, for he was in her, under her, over her and all around her. She smelled him and tasted him. He was her world as he rocked her.

He teased the nerve endings in her vagina until she could feel herself swelling around him. If she didn't burst, she'd go crazy. "Something is happening to me," she said, when a pumping and squeezing began inside her, her thighs trembled and she reached for the unknown.

"I know. And it's good. Concentrate on it." He increased his pace. "Am I in the right place now?"

"I don't know. I can't stand it. Warren, honey, I think I'm going to die."

"No you're not."

"I feel as if I'm going to burst wide open. I'm… I'm sinking… Oh, Warren." Where was he taking her, and what was he doing to her? She was dropping into nowhere. And then, she was losing herself, dying and then, incredibly, pure heaven.

"Warren. Warren. I love you. I love you." She flung her arms wide and gave herself to him.

"And you're mine now. Mine," he shouted, gave her the essence of himself, and collapsed in her arms. "I love you."

"Look at me," he said after a long silence, still locked inside of her. "We said a lot of things to each other tonight. Important things. Tomorrow or the next day when we're fully dressed and nowhere near a bed, we're going to have to deal with our feelings and with those words we said." He kissed her eyes, her cheeks and her lips.

"Are you happy?" he asked.

"Happier than you or I could imagine." But not as happy as she could be if no barrier existed between them. She knew it wasn't the time to tell him. "I didn't know that lovemaking could be like this."

He kissed her cheeks and the tip of her nose. "I'm aware of that. Sometime maybe you'll tell me about your first time, but if it's painful, I won't insist."

"There isn't much to tell. I was twenty-one, and he swore eternal love for me, but that one night with him was painful in more ways than one, and although I've been tempted and actually wanted to try it again, I couldn't make myself do it. I couldn't make myself trust another man that much."

"Then you're telling me that you trust me."

She felt her lips curve into a smile. "Yes, and it's a good thing, because the minute I first saw you leaning against that doorjamb talking to Ben, I wanted you."

"You're kidding. That's when I dropped anchor for you, and it must have shown, because Ben said, 'Don't go there. She doesn't fool around.' I remember hearing myself say, 'Fooling around is not what I'm about.'"

She wrapped her arms more tightly around him, and then she stroked his back, caressed his naked buttocks and kissed his lips. "Sometimes you're so sweet, and sometimes you seem tough and hard and serious, but you're always gracious to me, and so gentle."

Her fingers brushed over his hair, and she looked into his mesmerizing eyes and shivered at the desire blazing in them. Within seconds, he was hard inside of her, and when her lips parted in surprise, his tongue found its place insider her mouth. He wrapped her long legs around his hips and rode her to ecstasy.

Later he asked her, "Are you going to visit your father tomorrow?"

"No. I visit him every other day. If I go back tomorrow, he'll be suspicious. As sick as he is, nothing escapes him."

"I wanted our first time to occur in a place where we could spend the night together where we'd have the next day to ourselves, but it happened this way, and I wouldn't exchange it for anything."

"I want you to spend the night, but I'm not sure that walking out of here tomorrow morning is a good idea. I don't know who lives around here, and it would be my luck to run into somebody who's either an Allegory member or one of its employees."

After he left that night, Jackie sat up in bed, reliving the happiest moments of her life, yet fearful of the consequences of her double existence. She would love him forever, even if he walked out on her when he discovered her daytime life. She slid down between the sheets, rolled over to the place that retained the print of his body and put her head on the pillow that still carried his male scent. Frustrated with rising desire, she rolled over on her belly and began counting sheep.

* * *

Warren drove home slowly. Leaving her was one of the hardest things he'd ever done. And he was in trouble. Deeply in love with her, he would have to accept whatever came, and he knew that he was in for some surprises. To begin with, Jackie Parks was not a worldly woman. Her experience with men was practically nonexistent. She had taken him into her mouth almost out of curiosity, testing, to see what it would feel like. Then, she liked it and got greedy, almost making him ejaculate. He hadn't needed more evidence of her innocence. He wondered what kind of job that guy had done to make her, the hottest woman he had ever touched, spend the next twelve years of her life celibate. He blew out a long and harsh breath. She was also the most loving woman he'd ever taken to bed.

The last thing he'd expected from such an innocent with such a modest income were the satin sheets on her bed. Somehow, it didn't ring true. Her apartment not only showed the taste of an upper-middle-class woman, but so did its furnishings. But then, hadn't his parents taught him to buy quality and buy rarely rather than to buy cheap things and replace them constantly? Obviously, she had set herself up before her father became ill. He told himself to give her the benefit of the doubt and drop it.

The next day at noon, he drove to the clinic in Riverdale and asked to see Clyde Parkton. The receptionist examined his ID and called a guard. "Take this gentleman to see Mr. Parkton. You may remain with him."

Hmm. So the clinic had tight security. "Thank you, ma'am."

He introduced himself to Clyde and sat in the chair beside his bed, aware that the guard leaned against the doorjamb watching them.

"Hello," he began. "My name is Warren Holcomb and I'm a friend of your daughter Jackie," he said, and he saw that, immediately, the man tried to sit up straighter and extended his hand.

"Thank you for coming to see me. I wasn't expecting company today, but it sure is nice to have it. These walls get monotonous."

"Then do something about getting out of here."

Clyde frowned slightly and tried to brace himself in a better position. Warren could see that the man struggled to regain what had once been a commanding presence. "What do you mean?"

"I mean, you only have to give the doctor permission to operate, and you'll be home and walking around by Christmas."

Clyde turned his face to the wall. "It's not so simple."

"Yes, it is. Jackie is despondent, knowing that in a few months, you'll be gone from her forever, when all you have to do is have an operation that these surgeons have performed safely hundreds of times."

"Now, look here—"

Warren interrupted him. "Both of your daughters deserve better from you. They love you. Their mother is gone, and soon they won't have you, either."

"And where's she going to get all that money? This place has to cost a fortune, and with an operation to pay for on top of it, she'll be bankrupt for the rest of her life."

"She won't, because I won't let her. Besides, she told me last night that she has already saved enough money for your operation. Look, sir, don't you want to watch your grandchildren grow up? You're a young man. If the operation isn't successful, at least Jackie will know that she did all that could be done for you, but this way, she'll spend the rest of her life grieving about what might have been." He took the older man's feeble fingers in his. "Please don't do this to her."

"You seem to think an awful lot of her."

"Yes, I definitely do."

"You got any plans for those grandchildren you're talking about?"

"If she doesn't kill me for sneaking here and talking to you behind her back, there's a chance."

Clyde leaned back against his pillows, and let out a long breath. "You're a good man, and that's what she deserves, because she's first class."

"Will you reconsider, sir? Jackie is brokenhearted."

"I'll see when the doctor comes by today."

The guard walked over. "He's getting tired, Mr. Holcomb. Maybe you can come back tomorrow."

"Right." He shook Clyde's hand. "Goodbye, sir."

"You come back to see me, now."

"I will."

As he left the clinic, he pondered whether to tell Jackie about his visit and decided against it. He didn't want to raise her hopes. So it wasn't fear of the surgery as he'd thought, but an unwillingness to saddle his daughter with additional expenses. He got into his car and headed toward his Harlem Clubs thinking that after meeting Jackie's father, he was less concerned about whatever it was of her life that she hadn't told him. And the better he knew her the more certain he was that she still had much to tell him.

He parked in the small parking lot beside Harlem Clubs and went to his office. As he reached it, Allen walked out of the men's room. "What's up, friend?" Allen asked him, throwing him a high five. "Haven't seen you in a couple of days."

"I know. That Honolulu hotel is a hotbed of labor unrest. If I had a staff of men and hired a woman to supervise them, people would call me a hero, but I put a man in charge of housekeeping, and you'd think I dropped a bomb in the middle of those maids. They're just as chauvinistic as the men."

"Watch it brother. You can't speak your mind about some things, not even when you're telling the truth."

"How's Vanna?"

"She's upset about her father. He's adamant about not having an operation and—"

"I know. Jackie told me. I just left him, and I think I made a dent, but who knows. Don't tell Vanna I spoke with her father, but Jackie was so down that I had to do something. Alternately, I pleaded and shamed him."

"I hope it works. I'm going down to see Vanna Friday night, and I hope I can comfort her."

"Your being there will help."

"Man, I hope so. Vanna's usually so upbeat, but this thing has practically flattened her. See you later."

For the next three hours, Warren sat in his office checking the tutors' reports on the children's progress. He was going to have to do something about Charlie. The boy could become a champion swordsman, but he cared little for academic studies, and the rule at Harlem Clubs was no sports without academic improvement. Charlie thought that didn't apply to him. Warren went down to the gym and spoke with the man in charge of boys' athletics.

"Charlie is not to participate in any sport, including fencing, until he gets my permission. We've got enough empty-headed black athletes."

"But Warren, he's head of the fencing squad and captain of the tennis team."

"And he doesn't even know that he should begin a sentence with a capital letter."

"Gotcha."

He didn't feel good doing it, Warren thought as he returned to his office, but he would have to prohibit Charlie from participating in sports at the club. If Charlie refused to study, he would have to leave Harlem Clubs and, in accordance with the mayor's new rules, Charlie would probably be held over in the seventh grade. Why couldn't that boy understand that he was being given a chance he wouldn't otherwise have? He entered his office and pulled the boy's record.

Charlie had no idea who his father was, and his mother had been on welfare until recently. No one in his family had ever finished high school. The boy had no role model. He heard a knock on his door.

"Come in."

"You bounced me outta sports?"

"Sit down, son. Yes, I did, and you know why. You know who pays for all this? The city and the government don't give us one penny. This club is supported by concerned citizens and myself. Do you know why? Because we don't want to lose so many of our young people to the streets. And that's where you're headed. I want you to spend a day with me. I'll send your mother a note asking her permission."

"I don't need her permission."

"Really? Well, I do. It would be illegal for me to take a thirteen-year-old child and drive him around town without his guardian's written consent. I want to show you something. If, after we spend that day together, you still don't get it, I'll have to expel you from Harlem Clubs."

"But I'll do better. I promise."

"This is, let me see…the fourth time you've made that promise to me. I don't believe you." He folded the note, put it in an envelope and gave it to Charlie. "Give that to your mother. I need a written reply. After you give it to me, I'll call her to be sure she wrote the reply."

"Jeez, Mr. Holcomb."

"The way to establish trust, Charlie, is by living up to your word and doing the right things." The boy left his office, his shoulders drooping and with none of his usual self-confidence. "Better me than a warden," Warren said to himself.

He dialed Jackie's cell phone number and waited for the sound that would make his heart soar. "Hello, darling," she said, and he'd swear that his heart skipped several beats.

"Hello, sweetheart. Are you coming to work this evening? It's really cold outside."

"I'll be there. You can't imagine what a long day this has been."

"Oh, but I know it's been a long day. Minutes seem like hours."

Her laughter curled around him like the soft tail of a playful kitten. "If you're not there tonight, I'll be devastated."

"Let's plan right now to meet on 64th just beyond Fifth Avenue when you leave work. I'll get there late tonight, so that I don't have to wait so long for midnight."

"Where will you eat dinner?"

"I'll grab a hot dog or something. Anyhow, I don't always eat at the club. I like home-style cooking some-times."

"In other words, you're a big shot who hasn't forgot-ten his roots."

"You could say that."

"Can I have a kiss?"

He made the sound of one. "That merely whetted my appetite. I've spent a lot of time today thinking of the moment when you'll be back in my arms."

"Me, too. Bye, love."

"Bye, sweetheart."

He hung up and leaned back in his old-fashioned swivel chair. *One of these days, I'll ask her to marry me. As soon as we get her father well, I'll take her to meet Dot and Mom. I don't need their approval, but I'd like to give them a chance to like each other. But only the Lord knows what my mother will say to my bringing a cocktail waitress to see her. She isn't a snob, but she can be prudish as hell.*

Chapter 6

Jacqueline entered the lobby of the building that housed *African American Woman* magazine that morning, an escapee from the cold and numbing wind, and re-arranged her nearly frozen face just enough to smile at Jeremy and murmur good morning.

"It's a rough day, Dr. Parkton," he said, "but we're glad you're here." He took her briefcase and walked with her to the elevator as he usually did.

"You seem a bit down, Jeremy. Anything I can do?"

He took off the gold-braided doorman's hat and looked her in the eye. "I don't know, ma'am. When Mr. Zeigler makes up his mind about something—"

Her antenna came alive. "What has he made his mind up about this time, Jeremy?"

"He's given notice to the doormen and the concierges. He said he's going to install video cameras and buzzers, and if any of the staff has a visitor, you can come down to the front door and open it."

"Did he? Don't worry about your job, Jeremy."

Minutes later, Jacqueline sat down at her desk and punched the intercom. "L.Z., I need to see you," she said to Zeigler. "I'd like to come up right now."

"Sure. I'll send for some coffee."

She entered his office, said no to the coffee, sat down and crossed her legs at the knee. "L.Z., you have two concierges and five doormen working here, and all of them are between fifty and sixty years old. They've worked for you since you started this magazine, and that's…how many years? About twenty-five. Where do you expect a man that close to retirement to get another job?"

"Look, Jacqueline, I need to save some money."

"At the expense of those poor men and their families? The magazine is making money. Lots of it. And another thing. Neither I nor anybody on my staff is going down to answer that buzzer. We aren't employing them as doormen. Besides, anytime they wanted half an hour away from their desks, they'd be able to say, 'I had to go down and answer the buzzer.' That would also be the end of security here, because some people would push the button that opens the door and not bother to go down and see who it was."

"Look, I'm not doing anything a lot of other businesses haven't done."

"But those businesses are not running a magazine

for middle- and upper-middle-class women. It would cheapen our image. If you want to save money, all you have to do is remove alcoholic drinks from reimbursable items on the entertainment bills. And put an end to those extra hotel nights that some of our reporters put on their expense accounts. That will save you a bundle." She leaned forward. "I don't want to work in a place where the older workers are told that they are expendable and are then cast aside like old, worn-out shoes."

"All right. All right, already." He looked a little sheepish. "I see Jeremy got your ear when you walked in this morning. Tell him that the doormen and concierges stay."

"Thank you. You have no idea how relieved I am."

She took the elevator down to the lobby. "I spoke with Zeigler, and he told me to tell you and the others to forget it. He'll find other ways to save money."

"God will bless you, Dr. Parkton. I knew you'd help us. You always come through for us."

"I do my best, Jeremy."

She went back to her office and began looking through the slush pile for articles or short stories with a new twist, something to give the March issue some punch. She picked up a manuscript and was about to toss it back when she remembered that she'd done that twice because she hated the scent of hyacinths, and the writer had doused the manuscript with the offensive odor. She leafed through it and began to read when she recognized that it was a true story of a female German shepherd that rescued an abandoned newborn baby, took it home and watched over it until its master came home late that afternoon from work.

"Just what I need," she said, rang her secretary and gave her the manuscript. "I want a photograph of this dog, please, and I'd like you to get the author on the phone."

"What a day!" she said to herself later, as she prepared to leave her office. She felt tired, but satisfied. She had accomplished all that she'd set for herself that day and, best of all, she had salvaged the jobs of some of the magazine's lowest salaried, most needy and most likeable employees. Bracing herself against the west wind, she struggled over to Sixth Avenue, boarded a bus and was home in half an hour.

After a quick and refreshing shower, she dressed in a burnt-orange woolen suit and eyed her fur coat with longing. It would have to remain in the closet, because an ankle-length mink, although four years old, did not match her job as a cocktail waitress. Indeed, in her present circumstances with responsibility for her father's illness, it didn't match her lifestyle at all. Eager to get to the club and to see *him,* she ignored the bus, even though she saw it coming, and hailed a taxi.

Jackie had a seemingly interminable wait for Warren's call to a private lounge where she would see him at last. "Oh, hell!" she said at about nine-thirty when she remembered his having told her that he would arrive late at the club. "What a letdown!"

The blinking light indicated that she had a call from

Ben, and she picked up a tray and went to the bar. "What do you have for me?" she asked him.

"Sorry to tell you, but this is for Hornsby and he asked that you bring it."

"Something tells me I shouldn't. Is he in the main lounge or a private lounge?"

"He's in the Lincoln."

"What happens if I refuse?"

"He could have you fired."

"Then I'll take it, but if he makes one false move, he'll be sorry he ever messed with me."

"Be careful."

"I will, Ben, and so should he."

She put the drink, the pot of coffee and a coffee service on the tray, added a napkin and headed for the Lincoln, wondering if that would be her last night at Allegory, Inc. She knocked and went in. When Hornsby rose immediately and started toward her, she placed the tray on the serving table beside the door and waited. She wasn't taking one step farther into that room....

"Here's your drink and your coffee, Mr. Hornsby."

"It isn't the drink that I want, and you know it. Come here."

"If you come any closer to me, you will definitely regret it. From now on, Jack will bring your order." She turned to leave, and from her peripheral vision she saw him rush toward her. As he neared her, she opened the door and stepped aside, but he grabbed the doorjamb to prevent a fall. She didn't think she had ever seen a man so angry. His red, mottled face seemed to have swollen to twice its size.

"I'll have you if it's the last thing I do," he said, gritting his teeth just before he lunged at her.

"Never! You insufferable pig." She braced her weight on her left foot and then swiftly moved toward him, locking her outstretched hands on his forearm. The next second, he was flat on his back with his feet in the hallway and the rest of him in the lounge.

She dialed Ben. "Get in here this minute."

Hornsby tried to sit up, but she wouldn't allow it. "If you move an inch, I'll pour this pot of hot coffee in your face."

"You'll pay for this."

"Not as much as you'll pay."

"What the hell's going on here?" Warren stood over Hornsby with Ben at his side.

"Damn him. Did he hurt you?" He looked from Hornsby to her, his stance wide and aggressive and his breathing deep.

"No, but he got rough, and I gave him a judo demonstration. A couple of weeks ago, he offered me money to go to bed with him. Last week, he waited in his car and tried to lure me into it, but Ben came to my rescue. Tonight, he ordered a drink and asked that I bring it, then he attempted to manhandle me, and I let him have it." She saw that Arthur Morgan had joined them and had heard her explanation.

"Get up, man," Arthur said. "This is disgusting. The female staff are off-limits, and even if they weren't, you were out of order. Get up."

Hornsby struggled to his feet and sneered at her.

"You're lying, and you are not working here another minute."

"We'll see about that," Warren said. "This is not the only club rule that you've broken man, and I can prove it." He moved closer to Hornsby, but Ben stepped between them and put a restraining hand on Warren's shoulder.

"Right," Ben said. "I know a few of your infractions, and I can prove those, too."

Hornsby looked at Arthur. "Surely, you don't believe them. They're sticking together. What do you expect from these people?"

"The hole you're in is getting deeper," Arthur said. "You can be expelled for bigotry, and I'll have to report this at the next board meeting."

"I didn't touch her," Hornsby said.

Jackie folded her arms across her chest and glared at him. "No, you didn't. When you lunged at me, I stepped out of your way and threw your butt to the floor." She looked at Arthur. "And while you're making your report to the board, I want a different uniform. I hate this one, and I don't want to wear it anymore."

Arthur fingered his chin, obviously musing over her request. "It's kinda cute, and the guys like it, but I'll tell them what you said. I don't think a change will be popular, but…Warren, you'll have to support me in this."

"Be glad to. That dress is outrageous."

Arthur stared at him. "Man, you gotta be kidding."

Ben's head went back in a roar of laughter. "I know it's hard to believe, but he's sane," he said, winking at Arthur.

Jackie wasn't satisfied. "Is it understood, Ben, that I don't answer any more of Hornsby's calls?"

"Well, I don't see why you can't take them if he's in the main lounge. Otherwise, I'd say you don't have to."

"Come on, man," Arthur said, "Let the guy go to the bar, or let the waiter take his orders."

"I pay my dues like all the rest of you," Hornsby said, "and I'm entitled to—"

"Look fella, you'll be lucky if you don't lose your membership. And if you've got any sense, you'll leave this woman alone," Warren said.

"Yeah," Ben said. "Come on, let's break this up." He looked at Hornsby. "You realize I'll put a full account of this in my daily report?" Hornsby walked off without answering him.

"I didn't expect to find you in this mess," Warren said to Jackie when she delivered an order to him in the Reagan suite. "I counted the minutes till I'd get here and see you. I used a lot of self-control with that jerk to keep from breaking him in two. Expulsion is the penalty for fighting, no matter the reason."

Jackie couldn't help laughing. "You should have seen the look of surprise on his face when he realized he was flat of his back."

One of Warren's eyebrows lifted slowly. "He must weigh a hundred and ninety pounds. Where'd you learn how to do that?"

She almost said, my junior year in college. "In gym class. I was pretty good at it."

"You're still good at it," Warren said, his face bright

and smiling in that way that always made her feel as if she were melting. "Can we go somewhere later where we can just…be together and…talk?"

She had to get up early and go to work, but she couldn't tell him that. "Sure. Where can we go that we're not likely to run into an Allegory club member?"

He reached for her hand, and she stepped closer to him so that she could feel his flesh touching hers. "Smalls reopened a couple of weeks ago. Let's go up there for and hour."

And she'd get five hours sleep. "Fine, but I'll probably fall asleep on you."

His face transformed itself into what looked to her like a leer. "In that case, maybe I ought to take you home with me."

"Let's settle for a good-night kiss."

He tugged at her hand. "Are you saying you don't want to be with me?"

"Of course I do, Warren, but I don't intend to have an affair with you, and trust me, going home with you and not…touching you, that would be like having a candy bar in my pocketbook when I'm on a strict diet."

"Why would you go on a diet?"

"I wouldn't. That was a figure of speech."

His eyebrows shot up, and she knew at once that she had piqued his curiosity again. She had to be careful not to make him suspicious of her.

"I'd better get back to my station. By now, every man who's here tonight knows what happened between

Hornsby and me, and I expect I've got a few calls waiting for me."

"I'm sure of that," he said and stood. "Kiss me before you leave."

She kissed him and stepped back quickly before he could heat her up. "Any more of that, and I'd walk out of here the picture of guilt."

"I don't know why," he said. "That kiss was practically sisterly."

She grinned, wondering if he could see how happy she was. "You didn't say what kind."

Warren left the Reagan room, went out to the main lounge and joined two of the members in a game of pinochle. The club members hadn't heard of the game until he introduced it to them. Most preferred a four-hand game, but he favored three-hand cutthroat. He played the game without concentrating on it and his results showed it. He didn't want to grill Jackie on her life before he met her, because what he already knew about her pleased him. But he was leaning toward committing himself. It had cost him more willpower that he knew he had to refrain from punching out Hornsby, and he hadn't been in a fight since his junior year in high school. And the way in which she deported herself. He couldn't have been more proud of his sister. Yet, he wouldn't lie to himself. Something was missing, and it had never been *in* their relationship. He didn't think it wise to settle for what they'd found together, when he knew they could have so much more.

"You had that ace all the time and didn't use it?" one of the players asked him. "Wake up Holcomb. You're off tonight."

"Yeah," he said. "Do you think they'll unseat Hornsby?"

"Unseat him?" one player, an octogenarian, snorted. "He'll be damned lucky if the board doesn't recommend that we kick him out. I never did care much for that fellow. Something slimy about him."

"What gave him the idea that he could get away with it?" the other player, a man in his fifties, asked. "Jackie certainly didn't. She's pleasant, capable and impersonal. Very professional about her job. If a man's going to hit on a woman, he ought to at least wait till she gives him a reason."

"Yeah," the older man said. "That way he won't find himself lying on his ass looking like a fool. I'd have given anything to see her flip him over."

Warren thought about what his reaction would have been and let out a long sigh. "I have other questions about him."

"Me too," the older man said, "and one of them is why he and Mac are so tight. He shouldn't even know that Mac exists."

Warren spread his trump suit and a run in spades on the table. "I'll play it if you insist, but you two can't beat this. Hornsby introduced Mac to me and said, 'Get to know him. You'll be glad you did.' When it comes to people, I do my own judging, and I didn't bother to get to know Mac."

He glanced at his watch. Another forty minutes and he'd have her all to himself—if only for the fifteen-minute drive to the apartment building in which she lived. He knew he had a smile on his face, and he also knew that his two companions looked at him as if his sanity were in question. But he didn't care. He had a woman who loved him, and he didn't give a hoot about what anybody thought.

Jackie met him at their agreed place, and he drove her home, unable to rid his mind of the pleasure that awaited him when he last drove there. "I told you I wanted us to have some time to talk about last night, so I don't want you to forget how you felt and the way you expressed it to me. There's no way I can forget it."

"Nor I," she said. There it was again, but he couldn't put his finger on the reason that he would take exception to an expression that he ordinarily took for granted.

When he walked into his den at home, he saw that his answering machine flashed red and sat down to check the calls. The first one was from his mother, and he called her at once.

"I hope you weren't asleep, Mom. I just got in. What's up?"

"I'm wide-awake because I fell asleep after lunch this afternoon. It was the strangest thing. I dreamed I was sitting on our old back porch, and your father was lecturing to you about not paying attention. I don't know to what, but he was shaking his right index finger in your face. That seemed pretty odd, because your father was left-handed. I looked down in the pond—and you know we didn't have a pond—and there was algae on the surface, but underneath it the water was as clear as polished glass. He looked toward the pond and said, 'Your mother can see under all that, so why can't you?'"

Something akin to a chill raced through him. "You think that has some significance?"

"Could be. You would know that better than I would. Be careful and pay attention to everybody and everything around you."

"Thanks. I will. How's Dot, and where's Rob these days?"

"Dot's fine. I'm keeping the children tonight because she's reading a paper on the Moors of Spain at a convention in Raleigh. The little angels are asleep, thank the Lord. They're a handful. Isn't it about time you told me something else about the woman you didn't feel like talking about when you were here at Thanksgiving? That should be gelling by now."

He was not going to let her or anyone else push him into something that concerned his life. "Right, and as soon as it gels, I'll invite her to come with me to visit you. In fact, I've been thinking about doing that, even though it would be premature."

"Do what you think best, son. I doubt my dream had anything to do with her, but I'll be glad to see her whenever you bring her."

After hanging up, he phoned Jackie. "Sorry I'm a little late calling, but my mother had left a message on my answering machine. I had to call her back."

"How is she?"

"She's well, I'm happy to say." He thought for a minute. What the hell! It would make sense to check out a few things before he got in any deeper. The thought brought a silent laugh. How much deeper could he fall? "Let me know when you'll be able to spend a weekend with me down in Durham. I'd like you to meet my folks, and I suspect you want to know something about where I came from."

Her silence told him that he'd taken her by surprise. Good. That guaranteed an honest reaction.

"Gee, that's the last thing I expected to hear you say. Let me think about it, and I'll let you know."

He wasn't sure that response pleased him, but... "Why do you have to think about meeting my folks?"

"Oh, I don't have to think about *that*. The problem is when I'll be able to get away for an entire weekend. I'll speak with the doctor when I visit my father tomorrow."

"Good. Are you getting comfortable with the idea that you mean a lot to me?"

"I don't have a problem with that. The job facing me is getting comfortable with what you mean to me. That takes looking at myself and at life differently from the way I've seen myself over the last decade."

He slumped down in the chair feeling as if he'd taken a load of bricks on his head. "Tell me what it is about me that you find unacceptable or not up to standard."

"What? Warren, that couldn't have been a serious question. I've been accustomed to being a loner, to solving problems and dealing with issues on my own, except for occasional input from Vanna. Now, I have a feeling that you're there for me, and it is a comforting feeling. Yes, I know how to handle my affairs, and if I know a man is going to attack me, I can defend myself. But I have this feeling that I'm not alone, and getting used to it takes some doing."

"Sorry. I didn't read that correctly. You were sleepy an hour ago, so I'd better hang up. But I don't want to. Good night, love.

"Good night, sweetheart. Sleep well."

Jacqueline slept fitfully that night. Her conversation with Warren disturbed her, for she sensed that the closer to each other they became, the more demanding he would become. She loved him; she had no doubt of that, and it would sadden her if he terminated their relationship or if she had to do that. But her father still came first, and she did not intend to jeopardize her ability to give him the best of care.

She left home around ten o'clock that Saturday morning, shopped for stockings and toiletries and went to see her father. "Doctor Franklin wants to see you, Dr. Parkton," the receptionist said. "I'll tell him you're here."

She thought her heart had stopped beating. "Is…anything wrong with my father?"

The woman looked up from her computer. "Why no. Have a seat."

A few minutes later, the cardiologist walked over to her with his right hand outstretched. "Good morning, Dr. Parkton," he sang with all the joy of a mezzo soprano singing Mozart's *Jubilate*. "We have good news. Your father has agreed to have the operation."

She nearly jumped out of the chair. "He did? When? I can't believe it. He was so adamant with his opposition to it."

"That he was, but apparently that visitor he had the other day shamed him into it. He told me it hadn't occurred to him that he was being selfish, that he would deprive his daughters of a father. Best news I've had. He should be walking around by Christmas."

"But that's barely two weeks away."

"He'll be out of here well before the end of the year."

"I don't know when I've been so happy, doctor. I had stopped hoping."

She rushed to see her father, and the world seemed brighter and friendlier when he greeted her with a smile and with outstretched arms. "I'm so glad you came today," he said. "I signed those consent papers for the angioplasty this morning, and I knew that would make you happy. Be sure and call Vanna and tell her."

"You know I will, Papa." She scrutinized his face for evidence that he had deteriorated physically, and saw none. So why had he changed his position on the surgery? That was so unlike her father, who usually examined an issue thoroughly, made up his mind and thereafter didn't deviate, or at least she hadn't known him to change. As a child, she learned to accept her father's judgment and not to question him. But he was her responsibility now, so she had a right to know the motive behind his new decision.

She held his hand. "I'm so happy you're going to be all right, Papa, but how…what happened to make you change your mind?"

"It was that fellow who came to see me. Very persuasive. Between pleading and browbeating, he turned on the charm, but what got to me was his telling me that you and Vanna had lost your mother and I was going to deprive you of your father. He suggested that I was being selfish. Truth is, I didn't want to load that heavy expense on you, and I told him you'd be bankrupt for the rest of your life.

"He surprised me when he said he wouldn't allow that. Then he asked me if I didn't want to live to see my grandchildren. So I asked him what about giving me some grandchildren, and he said it was possible, but it wasn't up to him entirely. So—"

"You don't have to tell me anything else. I know who that was, but I didn't know he was coming here."

"Well, he's a fine man, and I want me some more grandchildren."

"Vanna has already given you three grandchildren. Why do you need any more?"

"Because I have two daughters, and besides, that man will make a first-class husband and father. He's got a strong sense of responsibility. Good-looking fellow, too."

She knew that Warren was resourceful, but how… She dropped her father's hand, got up, walked to the window and looked out on the Hudson River. So that was why Warren wanted to know her father's name and why he wanted to drive her to the clinic. Did he wonder why her name was Parks and her father's name was Parkton, and had he questioned her father about the difference? She blew out a long breath and walked back to her father's chair. The stress of two such incompatible identities was getting to her. She wondered when her bubble would burst and Warren would discover her deception and take himself out of her life.

If he doesn't mention it to me, I won't say a word about it to him until after this crisis with Papa, and I'm free of debt and can quit Allegory.

As soon as she left her father, she phoned Vanna at home and, getting no answer, dialed her sister's cell phone, but her good news had to wait. Vanna didn't answer. She went home, changed into a pair of jeans, a T-shirt and sneakers and got to work on a lecture that she was scheduled to deliver to students at a local community college. She had completed the outline when the phone rang.

"Hi, sis. Did you try to reach me? Ellis has to write a paper on health, and he decided to write about oranges, so this morning we all went to visit orange groves and talk to a grower. You'd think that at nine, Ellis wouldn't be hung up on the kind of chemical sprayed on the orange groves, but he was, and he and the man in charge of one of the groves talked until I was exhausted. What's up?"

Vanna never wanted for words. "Papa signed the paper permitting the operation, and the—"

"What did you say? Hallelujah! How on earth did that happen?"

"Papa said Warren went to see him and convinced

him he was being selfish. I haven't spoken to Warren yet, because I don't know what to say to him, but I'll call him after we talk."

"Well, thank the Lord. And Warren, too, of course."

"Yeah? Well, maybe you'd like to know that Papa told Warren he wants some more grandchildren. I wonder what else they talked about and how the question of reproduction arose."

"Now, if I'd been Papa, I would have reasoned that if the man thought enough of a woman to fight for her interest, I could ask him about his intentions, too."

"Lord, I hope Papa didn't do that to Warren."

"Why not? He's a man and he's got a penis, and where a good-looking single woman is concerned, Papa knows exactly what that means."

"Oh, Vanna, for Pete's sake!"

"Sorry, sis, but you're the only old-fashioned person in this family. Mama always said you were the most prim Parkton who ever lived, including our super-proper grandmother."

"I know. Just because I dropped a guy for swearing in front of her. He was getting on my nerves, anyway. Besides, Papa said I was right, that the boy should have shown Mama more respect. Bye. I have to call Warren."

"You make it sound like a chore. Honey, calling that man wouldn't pull no skin off my teeth."

"Trust me it doesn't pull any off mine. Say, have you heard from Allen?"

"Every single solitary night."

"Well, 'scuse me. You go, girl. Talk later."

* * *

Her fingers shook as she dialed Warren's phone number. She didn't know where they stood after his visit with her father, so she would have to take her cue from him.

"Hello, Jackie," he answered, having seen her number in his caller ID window. "What's up, sweetheart?"

She let herself breathe. So far, so good. "I just left my father. He's agreed to have the operation and has signed the papers. Warren, I'm ecstatic."

"I imagine you are, and I'm happy for you and for him. When will he have the operation?"

She couldn't pretend not to know his role in her father's decision. What would be, would be. She owed him honesty in this and in everything else. So she had to thank him. The rest would come later.

"Warren, my father told me about the man who visited him and made him see that, by refusing the operation and choosing the inevitable, he was being selfish. When he mentioned the part about grandchildren, I deduced that you were his visitor. You know that I thank you, but you will never know how much. It's a wonderful thing you did."

"I had to try. I suspected that he would react to a challenge, or that he would at least think hard and long if I laid a guilt trip on him. Let me know when the operation is scheduled."

"I will. Warren, you can't know what this means to me. I'm dying to hug you."

"No kidding. Did you eat lunch yet?"

"No. I can make you a Portuguese omelet, leek soup and hot buttermilk biscuits. You bring some ice cream. What about it?"

"Homemade biscuits? You're on! I'll be there in an hour."

"Wait. I can't cook the food plus comb my hair and stuff like that in one hour."

His laughter came to her through the wire and she wondered what he found humorous. "Just do the cooking," he said. "You can't possibly be anything but beautiful, hair combed or not. See you soon."

If would serve him right if she stuck her head under the shower and opened the door wearing her old jeans and—why not. Her jeans and sweater were clean. She ran the comb through her hair, put some gold hoops in her ears, set the table and went about making the biscuits.

He left the meeting of corporate heads interested in acquiring venture capital for a housing project that would help clean up East Harlem and offer desirable living places for the middle class. He meant to have a share in it, and he'd get back to them, but for the moment, his mind was on a sexy, long-legged brown beauty who had promised him hot biscuits.

When she opened the door, he wasn't sure whether it was the scent of buttermilk biscuits or the sight of her in faded jeans and a tight red sweater that rocked his senses. He knew that his face was one big smile. She hadn't bothered to pretend that she was always dressed at home, and he liked that. She seemed a bit diffident—not her usual demeanor—so he hastened to reassure her.

"You're a sight for sore eyes. Come here and give your man a hug."

She closed the door behind him, opened her arms and enclosed him in her embrace. "You're so precious," she whispered.

He knew better than to open himself to the kind of loving he needed right then, and of which she was capable of giving so generously, so he stepped back. But her inquiring look told him that she was harboring insecurity about something. He took her hand, headed for the kitchen and, to lighten the air, said, "I have to ask you something, but I don't want those biscuits to burn while we talk." She seemed to wilt, and he drew her into his arms.

"You seem as if something is bothering you, as if you're not sure of yourself. What's the matter? Tell me, sweetheart."

She drew herself up. "That's what you wanted to ask me?" He nodded. "I guess I'm humbled by your...your caring. I don't know how else to phrase it."

"Don't you know yet that you mean everything to me, and that your problems are my problems?"

"Stop it, or I'll cry, and I hate to cry."

He held her closer, loving the feeling of her softness in his arms. "Then don't cry. Here's the ice cream. Better put it in the freezer before it begins to melt." He handed her the bag. "I haven't had any biscuits since I was last home, and I love 'em. I hope you made enough."

She closed the refrigerator, turned and looked at him with an expression of awe. "I must have made about thirty. Will that be enough?"

Happiness suffused him as he watched her make the omelet, the stretch jeans more revealing than her waitress uniform and the red sweater outlining the shape of her firm, beautiful breasts. All that, in an intelligent, well-mannered, elegant, knowledgeable and beautiful woman who had just told him that he was precious to her.

He walked over and kissed her on the mouth. "You're precious to me, too."

She dropped the dish towel on the floor, parted her lips and sucked his tongue into her mouth. "Hold it, baby. I have to go up to Harlem Clubs when I leave here." He backed away from her, heat already spreading through his groin. He shook his head, puzzled as to why she so easily turned him on.

"If it's all right with you," he said after eating all of his lunch except the ice cream, "I'll leave the dessert for another time, and may I take some of these biscuits home with me?"

She wrapped the biscuits in aluminum foil and put them in a brown paper bag. "Heat them up in the foil, and they'll be fine. Can you stay awhile?"

He looked at the treasure before him and sucked in his breath. "Believe me, I want to, but I have to be in Harlem by two-thirty. Maybe we can see each other tomorrow. I'll call you." He gave her as stern a look as he could manage. "And you can call me. Thanks for the best lunch I've had in… I don't know when."

She walked with him to the door, kissed him on the mouth and looked down at her shoes. "Are you coming to Allegory tonight?"

"You bet I am. Bye for now."

Another five minutes, and he'd have been tempted to do something he didn't believe in doing, and that was, breaking an engagement merely because he had a more interesting alternative. In any case, he didn't need to knuckle under every time she trained those big, slumberous eyes on him. He hurried to his car, but a light sleet slowed his steps. At last he was on his way up the Henry Hudson Parkway, but he suddenly slowed, almost braking to a stop.

What had he said to himself back there in that kitchen? "An intelligent, well-mannered, elegant, knowledgeable... What the hell! Had he been describing a cocktail waitress? He didn't think so. Still, she might have taken the job because she was down on her luck. It was honest work, and it paid more than a lot of teachers made. So why shouldn't she do it? Topic closed.

When his phone rang early Sunday morning and he saw her number in his caller ID screen, his heart fluttered wildly. Had anything happened to her father?

"Hello, Jackie. Are you all right?"

"Hi. The doctor said Papa's having surgery tomorrow morning at seven-thirty. He called me a minute ago. I can't work till midnight and be in Riverdale by seven, Warren, so I'll have to call Ben and tell him I won't be at work tonight or Monday. After that, we'll see. I hope I don't have to miss too many nights from work."

"Look here, woman, if you need anything or if your father needs anything, tell me. If you don't, you won't see much of me in the future."

"Thanks, Warren, but so far there isn't anything that I can't handle. Knowing that you're there for me…is what I need right now."

"And you can count on that. I'll be in front of your building tomorrow morning at six. If you need me before then, you have my cell phone number. If I can't share this with you, Jackie, I will conclude that I don't mean much to you."

Chapter 7

She stepped out onto West End Avenue, tightened her scarf around her neck, looked around and saw Warren walking toward her. "My car is right down the block," he said, taking her arm and tucking her close. "Hopefully we won't encounter much traffic, and we'll have time for coffee or something."

"You're an angel to get out so early in order to be with me. I can use some coffee."

In the car, her teeth chattered, and she hoped he didn't notice, but he must have because his next words were, "You're not to worry. These doctors know what they're doing. Now, I want you to put your head back and rest. I'll wake you when we get there."

She rested her head and closed her eyes, but she didn't try to sleep. How could she, as ridden with anxiety as she was? After a time, the car came to a stop, and she felt his arm around her shoulder.

"We're early. We have time for breakfast," he said, "so I suggest we stop here." He ate a hearty breakfast of fresh fruit, waffles, bacon and scrambled eggs, but she could barely manage to consume a small glass of orange juice and a little bowl of cereal. He chided her for not eating more, and she knew he had her interest at heart, but she couldn't force down another bite.

"I'll have some coffee," she told the waitress.

Later he drove the three blocks to the clinic, parked in the parking lot, took her hand and walked with her to the receptionist. *I can do all this myself,* she thought, *and I would if I was alone, but it's so good that he's here.*

"You may follow me," a nurse told them, and took them to a small waiting room on the fourth floor of the building. "He's already been prepped for surgery, so you can't see him. It'll be a good while. I'll be back."

The hours passed. Why didn't they take that clock off the wall in the waiting room? She closed her eyes, wrapped her arms around her middle and rocked. "What's taking them so long?" she asked Warren. "Can't they just come out for a minute and tell us something?"

He tightened his arms around her. "Have faith. The nurse told us it would be a while."

"But he's been in there almost six hours."

"I know, and I hurt for you, but try to be patient. They'll be out soon."

Her cell phone rang and she rummaged around in her

purse, couldn't find it and gave up. "It may be your sister," he said. "Want me to look?"

She didn't want to seem to fall apart, so she opened the bag, dumped its contents into her lap, got the cell phone and answered it. "Hi, sis. No word yet. What? Warren's with me. I'll call you as soon as we know how he is, okay? Right. Bye."

At two, seven hours after their vigil began, a doctor appeared. Both Warren and Jackie jumped to their feet and ran to the doctor. Warren stood beside Jackie, holding both of her shoulders, and neither of them spoke. Their faces spoke for them.

"He'll be as good as new," the doctor told them. "Fortunately, he's healthy otherwise. It was a long and tedious operation, but we expected that. He's in intensive care now, and I'd think you ought to be able to see him in a couple of hours, though I doubt he'll have come out of the anesthesia by then. Go get some rest."

For a few minutes, she thought she would faint. "Thank you, Doctor," she managed to say. "I don't know when I've been so relieved."

"You're very welcome," he said. "It always gives me pleasure to bring a family good news."

"You're exhausted," Warren told her as they rode the elevator down to street level, "and I think it would be a good idea if I took you home, and you rested until about five. I'll be at your place at six and bring you back here. By then, your father should be out of the anesthesia. What's Vanna's phone number?" Good grief. She'd forgotten to call Vanna. She gave him the number.

"Let's sit here in the lounge for a minute and see if we can get her on the phone." He used his own cell phone to make the call.

"Hello, Vanna, this is Warren. You father's fine. She's here beside me, but the ordeal of that seven-hour wait practically knocked her out. The doctor said your father will be as good as new. You're welcome. We'll visit him this evening, and then let you know how he's getting on," he said and handed the phone to Jackie.

"I'll talk with you later, Vanna. I didn't sleep a wink last night, and I got up early this morning, so I'm going home to get some rest. Yes, I'm happy too. We'll talk later."

She hung up and handed the phone to Warren. "Thanks."

He got up and extended his hand to her. "Come on, sweetheart. You must be a wreck."

At her apartment door, he kissed her on the cheek. "I won't ask to come in, because you need some rest, and rest wouldn't be on my mind."

She looked at him, and her amazement must have been obvious, for he laughed. "When I'm around you, rest is the last thing that pops into my mind."

She laughed for the first time that day. "You're a nut. A positively wonderful nut. See you later."

"I'll be here at six, and the way things look now, if you're as smart as I think you are, you'll be fully dressed with your coat on."

Now what did that mean? Suddenly, following his train of thought, she snapped her finger. "Anything to do with…uh…rest?"

Exposing his white teeth in a wicked grin, he said, "You got it," pressed a kiss to her lips and left.

She made coffee, took a cup of it to her bedroom, sat on the edge of the bed and kicked off her shoes. "I'd better get undressed, because I'll fall asleep in a minute." After crawling into bed and resting her back against the headboard, she telephoned Vanna.

"I was going to wait and call you after we visit Papa this evening, but I'm just so overjoyed that I had to share it with you. Imagine after all these months, Papa will be his old self again, fishing, playing golf, taking trips, writing and lecturing... I can hardly believe it."

"It is wonderful," Vanna said. "Let's hope he follows the doctor's orders and gets well. You know how hard-headed he is. Is Warren going back to the clinic with you tonight?"

"Yes. He's taking me there."

"Girl, you and Warren are getting pretty tight. He's acting like he's really in love with you. Sis, please watch your step and come clean with him. I don't understand this secrecy. You don't have anything to be ashamed of; in fact, you can be proud of what you've accomplished. Not many thirty-three-year-old women are as success-ful as you are. He'll be glad to—"

She interrupted Vanna. "He won't be glad to know that I'm a reporter and a senior editor of a popular women's—" She stopped short, realizing that she had almost told Vanna she was working nights as a cocktail waitress. She wouldn't mind her sister knowing of her nighttime job, but she didn't want her to feel guilty for not being able to help financially with the cost of their father's care.

"Say what?"

"Uh… Some men don't like smart women," she said, covering her blunder.

"Nonsense! Warren doesn't like bimbos and wouldn't go two feet with one. But he's your man, and you know him better than I do. Just make sure he's still around when you turn seventy. Give him a hug for me."

She hung up, and instead of going to sleep, she got out her bank books and her accounts ledger. An hour later, she figured that if she worked at Allegory until the end of January, she'd have paid the clinic and the doctors, and she could go back to living a normal life. *But would she still have Warren?*

That evening, she sat with Warren at her father's bed, rejoicing that he recognized them both and talked a little. "Did the doctor say when I could get out of here?" he asked.

Warren leaned toward him as if to make sure that he heard and understood. "We just finished thanking the Lord that you're going to be good as new. Neither we nor the doctors are much concerned right now about when you're going home. We'll tackle that in a couple of days."

To Jacqueline's amazement, her father said, "I guess you're right."

Later, she told Warren, "He would have given me an argument. You have a way of sounding so authoritative that the temptation to question your reasoning doesn't arise."

"Not so," he replied. "My voice is deep, and I guess

that impresses people, although I'm careful not to equivocate when I talk. I know you want to spend as much time as possible with your father this week, but how about going with me to Harlem Clubs Saturday afternoon? We can stop by the clinic to see your father on the way back."

"I'd love to. Anything special going on up there Saturday?"

"Not special, but a lot of activity. We focus on tutoring Monday through Friday, and Saturday is devoted mainly to sports and drama."

"I'll look forward to it.

"Why don't you visit with the girls' drama group for a while?" Warren said to Jackie as they entered Harlem Clubs that Saturday afternoon. "I'll walk over there with you, and then I'll check out the boys' fencing class."

She nodded, and pasted a smile on her face. Her only experience with young people had been with college youth who disciplined themselves, at least when she was with them. They entered a small theater in which approximately a dozen and a half girls aged fourteen to eighteen milled around, arranging and rearranging themselves as suited them.

"Girls, Ms. Parks will work with you for a while. Go ahead with your rehearsal. I'll be back later."

She knew enough about young people to realize that if she didn't take command at once, they would become unruly. "What's the name of the play?" she asked, "And who wrote it?"

"*Who's Afraid of Virginia Woolf?*" a tall girl who appeared to be about fifteen responded.

"I know that one. Albee wrote it," Jackie said. "Who's playing the husband?"

"I am."

"No, you're not. You bucktoothed tart," an older girl yelled, adding a barrage of obscenities to her insults. Jackie blinked rapidly, aware that, in her amazement, she had allowed her lower lip to drop. But she recovered at once, strode into their midst, and locked her knuckles to her hips. "None of that in here. This is the place where you come to rid yourselves of that self-defeating language and behavior. You come here for an opportunity to improve your chances of having a happy and productive life.

"Why can't you discuss your differences while showing respect for each other? Each of you could one day become mayor of this city, or governor of this state, or secretary of state of this country. In this twenty-first century, you can be anything you want to be, but not unless you learn how to behave."

She faced the girl who had used the offensive language. "Will you teach your children to behave as you just did?" The girl shook her head. "Then I'd like you to apologize to the entire group for your behavior. You're a beautiful girl, but no one will notice that, if you act ugly. I'm waiting."

"I'm sorry, everybody."

"Good. We all accept your apology. Now, what do you know about Virginia Woolf? The real one, I mean?"

When none of them seemed to know about the famous late-nineteenth and early-twentieth-century English novelist, Jackie put an arm around the girl who had made the offensive remark and said, "Okay. Let's sit over here, and I'll tell you about her."

She could hardly believe how attentive they were as she told them about the novelist's life and work and then informed them that the play was not about Virginia Woolf.

"We did a play by Lorraine Hansberry, but I forget the name of it," one girl said.

"A Raisin in The Sun," Jackie said. "Hansberry took the title from a line in a poem by Langston Hughes that reads, "What happens to a dream deferred? Does it dry up—like a raisin in the sun? Or fester like a sore—and then run?"

She looked around at the eager faces. "I would have loved to see you do that play."

Warren leaned against the entrance to the theater, stunned. He had stood there unseen by anyone in the theater from the time Jackie asked the name of the play the group would perform. Deciding that he didn't want her to know he'd been there, he rushed down the hall, turned the corner and went into his office as quickly as he could. Feeling like a thief who had absconded with something precious, he let the wall take his weight and released a long breath. Who was Jackie Parks? One thing was certain: She was a very well-educated woman with values and attitudes similar to his. He remembered telling her the first time they talked at length that she

and her job as a cocktail waitress didn't match, and now
he marveled at his wisdom. She was keeping something
from him, but at the moment, that didn't concern him
too much; if he added the woman he had just witnessed
to the one he already knew, she was a rare prize, and he
meant to have her for himself. Jackie Parks was an
enigma, but not for long.

"How'd you enjoy that session with the drama
group?" he asked her later as he drove them to the clinic.

"They tried to test my mettle," she said, "but we
parted friends. That's a very interesting group. I learned
something from them, and I hope they learned something from me."

"Will you come back?"

"As a regular volunteer? I'm not sure that would
work, but I'll go often, if you want me to."

"I want you to."

He stopped for the red light and patted her thigh, a
deliberate act of intimacy, and he watched her from his
peripheral vision to get her reaction. She glanced at him
but said nothing, and he allowed himself an inward
smile. The lady had some boundaries, and he'd just
crossed one and intended to cross any others she might
have that would interfere with his getting as close to her
as a man could get. She had made love with him once
but she'd made it clear in subtle ways that, although she
cared for him, she was not readily accessible. Slowly,
but definitely, a picture of the real Jackie Parks was
forming in his head. But why was she working as a
cocktail waitress, and what had she done before she

took that job? The light changed, he squeezed her knee and drove on.

"We don't have to stay long," she told him as they entered the clinic. "You've been devoting all your free time to Papa and me."

He pushed the elevator button. "How do you manage to say things like that? When I was four years old—and that's as far back as I can remember—getting me to do something I didn't want to do was practically impossible. You can figure out how easy that would be now that I'm forty. You're my number one priority, lady, and whatever concerns you is my concern, too." He ran his right index finger down her nose. "Got that?"

They stepped into the elevator, and she kissed his cheek. He wanted to ask her if she loved him, or if she had merely said so at that moment of orgasm, but it wasn't the time. He'd promised her that they would talk about that night, and he had to arrange it soon, for as time passed, the wonder of it became increasingly vague. The elevator sped to the fourth floor and, as badly as he wanted her in his arms, he took her hand and walked down the short corridor to the intensive care unit.

"Your father's been resting comfortably in his room," a nurse told Jackie. "He's been sitting up and ate a good lunch," she said. "And is that man ever a charmer!"

"Oh, yes," Jackie said with a broad grin. "He's known for that, so watch out."

They went back down to the second floor and to her

father's room. "How are you, sir?" he asked Clyde, but he could see that the man had improved greatly.

"I'm glad to see you," Clyde said. "Where's…" he asked as Jackie walked over to him, "Oh, there you are. I see you're spending a lot of time with this fellow."

"I'm glad to see that you're doing so well," Warren said.

"Well, you pushed me into it. What's going on between you two? I've been trying for years to get my daughter to settle on a fine young man, but something is wrong with every one she meets."

"Papa—"

"Well, it's true. As I was saying, Warren, she's seen you at least three times, and I'll bet that's a record."

"Papa, you're talking out of school."

"When are they going to let me go home?"

Jackie's facial expression was a call for help, so he said, "We'll have to ask the doctor, but I'm sure that if your progress continues this way, it shouldn't be long."

"He said I'd be walking by Christmas, but I walked twice today already. I want to be out of here by Christmas." He looked at Jackie. "How long before Christmas?"

"A little over a week," she told him.

There was his chance, and he was nothing if not an expert at taking advantage of opportunities. "Tell you what, sir. Jackie is very tired these days, and I'd like to take her away for a weekend of rest and relaxation. If we can do that, I'll ask the doctor if you can at least have Christmas dinner at my home with Jackie and me. What do you say?"

"You're a good man. If she's exhausted, I'm not surprised. A weekend of rest will do her good. Just let me know, so I won't expect her."

"But Papa, I wouldn't go off anywhere while you're convalescing."

"I want to have Christmas dinner out of this place, and I just made a bargain that I plan to keep. He's a gentleman, so what are you afraid of?"

"I know Warren's a gentleman, Papa."

"Good. I'm glad to know you've got better judgment that Vanna."

He could get to like the man, who reminded him in some ways of his own father. "Do you need anything, sir?" he asked Clyde.

"Thank you, but they give me everything here, even the daily papers, and I know it's costing a fortune."

"You're not to worry about that, Papa. I'll see you after church tomorrow."

"It's good to know you still go. Your mother would be pleased."

Warren parked the car in front of the building in which Jackie lived, cut the motor and turned to her. "I want you to go away with me this coming weekend, so could you please wrap up your plans and your Christmas shopping so we can have a couple of days to ourselves? Tell Ben you need Friday, Saturday and Sunday off. You're entitled to paid leave."

"But it's Christmastime. What if he says no?"

"He won't. Ben is very fond of you, and he knows you haven't had a vacation in at least a year."

"All right. I'll tell him. Where will we go?"

"If you ski, we could go up to Vermont." He didn't know why he had assumed that she skied, but the sport seemed compatible with what he now knew about her.

"Okay. I haven't skied for a couple of years, but I ought to get back into it easily."

"Would you mind showing some enthusiasm?"

She lifted her shoulder in a careless shrug. "I've never had a tryst with a man. I'm not wary, but I didn't think I was supposed to let you know how eager I am to be with you. Am I?"

She had a way of knocking him off balance. He swallowed a mild expletive and let the laughter roll out of him. "Damned right you are. My ego loves buttering as much as the next guy's. What time next Friday can we leave your house?" She thought for a long minute. "As early Friday morning as you'd like."

"Great."

Jacqueline could hardly wait for Friday. After announcing that she wouldn't be at her office on Friday, and getting Ben's permission to take time off from Allegory, she did something that she hadn't done since she was a teenager. She went on a shopping spree and bought sexy lingerie, a pair of white silk-satin pajamas—if he didn't like them, he could do something about it—a bathing suit, knee-high brown leather boots and a matching set of woolen gloves, scarf and cap. Her ski things didn't require replacement.

"Lord," she said to herself Thursday night, as she crawled into bed, "I feel like a wanton woman. I'll have him all to myself for three whole days." Giddy with excitement and yes, happiness, she tossed in bed for an hour unable to sleep. And then, Vanna's words came back to her. *Watch your step and come clean with him.* She prayed that nothing would happen to take Warren Holcomb from her and destroy the greatest joy she'd ever known.

Their flight to Burlington left LaGuardia at nine-twenty that Friday morning. She wasn't used to flying first class; on her trips for the magazine, she had business class accommodations.

"Thanks for the comfort," she said to Warren shortly after takeoff. "It's a short flight, so it hadn't occurred to me that you'd—"

"Jackie, I can afford the best, and I wouldn't consider less than that for you, not in this or in anything else."

Unable to respond, she merely squeezed his fingers, and that seemed to satisfy him, for his face brightened in a smile. "Did you tell Vanna where you're going?"

She hadn't felt comfortable doing it, but she had, mainly because of their father. "Yes, I told her, and not because I thought it was any of her business, but she needed to know how to reach me in case Papa needed me."

"Hmm. Allen seems quite taken with Vanna. What do you make of that?" He changed the subject, and that suited her. "It's obviously mutual, and it happened when they met."

"There is more to Allen than meets the eye. If you need a friend, he's the best man around."

The stewardess passed the breakfast menu, and after

they made their selections, Warren unbuckled his seat belt and turned to Jackie. "You don't have to share the answer with me, but I'd like you to answer this in your mind. Your behavior will give me your answer." She supposed that her face reflected her puzzlement, for he raised a hand and said, so softly that she barely heard him. "It's just between us, love. Are you spending these few days with a man you like a lot, a man you love or a man who happens to be your lover?"

She looked at him, searching for a reason behind the question, but finding none. "I'm not sophisticated enough to make the distinction between two and three."

"Meaning that a man wouldn't be your lover if you didn't love him? Is that what you're telling me?" His face, the tone of his voice and his whole demeanor bespoke hopefulness, or was it anxiety?

She looked out of the window, away from the dark, penetrating eyes, eyes that seemed to look through her soul. "Ask me that same question again when I'm... when you have me in a more vulnerable position."

"Maybe I'm moving too fast. I shouldn't rush you. As it is, I'm happy that you agreed to spend a few days with me."

Their breakfast arrived, and she consumed all of hers, aware that he occasionally observed her from the corner of his eye.

"I'm fine," she told him as she sipped coffee after a period of silence. "Stop worrying about what I'm thinking, Warren. I have only good thoughts of you."

He leaned back and rested his head against the leather

seat. "I'm not overly worried, but I want you to enjoy this. I want it to be perfect."

The fingers of her left hand trailed down his cheek, barely touching his skin. "I'm with you," she whispered, "so how could it not be perfect?"

His hand shot out and gripped her hand that caressed his face. "When you say things like that, I want you all alone, to myself, where I can love you until we shatter the earth."

She looked at him, lost in his gaze, mesmerized. *I'll always be in love with this man,* she thought. *I'll always need him before and above anyone or anything else.*

And as if he read her thoughts, he put his left hand over his heart and said, "You're locked in here, and I don't think you'll ever get out. I don't want you to get out."

Tremors raced through her, shaking her to the core of her being, and when she couldn't contain the trembling, he gathered her in his arms, settled his mouth over hers, plunged his tongue into her for a second, and released her. His sigh reminded her of someone seeing the light when coming out of a long, dark tunnel.

"This is why we needed this time together," he said. He reclined their seats, put his head on her shoulder and was soon asleep.

When the plane landed at Burlington International Airport, she awakened him with a kiss on his lips. "Wake up, hon. We're in Burlington."

He stretched languorously. "I wouldn't mind hearing that every morning."

Stunned, and unsure as to how she should react or

what kind of response he expected, she attempted to finesse the remark. "You want to wake up in Burlington, Vermont every morning?"

He captured her with a reprimanding stare. "Don't pretend to be dense. You know what I meant."

The rental car awaited them, and they soon arrived at the Skyline Hotel. He wondered why she hadn't asked about their room accommodations. After they registered and remained in the posh lobby waiting for the bellhop, he said to her, "It surprised me that you didn't ask what arrangements I made for us."

Her eyebrows lifted sharply. "Why? You're a man who possesses class. It never occurred to me to ask you."

"Thanks for the vote of confidence." Her comment told him a lot about her. She was a lady accustomed to being treated as one. A point in her favor, and a puzzle piece in the enigma that was Jackie Parks.

"This one's mine," he said when they reached suite 7R. "If you like, I'll open your door and see whether everything is in order." He opened the door to suite 7S, looked around and said, "Come on in." Then, he handed her the card-key to the door that led to the public hall. "This one," he said, showing her a metal door key, "locks the door that joins our rooms. I don't have one of these." He gave her the key. "But I'll welcome a visit whenever you get lonely, or any other time, for that matter."

"Thanks. I…uh…I think I'll rest for an hour. Can I…have a little kiss?"

He looked down at her, unsure as to her mood,

though he had no doubt about his feelings, and he knew where teasing his libido with her sweetness would lead.

She gazed up at him, expectantly, and suddenly she read him as if he had been a printed page, stunning him with the accuracy of her observation. "Okay," she said, "not a real kiss, just a peck on the cheek. It's too early in the day for the heavy stuff."

Some might say that his stare was blatantly brazen, but so be it. In all his life, he had never wanted anything or any woman, as badly as he wanted her that minute. He brushed her cheek with his lips, barely allowing himself to feel her smooth, warm skin, and then he walked out of there. Thoroughly drunk on her, he entered his room and had made himself start unpacking when the telephone rang.

"Yes."

"What are you going to do? I need to know what to put on when I wake up."

She was kidding. She had to be. If there was anything he didn't care to entertain right then, it was the thought of her in a bed. "It's best to go out on the slopes in the mornings. Would you like to eat lunch and then ride around the city? Or we can swim before dinner."

"Let's do all that."

A look at his watch told him that, if she slept for an hour and spent half an hour dressing, he wouldn't get lunch before two o'clock. "Sweetheart, do you *have* to go to sleep?"

"No, and it's starting to look like a bad idea. I'll be ready for lunch in about forty-five minutes. Okay?"

"Perfect." She could probably hear the relief in his voice. In his work and in his private life, to the extent possible, he surrounded himself with reasonable people, and Jackie was, if anything, reasonable. For that, he was thankful.

Jacqueline moseyed through the suite, admiring the antique-gold decorated living room; the little chrome kitchen; the elegant dining room with its Royal Bakara carpet and crystal chandeliers; the wonderfully feminine bedroom that had a canopied bed and chaise longue done in gold silk taffeta; and a Regency desk, chair and television cabinet. A bowl of yellow and red roses sat on a night table beside the bed.

She sat down on the edge of the chaise lounge, blinking her eyes to keep from crying. How had she managed to back herself into such a hole? He would never believe that a reporter worked as a waitress in that posh men's club for any reason other than to spy for story material. He would think her dishonest, and he wouldn't forgive her. But without her job as a waitress, she couldn't have paid her father's hospital and doctor bills or helped her father care for her mother after he exhausted all of his own resources. If Warren walked away from her, she would survive, but the light would go out of her life.

She dressed, picked up her coat and pocket book, locked her door and rang the bell at suite 7R.

"What's the matter?" she asked when he opened the door, unaware that the more intimate they became, the more she showed him Jacqueline Parkton instead of Jackie Parks. "Your expression says you're not happy. Don't you like your room?"

"It's perfect," he replied. "How's yours?"

"I love it. It's wonderful, Warren." She looked closely at him. "Aren't you going to answer my question?"

A smile formed around his lips. "As you said a few minutes ago, it's too early in the day for the heavy stuff, and that's what's on my mind right now. What do you say we go to a seafood restaurant at the edge of the lake?"

"I'm in your capable hands." She meant to follow his suggestions as to where they ate and what they did for recreation and entertainment, for she didn't want him to think her a gold digger. She'd have been content with a four-star hotel, instead of the palatial suite that he chose. She suspected that he lived well, but no one could make her believe that he was extravagant.

He locked the door of his suite, put the key in the pocket of his fur-lined, leather storm jacket and, with an arm around her waist, headed for the elevator.

"Women have a sneaky way of putting a man on his honor," he said in reference to her comment. "It works with some of us."

An expression of surprise covered her face. "And not with you? I wouldn't have thought it."

He rubbed her nose with the tip of his right index finger. "I do not remember saying that. I do my best to get what I want the honorable way."

The slow wink of her left eye sent hot blood charging to his loins, and when she said, "That definitely works with me," he stuck his hands in the pockets of his jacket to keep from grabbing her right there on the elevator.

Seconds before the elevator door opened, she reached up, kissed him on the mouth and said, "You're so sweet."

"Damn!" he said aloud, thoroughly discombobulated and not bothering to hide it.

After a satisfying lunch of grilled, fresh lake trout, roasted red and yellow peppers, corn muffins and a hot cranberry turnover, his libido still tortured him. Maybe if they walked a few blocks in the freezing temperature, he'd cool off in more ways than one.

"Let's walk along the main shopping drag," she said as if she were clairvoyant. "Maybe we can look at some antique shops."

He guided her to Church Street Market Place, though it had been his experience that New York offered the best in shopping no matter what you looked for. "So you like to shop," he said, hoping that he was wrong, for he considered shopping for shopping's sake the height of frivolity.

"Me? I detest shopping, but I love to browse for antiques."

"I don't recall any antiques in your apartment," he told her after an hour of strolling in and out of shops. "Let's sit over there by that fireplace and warm up a bit."

"I can't afford genuine antiques, but I enjoy looking at them."

He made a mental note of that. "We ought to head

back if you still want to swim," he told her, not that he was eager to give his libido more of a beating while he watched her in a bathing suit.

"I'll meet you at the pool in half an hour," she told him when they reached the door of her suite.

"Can't we go together?"

"We could, but it's best that I meet you there. Okay?" With a wink, she disappeared into her room. Meet him or go there along with him, he didn't see the difference, but he wasn't going to massacre his brain trying to figure it out. He was beginning to understand why his father's most frequent response to his mother had been, "Whatever you say, dear."

Long before she reached him, she saw him stretched out on a white beach lounge chair wearing swim trunks. He stood when he saw her, and she stopped short. Lord, but he was one beautiful man. Tall, lean and muscular, rippling flat belly and tight buttocks. She caught herself when she started fanning, and she couldn't close her mouth as he ambled toward her, slowly and lazily.

"You planning to swim in that thing?" he asked of the white, terry cloth robe.

Speechless, she could only stare at him, a perfect example of God's handiwork. His wicked grin seemed to singe her nerves as old devil desire slithered through her system. "Like what you see?" he teased.

Both of her hands went to her hips, but quickly fell to her sides. "Damn straight, I do," she replied, annoyed at being caught out, and he raised an eyebrow. She dropped the robe on a chair and was about to wade into the pool. *Oh, what the heck*, she thought and dove into the deep end, leaving him staring as if he'd been poleaxed. He dove in behind her, and they swam and frolicked in the water until he suggested that they get ready for dinner.

When she stepped out of the pool, a good-looking blond man attempted to waylay her.

Within seconds, Warren was out of the pool, and she could feel him behind her, hear his breathing and sense his rising anger.

Standing behind her with his hands gripping both of her shoulders, he said, "Don't even think about it, buddy."

The man saluted. "Sorry, pal. You're not the only guy who can see."

She turned to Warren, "Next time, give me a chance to tell the man that I'm with you."

He gazed down at her, but she didn't blink. "Sorry," he said, "but I hated the way he looked at you."

"I didn't notice, Warren. I barely noticed *him*. I have to dry my hair, so if you want to have dinner anytime soon, shouldn't we go?"

"There's a club just off the lobby," he said to her after their dinner in the hotel's restaurant. "Want to go?"

"I'd love to." She wanted to prolong the day. The night would take care of itself.

"You're so beautiful," he said after a waiter seated them in the hotel's Skyline Club. "And that dress suits you perfectly."

"I'm glad you like it. I love the way you look, too."
She had thought he would smile at that, but he didn't.
A mournful-sounding alto saxophone pealed forth with
"You Belong To Me." Wordlessly, he stood, opened his
arms, and she stepped into them. She hadn't danced in
years, but her body moved to him and with him as if she
had danced with him all of her life.

He didn't talk. Nor did she. There was no need; their
bodies spoke for them and to each other. The music
ended, but its sensual message remained in them, and
he stood there, still holding her, seemingly oblivious to
all in the world except her. She looked into the dark
pools of desire that his eyes had become and stared,
mesmerized, as he possessed her.

"Do you want to leave?" he asked her.

"Yes."

They didn't speak again until they reached the door
of her suite. "Would you like to come in?" she asked,
handing him her key. His answer was to open the door.
Within a second, he had his tongue deep in her mouth.

He stepped back from her. "I've been insane for you
since before that plane left New York. If you don't
want to make love with me, I'd better say good-night
this minute."

She wondered how a woman slowed a man down.
"What's the hurry?" she asked, aware as the words left
her mouth that they were the wrong ones.

Both of his eyebrows shot up. "How would you
feel if I picked you up, put you in that bed and
ravished you?"

It was her turn to raise an eyebrow. "I don't know. Why don't you try it? Sounds very exciting."

The last thing she expected from him was his lusty laugh. "I love you."

As if she didn't hear those words, she turned her back to him and said, "Which would you rather do, have a glass of wine or unzip this dress?"

"Where's that key?"

"Sticking in the door."

He picked her up, unlocked the door to his suite and put her in his bed. Excitement possessed her as she turned to her side and reached for the zipper. Immediately, his fingers covered hers, and he eased it down. She rolled over, stood and stepped out of the short, red dinner dress. His gasp matched the glimmer in his eyes as she revealed the low-cut red bra and matching bikini panties.

Her nerves began rearranging themselves in her body, and butterflies flitted around in her belly as he gazed at her.

"Warr—"

He swallowed the remainder of his name in a kiss, and as his hands roamed over her naked flesh, that empty space within her screamed to be filled. She wanted him inside of her and when she grabbed his buttocks and pressed herself to him in desperation, she felt him harden. Eager for all he could give her, she pressed his hand to her breast.

"What do you want? Tell me."

The urgency in his voice increased her excitement.

"I want your mouth on me. I want to feel your lips pulling on my nipple."

As eager for it as she, he put his hand inside of her bra, freed her left breast, and bent to it.

"Ooh," she sighed when his warm, moist mouth covered her nipple and began to suckle.

"Put me on the bed," she moaned, "and get in me."

He placed her across the bed, removed her bra and panties, stripped himself and knelt before her. With her legs hooked over his shoulders, he found his target with his talented tongue. She didn't try to restrain herself, as she bucked in response to his nipping, twirling and sucking, and her cries of pleasure filled the room.

"I'm going to explode," she moaned. "Get inside of me. I want you inside of me."

"All right, sweetheart." He eased her body to the edge of the bed, leaned forward and found his home deep inside of her. She thought she would die from the pleasure of his penis filling her, setting her on fire, possessing her. She was his, and he had to know it.

"How do you feel?" he whispered. "Am I hitting the right spot?"

"Yes. Oh, yes," she shouted. His face brightened into a smile of joy, and he began to move faster, bringing her to the edge, leaving her there, and taking her back again. Over and over he teased until she screamed, "I can't stand this. I'll go crazy!"

"Do you love me? Tell me."

"You know I love you. Only you," she said.

He sucked her left nipple into his mouth, feasted on

it voraciously, increasing the pace of his thrusts and rocking her until she screamed. "Don't you do this to anybody else."

"No, never. You're all I want. All I need. Give yourself to me."

Tremors shot through her and she could feel heat at the bottom of her feet and up her legs until her thighs shook. "I'm so full," she told him. "I need to burst."

"You will, sweetheart. Let yourself go." He put a hand beneath her hip and quickened his thrusts. "I want all of you."

She tightened her hold on him, braced herself on her heels and moved with him until suddenly the clinching and squeezing began in her vagina, gripping his penis, whirling her into a pit, dragging her back and flinging her into ecstasy as she burst wide open, and her scream pierced the air.

"Jackie!" he groaned, and gave her the essence of himself.

For a long time, neither spoke. She waited to come back to earth, to find herself still wrapped in his arms. Then, his arms gathered her close and she opened her eyes and looked into his brilliant, smiling face. Happiness seemed to envelop him, for his eyes shone as she'd never seen them.

"I've always prided myself in an ability to articulate my thoughts, but I don't have words to tell you what I'm feeling right now," he said. "I needed you so badly, and you gave and gave and gave. Do you really love me?"

"I don't know what else to call how I feel about you."

His lips brushed hers, barely touching, but they left a trail of fire. "You told me that you love me," she said. "Do you?"

"Yes, I love you, and I'm certain now that I've never loved any other woman." He separated them. "You sapped all of my energy, and I don't think you want to bear the weight of a hundred and ninety-three pounds."

"Hmm. I was doing all right a few minutes ago. Could I borrow your pajama top?"

"What pajama top? I'll get you a bath towel. Where're you going?"

"To my room. I'll be back."

Wrapped in a towel, she went to her room, brushed her teeth, removed her makeup, washed up, put on the white silk pajamas and went back to Warren.

He sat up in bed. "What's that?"

"You mean my pajamas? You don't like them?"

He stared at her. "You're joking. Did you go in there just to put on these...things?"

She threw the towel across the chaise longue. "No. I put them on because I like them. I figured if you didn't like 'em, you knew what you could do."

"And what's that?" he growled.

She lowered her gaze. "You can pull 'em off. You're...uh...not too sleepy, are you?"

He bent over laughing. "There is no way that you're going out of my life."

Shortly after one-thirty, Jackie slid out of bed, slipped on the top of her pajamas, found her bedroom shoes and went to her room. He would probably feel deserted, and perhaps he had that right, but she had never spent a night in bed with a man, and she didn't intend to do that until she was married. She just didn't think she'd feel comfortable waking up and staring into a man's face, not even Warren Holcomb's. Besides, she reasoned, as she crawled into her bed, feeling like a sneak, it would be the beginning of an affair, and she didn't want that. Warren Holcomb could get most any woman he wanted, and he probably knew it. She had enough problems facing her when their day of reckoning came, being easy to get shouldn't be one of them. All the same, she hated the loneliness that swept over her making her want to go back to him and nestle into the curve of his strong arms.

Chapter 8

Warren sat up in bed, trying to push aside a feeling to which he was unaccustomed. He hadn't failed her. Of that, he was certain. They came together, like the stars and stripes, blending to perfection. He had opened himself to her as he'd never done with any other human being, and she had reciprocated. How could she leave without a word? He turned on the light beside his bed and looked at his watch. Rubbing his scalp with the pads of his fingers and insensitive to the pain of it, he tried to come up with a reason why she would leave him. He'd loved her with his heart as well as his body, and she should have felt it.

"I'm not going after her," he said aloud, but he told himself to keep an open mind. And that wasn't easy, because he hurt. He got up, went to the window and gazed out at the night, made bright by the snow-capped mountain in the distance, and stared at the dark waters of Lake Champlain, the clear, star-encrusted sky above and the cold, unfeeling moon. Had he invested too much of himself in her? As much as he'd learned about her, he couldn't shake the feeling that he still knew nothing important of her life.

Oh, hell. Maybe I'm being unfair. Maybe she needs some privacy. She'd better have a damned reasonable explanation for loving me senseless and then leaving me without saying a word.

The more he thought about it, the uglier the scenario and the worse he felt. As tired and as miserable as he'd ever been, he crawled back into bed. She wanted him. Nothing anyone would say could make him believe otherwise. She went at him like a wild woman, giving until he thought she had no more to give, but then she crawled on top of him and made love to him until he nearly went out of his mind. And she loved him. So where was she? He started counting sheep.

Sometime later, he sniffed and turned over, but the odor of freshly brewed coffee still tantalized his nostrils. He opened his eyes, tentatively, for he wasn't sure of his whereabouts. He knew he wasn't home, because he wouldn't smell coffee in his house if he was in bed. If he smelled it, he'd made it.

"Wake up, sleepyhead. It's almost nine o'clock. Here. I brought you some coffee."

"I don't want any…" He sat up. "Jackie, for Pete's sake." He told himself to get it together, focused as best he could and looked hard at her. "Why did you leave me last night?"

She put the coffee on the night table and took his right hand in both of hers. "I've never spent the night with a man, Warren, and I…I didn't know how you or I would feel this morning. I also had no idea how I was supposed to behave this morning. Anyhow, I was terribly lonely after I left you, and my heart wanted me to come back here and curl up as close to you as possible. But if I did that, I'd need you all the time and my head doesn't want to start an affair with you. Maybe I should've said good night or something, but if you had so much as put an arm around me, I would've stayed."

He was fully awake now, trying to follow her reasoning, but having a difficult time doing it. "You're saying you left me because you didn't know whether I'd still care for you this morning? Woman, I hurt the rest of the night, and I didn't fall asleep until broad daylight."

"I'm sorry. I'm thirty-three years old, but before you there was only one man. *Once.* And that was terrible." Her hand caressed his cheek. "Do you understand what I'm saying?"

She'd said plenty. "Yes, and what you didn't say, too. But since I hurt all night, you have to kiss me and make it better."

Her lips brushed over his mouth in something less than his idea of a kiss. "While I'm telling the truth, I may as well say the rest. You can have any woman you want, but you seem to want me, and I'm happy that you do. But I'm not going to fall out of character. I have to be myself."

He also understood what she left out of that last statement. She intended to be herself without regard to his wealth and position, and that suited him perfectly. A thousand women would gladly love him for his money, and he wanted none of them. Because she loved him for himself, she was that much dearer to him.

He reached for the container of coffee and took several swallows. "Thanks for this. It's a treat to have it in bed." He finished the coffee, put the cup aside and looked at her. "You're so feminine and so sensual, yet you've spent years as a celibate. That guy must have wounded you deeply. Are you over it?"

She gazed steadily at him, giving him the impression that she wanted her words to sink in. "I've been over it mentally for a long time and, thanks to you, I'm no longer victimized by it emotionally."

He drew up his knees and locked his hands in front of them, his gaze still pinned on her. "Thank goodness for that." He hadn't understood how complex she was, and he was grateful that he hadn't made a major error with her. He lifted her to the bed and put an arm around her.

"Jackie, the night we made love in your apartment, you and I said some things to each other at the height of excitement that need substantiating. We did the same last night, only with a great deal more feeling.

"I'm not inside of you right now, and I'm telling you I love you. The more I see of you, the more you mean to me. How do you feel about me?"

To her credit, she didn't hesitate, didn't play a

game with him. "I'm in love with you." She poked out her bottom lip, and that perplexed him until she added, "I told you that on the plane coming up here. Don't you remember?"

As he hugged her close, he couldn't restrain his laughter. She never missed an opportunity to defend herself. "You mean you allowed me to figure it out on the basis of something else you said."

Rubbing the end of his nose with the tip of her right index finger, she said, "You're smart, so I figured I didn't have to paint you a picture."

Her arms tightened around him, and he held her close in one of the sweetest, most loving moments of his life. His heart seemed to swell in his chest, and he had an urge to hold her forever and to protect her from everyone and everything.

"I don't want to see any other women. I want us to get to know each other, to see if we can make it together. Is there another man in your life?"

When her face creased into a frown of disapproval, he realized that he may have surprised her, and he was certain of it when she said, "Of course not!"

He held up both hands, palms out. "I know. I know. Then, will you agree not to see other men while we work on our relationship?"

With a serious expression she said, "I agree. Does that mean I'm semicommitted to you?"

If that was the way she read it, fine with him. "You could say that. As soon as you can manage it, I'd like you to meet my folks. I've met yours."

For a second, he thought she'd wandered away from him again, but she said, "I'd love to meet them. Maybe in a couple weeks when I have my next long weekend." Then, as if she suddenly remembered that she had a watch, she focused on it. "Are we going to ski this morning? It's nearly ten."

"I'll be ready in half an hour, so go put on your ski clothes."

"Okay. That'll give me time to chat with Papa."

Standing at the door of her apartment that Sunday night, he said to her, "I hope this weekend has been as meaningful for you as it has been for me."

"They were the most important three days of my life," she told him, although she hadn't realized that until she heard her words.

A frown creased his forehead, and she thought he seemed hesitant about something. She supposed she noticed it because hesitancy was not a trait that she associated with him.

"Be careful at the club. I am not a man given to settling things with my fists, but Hornsby doesn't have any sense and… Well, just be careful, please."

She was worried enough about Hornsby without having Warren tell her that he also had concerns. "I won't give him cause to approach me, but if he does, I will defend myself."

A half smile played around his lips. "Poor fool. I hope he has already learned a lesson. Kiss me. I'll call you when I get home."

She opened her arms, parted her lips and took him in, enraptured by the joy of loving and being loved.

Jackie had never been more grateful than when Hornsby failed to appear at Allegory that Monday night. "I think he's ashamed," Ben said of Hornsby. "But if I read him right, he'll be back. He'd pay a million dollars to keep this membership. If he gets out of hand, just let me know. He broke one rule when he hit on you, and a couple of the members are anxious to expel him."

"What's the chance of getting Christmas off, Ben? My dad's anxious to have dinner away from the clinic."

"The board voted to close from the twenty-third to the twenty-sixth. It's posted on the bulletin board. My wife and I are leaving Thursday morning for Atlanta. You spending Christmas with Warren?"

She stared at him. "What?"

"Very little gets past me, Jackie. He's a fine man. One of the best."

With shaking fingers, she picked up the tray of drinks and walked with hesitant steps to the main lounge where several men played chess. She managed to serve the drinks without spilling them and returned to her station. Who else knew about her relationship with Warren? A liaison that was against club rules. Should she tell Warren?

It wouldn't make his mother happy, but it was the best he could do. "I'll be at your place Christmas morning around eleven," he told Jackie, "and we'll drive up to Riverdale, get your father and bring him to my place for Christmas dinner."

"How are you going to manage this if you're spending Christmas Eve with your folks in Durham?' she asked him. "We could have dinner at my place."

"Not to worry. I'll be back in New York at five after nine Christmas morning, and dinner's taken care of."

"When am I going to meet her?" his mother asked him as he was about to leave her home on Christmas morning.

"In two or three weeks. As soon as she can get time off from work."

"I'm looking forward to meeting her, son. I'm not interested in judging her. I just pray that she and I will love each other. That's all I want."

He wrapped his mother in his arms, hoping to calm the fears that reached him in the tremors that laced her voice. "If you greet her with open arms, Mom, she'll love you. I'm not concerned about that."

His mother gazed into his eyes. "Do you love each other?"

"We love each other."

"That's all I need to know."

Later that day Warren walked out of New York's La-Guardia Airport, got into his car and headed for West End Avenue in Manhattan. To his delight, he arrived at Jackie's address just before ten o'clock, parked and phoned her.

"Hi. Merry Christmas. I'm parked outside your building. How soon can you be ready?"

"Merry Christmas. As soon as I get my coat."

He met her at the front door of the building, and took the parcels that she carried. *Why am I so excited?* he asked himself, as he fastened her seat belt. Before putting the car in Drive, he leaned over to kiss her mouth and stopped as shock reverberated throughout his body. He had practically told his mother that he intended to marry Jackie Parks. Slowly, he bent to her mouth and lingered there savoring the sweetness that she offered.

"My mother sends you her love," he said as he moved the Town Car from the curb and headed for Riverdale.

"Thank you, Warren. I want to meet her, but I confess I'm a bit wary."

"She wants the two of you to like each other. You see, I've never taken a woman to meet my family."

He could see that Jackie was taken aback. "Don't worry," he hastened to add. "You two will get on beautifully." He refused to imagine that they wouldn't. At the moment, he had to concentrate on dealing with her father.

"You're early," Clyde Parkton said when they walked into his room. "Merry Christmas." He extended a hand to Warren. "And thanks for getting me out of here at least for today. It's the best Christmas gift I could get."

Clyde Parkton had once been a figure of a man, and when he stood, tall, lean and dressed in his gray pin-stripe suit, gray dress shirt and blue paisley tie, he looked to Warren as if he were a university professor, and Warren said as much.

"I've flunked a few students in my day," he said,

"but I never enjoyed it. My pleasure came from those who excelled."

"We're having dinner at my house," Warren said.

"You said we would, and that's what I expected," the older man said.

"How do you feel, Papa?"

"Better than I've felt in years. I wish I'd had that surgery earlier. Where do you live, Warren?"

"Brooklyn Heights, sir, and we'll be there shortly."

He double parked in front of his house. "Sweetheart, would you sit here while I take your father inside?" He nearly leaned over and kissed her, remembered who sat in the backseat, got out and assisted her father inside the house and to his living room. "Have a seat, sir. I'll be back with Jackie as soon as I put the car in the garage."

"Thanks. How far away is the garage?"

"It's attached to the house."

"Hmm, and this is a fine place you have here."

"Thank you." He went through the dining room on his way to the kitchen. "Mrs. Ross, is everything all right?"

"Yes, indeed. Right on time. You might want to put a couple of logs on the fire in the living room. I've been too busy to take proper care of it."

"The table is beautiful," he told his caterer, "and the house smells wonderful."

He rushed back to the car, drove it into his garage and turned off the engine. Before he could reach for her, she lifted her arms to him. "Go easy, sweetheart. You've consigned me to celibacy, so please don't raise the heat level."

As if she hadn't heard him, her lips parted, and with

his tongue deep in her mouth, his libido began its dance. He pulled away and gazed down into her face. "I know you don't want us to have an affair, but we're having one, so keep it between the lines, sweetheart. I'm human."

She reached up and kissed his nose. "I never would have thought it. Let's go inside before Papa thinks we're off some place making out."

"Aren't we?" They entered through the kitchen and, after introducing her to his caterer, he led her to the living room where her father awaited them.

"Warren, what a delightful place this is. Your home is lovely."

"Don't tell me this is the first time you've been here," Clyde said to his daughter. He looked at Warren. "Have you ever been to her apartment?"

"A few times. Would you like to rest awhile?"

"I had thought I'd be tired, but I'm fine."

Warren roasted pecans, chestnuts and hazelnuts at the edge of the fireplace, and the odor of the roasting nuts mingled with the scent of pine and bayberry tantalized his olfactory sense. He breathed deeply as he shelled nuts for his guests.

I've lived alone too long, he thought to himself. *I've never before been this happy in my house.*

"I'm surprised you didn't dress a tree," Clyde said, interrupting Warren's thoughts.

"It's in the den. We'll go in there after dinner."

Clyde looked at Jackie. "How was last weekend?"

She gave the impression of having forgotten his bargain with her father, promising him Christmas dinner if he would excuse Jackie for the weekend. "The weekend? Oh. I had a wonderful time."

"Good," Clyde said. "I knew you would."

Mrs. Ross entered the living room. "Dinner is served, Mr. Holcomb."

"I should have known that you have a housekeeper," Jackie said to Warren.

"But I don't. Mrs. Ross is a caterer and party planner. She's also a great cook." He didn't know Clyde's preferences, but he was at his table in his house, and he'd been raised to say the grace before meals. He reached for their hands, bowed his head and said the grace.

When he had finished, Clyde leaned back in his chair and looked at him. "The more I see of you, the happier I am that you are a part of my daughter's life."

He hadn't expected that, but he appreciated it. "Thank you."

After a dinner of oyster stew, roast turkey with gravy, cornbread dressing, red cabbage with chestnuts, glazed winter squash, cranberry relish, arugula salad, stilton cheese and lemon meringue pie, Warren felt like royalty.

As Clyde savored the pie, he said, "I've a good mind to ask Mrs. Ross if she's already taken. Food can't get any better than this, especially after eating hospital food all these months."

"Let's go into the den," Warren said, and led his guests into the wood-paneled room where fire crackled in the huge stone fireplace, and a ceiling-high fir tree sparkled with lights. Beautifully wrapped packages lay on the floor beneath it.

He was glad to have Jackie's father with them, because Jackie seemed so quietly content, he'd even say she radiated happiness, but he yearned to be alone with her and to show her his home from the basement to the attic. She sat in a beige-leather wing chair, leaned back and crossed her knees, comfortable and relaxed. He stood over her, looking down at the reflection of the dancing flames on her face and in her eyes. No doubt about it, she belonged in his home and in his life.

"Sorry to cramp your style," Clyde said, "but a little discipline is good for everybody."

Warren's head snapped around. He could hardly believe the satisfied glint of wickedness in the man's eyes. "Besides," Clyde went on, turning the knife, "if this is her first time in your house, you haven't been very eager to get things…uh…going. This place would impress any woman."

He mused over those words for a few seconds before deciding not to respond. If the man was fishing for information, he'd have to ask a direct question. "Let's have some Christmas music," he said. "From the time I was growing up, I could count on three things in our home at Christmas time—religious music, family prayers at the table and, most especially, a lot of happiness."

"Sounds like the way I grew up," Jackie said. "We had the traditional food and presents, too, but they were never the focus."

Soon, the sound of the Mormon Tabernacle Choir singing carols filled the room, and he noticed that

Jackie's father had closed his eyes, crossed his knees and begun swinging his right foot. He couldn't resist leaning down and kissing her. He flicked his tongue across the seam of her lips, and his heart bounced in his chest when she reached up, grasped his head and parted her lips. He plunged into her, stifling a groan as he did so. However, she broke the kiss quickly.

"Nothing this wonderful can possibly last," she said with a worried look on her face that stunned him.

Just my imagination, he thought, walked over to the tree, picked up a package and handed it to her father. "Merry Christmas, sir."

Clyde opened his eyes. "You're a very gracious man. Thank you." He opened the package and took out a state-of-the-art iPod. "Well, well. This is something I've wanted. Yes, indeed. Thank you so much." The smile on the man's face told him more than his words did. Warren had spent hours thinking about the gift and had settled on the MP3 player, because he could exchange it if the man already had one. His eyebrows shot up and his mind became a whirlwind when Clyde opened his daughter's gift of three leather-bound volumes containing the works of Greek, English and German philosophers. Clyde's hands caressed the volumes with the gentleness one would use when touching a newborn baby.

"I see you intend to keep me mentally active," he said to her. "You know how I will cherish these."

Next, Jackie handed Warren a box wrapped in gold foil with a green star-spangled ribbon. "Merry Christmas, love," she said, and he relished the fact that she hadn't allowed her father's presence to deprive her of the opportunity to greet him as she wished.

In response he leaned down and kissed her quickly on the mouth. "Thank you for thinking of me," he said, and handed her a small red box tied with a red velvet bow. "Merry Christmas, sweetheart."

A grin spread over his face when he saw the brown leather travel kit with WH in gold letters. His taste precisely. He held his breath while she stalled for time, opening the box he handed her.

"Good Lord," she gasped. "Papa, would you look at this!" she exclaimed of the diamond tennis bracelet. "Warren, this is the most beautiful thing I've ever had." To his amazement, she jumped up and hugged him. He fastened it on her arm, and she walked over to her father. "See?"

"It's beautiful," Clyde said. "I hope the two of you will show the Lord proper appreciation for this gift he's given you." He looked at Warren, "And I remember your telling me I had to get well so I could see my grandchildren. I'm not saying any more, but you're a smart man."

A glance at Jackie told him that she was appalled at her father's bluntness, but he wasn't. He needed all the support he could get. If Jackie ever entertained the thought of a life with him, she hadn't shared it with him, although he'd put out feelers more than once. But it seemed that he had her father's good wishes, and he meant to make the most of that.

"Do you play chess, sir?" he asked Clyde, pretending to have ignored the comment about grandchildren.

"Do I play chess? Indeed! Trouble is I can't find anyone who can play."

"Then would you play with me on, say, Monday afternoons?"

Clyde sat forward. "I'd love to, but don't you work?"

"Yes, I do, but when you're up to it, maybe you can come up to Harlem Clubs and give me a hand. I'll bet you could get those kids interested in the classics."

"I can get anybody interested in the classics. Next time we meet, I hope you'll tell me more about these clubs." He looked at Jackie. "And when I see you again, I hope you'll tell me why you're dragging your feet with this fellow."

She looked him in the eye. "I will if you tell me why you're embarrassing me. I thought the time had passed when fathers tried to palm off their daughters on the first man to come along." Warren looked from father to daughter and back, detected no animosity and relaxed.

"I know a good man when I see one," Clyde said with a broad grin on his face.

"I know this will surprise you, Papa, but I do, too. After all, I've had a good example all my life." She grinned when she said it, and Warren couldn't hold back the laughter, for their physical resemblance was so strong, and he could see that their likeness in regard to personality was just as strong. He got a bottle of his best brandy, poured three glasses and gave one to each of his guests.

"I get a wonderful feeling being with you two, and I think it calls for a warm drink."

Clyde Parkton held up his glass. "Here's my wish for many more evenings like this one."

Warren didn't like Jackie's wistful look, but he drank to the toast. "Amen."

She drank, but said nothing.

"Aren't you getting tired, Papa? I don't think we should overdo it."

He drained his glass. "I probably am, but I'm enjoying being a normal person for the first time in over a year. This has been wonderful, Warren." He stood, clutching his gifts, and looked around. "The one thing missing in this fine house is books."

"They're upstairs in my study. On your next visit, I hope you'll feel like taking a look up there."

"So do I," Clyde said. "So do I."

"Good evening, sir," the receptionist said to Clyde when they returned to the clinic later that evening. "Did you have a lovely Christmas?"

"Indeed." He hugged Jackie and then turned to Warren. "Thank you for a delightful day. I'm looking forward to seeing you Monday at four."

"I'll be here."

Jackie and Warren said little to each other on the drive to Jackie's apartment, because he couldn't shake the feeling she had withdrawn. He parked across the street from the building in which she lived and accompanied her to her apartment.

"Would you like to come in?" she asked him.

He wondered at the question, for she had to know how hungry he was for her. "I want to, but you'll send me packing before morning," he said, taking in her plaintive expression. The look on her face nearly brought him to his knees, and he took the key from her, opened the door and entered the apartment holding her tight in his arms.

"Kiss me, Jackie. Kiss me like you mean it."

She didn't understand why he had to say that, but she knew he needed her, had known all day that his need for her was as great as hers for him. She opened her arms to him and parted her lips for the thrust of his tongue, but nothing, not even their previous lovemaking, had prepared her for the driving, powerful need that the trembling of his body communicated to her.

"Warren, what is it? What's the matter?"

"Just love me. Let me know that I'm all you want and need."

She struggled out of her coat and then shed her jacket, letting them fall to the floor. "You don't need me any more than I need you," she told him. But even as he crushed her body to his, she realized that it wasn't enough for him. He picked her up, carried her to her bedroom and set her away from him, his eyes ablaze with fierce intensity.

"You said you needed me."

Something had given him a feeling of insecurity about her. The only experience she'd had with making love to a man had been with him. With only her instincts to guide her, she slipped the knot in his tie and pulled the tie over his head. Her fingers shook as she unbuttoned his shirt, drew it from his broad shoulders and put it across a chair. Perspiration moistened her forehead as she unhooked his belt and began unzipping his trousers.

She didn't glance up at him—she couldn't; but suddenly she felt his finger beneath her chin, looked up and thought her heart would break when she saw the smile that blanketed his face. His arms went around her, and his lips brushed her forehead, eyes, nose and cheeks. She held him so tightly that her arms began to ache, but she didn't relax her grip. He unzipped her dress, and she stepped out of it, leaving herself bare to him but for her little bra, garter belt, stockings and bikini panties.

"Do you always wear red underwear?" he asked her, lifting her and putting her on the bed. She didn't answer, only raised her hips as he removed her panties.

His gaze roamed from her head to her feet and back, and she grabbed a pillow to cover her body. But he wouldn't allow it. "You're as beautiful as a woman can be, and I love to look at you." She knew his passion was rising when he swallowed so heavily that his Adam's apple seemed to dance in his throat. Her blood responded with a wild ride straight to her loins, and she crossed her legs, but almost simultaneously he grew erect to full readiness. She swallowed the liquid that accumulated in her own mouth, held out her arms to him and said, "Come here."

He moved so quickly, that he nearly fell onto the bed,

ripped off his underwear and covered her with his body. She parted her lips for his kiss, but he stunned her, sucking her left nipple into his mouth and sending his talented fingers down to create a fire in her vagina. He teased, rubbed and stroked, playing her with the skill of a lyrist playing a lyre.

Her hips began to sway out of control, and she spread her legs for his entry, but he demurred, teasing, sucking and nipping at her breasts and bringing her near to completion with his dancing fingers. "Do something," she moaned. "Get in me, or I'll go crazy." But he charted his own course until, exacerbated with desire, she pushed him over, mounted him and took him. Screams poured out of her as she climaxed again and again until, spent, she collapsed on him. He rolled her over on her back, increased his pace with a furious pumping until he splintered in her arms.

He had made love with her, but he hadn't possessed her, and even as he remained locked inside of her, he sensed a growing distance between them. "Jackie, open your eyes and look at me."

Her eyelids seemed to move at a snail's pace, and at last he confirmed in them not the warmth he would have expected in the eyes of a sated woman but the look of wariness. If there had been a reason for it, he would call it fear. He separated them, but linked his fingers through hers and settled on his back.

"Do you have anything to tell me?" he asked her. "Twice at my home, I couldn't reach you...you were in a distant world, and I'd swear you were worried. We've just made love, but I detect a barrier between us, and I didn't put it there. Don't tell me it's my imagination. It isn't."

She sat up in bed. "Forgive me, Warren. You made it a wonderful Christmas for my father and for me, but this is the first Christmas I've spent without my mother. Please don't read anything into this."

He wanted to believe her "But if you're lonely for her, it seems you'd feel closer to me." Possible explanations whirled around in his head, and suddenly his heartbeat seemed suspended. "You're not pregnant, are you? I've tried to take precautions." He had to lean over her to hear her words.

"I haven't had any indications of that."

"How would you feel about it if you were?"

"Pregnant with your child?" Her voice was stronger now. "Given the right circumstances, I'd be deliriously happy." She turned on her side with her back to him.

"Wait a minute here," he said. "You can't drop a bomb like that one and then clam up with your back to me. Do you want a family?"

"Uh-huh."

"Then what…?" He grasped her shoulder, turned her onto her back and looked down into her face. "Sweetheart, what's the matter? You're crying. Can't you have children?"

"As f-far as I kn-know."

"My Lord." He gathered her into his arms. "If you

can't tell me about it, at least tell me whether it will ever be all right."

Her arms gripped him so tightly that he wondered where she got the strength. "Things will straighten themselves out when Papa is discharged from the clinic and settled again."

"Are you worried about money? Why would you be when you know I've got plenty of it?"

She shook her head. "You've given me more than money can buy, and my father, too. I wouldn't accept money from you, Warren. I don't want that kind of relationship with you or with any man."

He'd thought that, and it pleased him to hear her say it. "But if you have a problem, don't you know that I'm here for you?"

"Yes, I know it. Oh, Warren."

Was it a cry for help or a plea for understanding? He didn't know which, only that she needed him. A strange weakness stole over him, and he trembled with a harrowing need to give himself to her. Her fingers stroked his cheek, and then grasped his nape in a message that he'd come to understand, and he thrust his tongue into her mouth. But she wanted more, and within minutes he was surging inside of her.

"Do you love me?" he asked her. "I want to hear you say it."

"Yes, I love you. I'm yours. Yours," she shouted.

"And I'm yours," he said as she erupted around him, and he gave her the essence of himself.

At midnight, he still lay on top of her, wrapped in her

arms. Several times, he had made a gentle attempt to move, but she had tightened her hold on him. "If I go back to sleep," he warned her, "I'll be here in the morning."

"Are you coming to the club tonight?" she asked him.

"Yes. If we don't get a chance to talk privately, let's meet and I'll drive you home. The forecast is for snow. If it comes, we'll make other plans." He got up and began to dress.

"Do you feel better about…about us?" she asked him.

He put his tie in his pocket and sat on the edge of the bed. "As long as you're straight with me, nothing will come between us. I'm in this for the long haul, Jackie, and I'm in deep. Don't forget that."

She had never been so close to falling apart as when he asked whether she had something to tell him. If he only knew. *I can't go on like this. I lied to him, and I've always prided myself in being truthful. He no longer talks with me at the club or places an order in a private lounge, and I know it's because he doesn't want to break club rules. If I had enough money to pay the surgeon's bill, I'd quit the club.* Her upcoming lecture at the Alexandria Police Academy wouldn't net her enough to make a dent in the surgeon's bill.

She refused to worry herself sick about this. He'd either break up with her or he wouldn't. Her duty was to take care of her father, and she was doing that honestly. With that thought, Jackie went into the bathroom, showered and got ready for bed.

* * *

She arrived at work the following morning to find a sealed note taped to her office door. She detached it, opened her office and went inside reading the note as she walked.

"Dr. Parkton," she read, "would you please join us in the third-floor conference room at three today? Thank you, Junior Staff."

She wondered if there was a problem, but decided to wait until three o'clock to find out. She'd been working on a story about adolescent girls in low-income neighborhoods, spurred by her visits to Harlem Clubs, and she spent most of her working day polishing it. At a few minutes before three, her secretary buzzed her on the intercom.

"Dr. Parkton, are you coming to the third-floor conference room?"

"I'll be there in a couple of minutes." She cleared her desk, locked it and headed for the third floor.

A chorus of "Jingle Bells" greeted her when she opened the conference room door. A lighted Christmas tree stood in a far corner, the conference table was laden with food and wine, and a potbellied Santa Claus ushered her to the center of the room. Her first thought was that she was the only senior management person present, not that she minded.

"Dr. Parkton," Santa Claus began, "it gives me great pleasure on behalf of the entire junior staff of *African American Woman* magazine to present you with this small token of our appreciation for your kindness to us.

Your devotion to fairness and honesty makes working here a pleasure."

"I don't know when I've been more moved," she said. "Thank you. I'll cherish this." Realizing that they wanted her to open it, she did and, to their delight and applause, gasped at the sight of a two-ounce bottle of her favorite perfume. "This certainly won't go to waste," she told them. She sampled the food, but skipped the wine, for Allegory club rules forbade her to drink while working, and she didn't want the scent of alcohol on her breath. She thanked them again and left to prepare for her evening job, somewhat surprised that the junior staff regarded her as their favorite among the more senior staff.

She had an eerie feeling entering Allegory that evening, and it wasn't due to the inclement weather. As soon as she changed into her uniform, she went to the bar. "How's everything, Ben?" she asked him. "I hope your Christmas was as pleasant as mine."

"Couldn't have been better, thanks, but all hell's threatening to break loose here. Hornsby's on the warpath. He wants you fired, and there's going to be a big fight about it."

"But Ben, I need the work."

"Act like you don't know anything about this. He'll have to get around three of the members and me. And I remember I had to walk out of here with you one night to protect you from him. Not to worry."

She went back to her station with a gnawing ache in her belly and a fear that she could cause a problem for Warren if he chose to defend her against Hornsby's complaints. All she had done was force him to keep his hands off her. If she had to do it again, she'd pitch him down even harder.

She answered the telephone, surprised that the call wasn't coming through the intercom. "Service. Jackie speaking."

"This is Hornsby. I want to see you in the office this minute."

She took a deep breath and thought rapidly for a way out. "In a minute, Mr. Hornsby." She rushed to the bar. "Ben, Hornsby just called and ordered me to his office."

"Wait here. I'll go with you."

She walked into the club office with Ben right behind her. "Yes, Mr. Hornsby," she said.

"You thought you were so clever with your tricks, did you? Well, as president of this club, I'm firing you. You'll get your pay in the mail."

"And as manager of this club, I'm the only person here who has the right legally to hire and fire the employees. You're out of line," Ben said. He turned to Jackie. "Go back to your station. I'll take care of this. It's a matter for the board."

She went back to her station, but her uneasy feeling about Hornsby wouldn't leave her. At midnight, she changed into her street clothes, left Allegory by the Fifth Avenue exit, mostly to foil any attempts at revenge Hornsby might make and headed for her meeting with Warren.

When she was seated in his car, Warren leaned over,

kissed her quickly on the mouth, too quickly to satisfy her, and moved away from the curb.

"I know what's going on," he told her, "but you needn't worry. The board meets tomorrow, and tomorrow will be Hornsby's last day as club president. We're supposed to be a civilized group of men, and Hornsby has begun to pop the cork. What do you say, you and I spend Saturday and Sunday in Durham? This is your long weekend off, and you'd still have Monday and Tuesday free."

It wasn't the time to meet his family, but she remembered that on Christmas night he'd been suspicious, and if she put him off, he would demand an explanation. "All right," she said, aware that she sounded anything but enthusiastic. "What's your mother like?"

"Down to earth. Biscuits and cornbread, and I'm the apple of her eye."

That last part was precisely what she feared. "You... uh...think she'll approve of your being involved with a cocktail waitress?"

"I haven't told her what you do."

"But she'll ask me, Warren, and I am not going to lie to her."

He parked at her address, turned and looked her fully in the face. "I said my mother is down to earth. I did not say she's stupid."

Jackie didn't know how to take that, so she didn't comment. As he walked with her to the elevator, she realized that her distraught feeling had nothing to do with her impending meeting with Warren's mother and everything to do with the fact that she couldn't share with him the honor that the magazine's junior staff had paid her earlier in the day. She had another life of which he knew nothing, and that life was the most important part of her.

"You're on another planet again tonight," he said when the elevator arrived. "One of these days you're either going to take me wherever it is that you go or I'll be gone when you get back. I'm praying that it doesn't come to that." Her eyes widened, and she didn't part her lips when his mouth pressed hers, startled as she was by the harshness of his kiss.

"You want to explain that kiss?" she asked him.

"Chalk it up to frustration." His arms eased around her and, for a minute, he held her tenderly. "See you tomorrow night."

Chapter 9

Jacqueline regarded royal blue as a conservative color, and she looked good in it, though not her best. Nonetheless, she dressed in a woolen suit of that color. As cold as it was, she would have loved to wear her fur coat, but that coat belonged to her life as Dr. Jacqueline Parkton. Jackie Parks wore a gray tweed coat. With her left hand held tightly in Warren's right one, Jackie stood at Jayne Holcomb's front door with her heart near the pit of her stomach. She'd never been so scared in her life. The door opened, and a tall matronly woman looked directly at her, and after a second, the woman's face creased into a warm and welcoming smile. Then, she looked at Warren, reached up and hugged him.

"Mom, this is Jackie Parks. Jackie, my mother, Jayne Holcomb."

Jayne Holcomb opened her arms, and Jackie walked into them. She knew at once that Jayne's hug was anything but perfunctory, for she felt the woman's fingers—the fingers of a loving mother—caress her shoulders. She didn't want it to be one-sided, so she stepped back and looked Jayne in the eye.

"Thank you for greeting me so warmly. I didn't know what to expect, and I confess that my nerves are a wreck."

"No need for that," Jayne said, still smiling. "This house is and always has been filled with love. Put her bags in the guest room, son."

She took Jackie's hand and walked into the spacious living room. "I know this isn't easy for you, because you feel as if you're on trial. You are not. I want my son to be happy, and he will be if you and I learn to love each other. He didn't tell me that you're so beautiful and so elegant. What do you do?"

There it was, and she would meet it head on. "I'm a waitress at Allegory, Inc. That's where I met Warren."

Jayne appeared skeptical. "Waiting tables is good, honest work, but somehow, it doesn't seem to fit you. I'd have sworn that you're an executive." Her quick shrug said it didn't matter, and her words confirmed it. "Whatever. I'm glad you're here. You've made my son happy, and that's what matters to me. I hope you'll come to see me often, and that you and I will become close."

Jackie looked at the woman who had given life to the man she loved and smiled. "No wonder Warren is such a fine man. I'm glad I came."

"I wasn't eavesdropping," Warren said, "but I must say that what I heard doesn't surprise me." With an arm around Jackie's waist, he kissed her cheek. "She's very important to me, Mom."

"I know, and I'm happy for you."

Later, as they strolled hand-in-hand along the edge of Amber Brook, she told him, "I like your mother."

"I knew you would. With Mom, what you see is what you get."

"She asked me what I do, and I told her I'm a waitress at Allegory. The question surprised me, and so did her reaction when I told her. She really didn't seem to mind."

He pushed his hands into his trouser pockets, and kicked a tuft of moss. "Why should she mind? Anyhow, she probably doesn't believe you. If I didn't know better, I'd swear you were a university professor." He paused as if waiting for her reaction to that remark, and she knew the thought had crossed his mind before. She didn't comment.

"Let's sit over here. I like to feed the ducks." He broke off a few pieces of bread and threw them into the brook. "I've done this since I was a boy."

The birds crowded at the edge of the water, catching the bread crumbs as he threw them. "Back then, this area was dense with trees, hedges and wildflowers. Now, it's a public park. Nice, but different from the paradise of my youth where I wandered and dreamed."

He pointed to a tree whose girth proclaimed its considerable age. "I'd sit there with my back against that tree counting the birds that flew overhead, listening to the wind whistle through the trees, hearing the ripples of this brook play all kinds of tunes in my head. This was my Eden. From here, I traveled the world and accomplished all kinds of feats. And this is where I vowed to go to Massachusetts Institute of Technology. But when I was admitted to MIT, I quit dreaming and got down to business."

"You mean the place lost its attraction for you?"

"Oh, no. I was sitting over there when I decided to build a home for my parents, made plans to buy my first hotel and drew up the basic plan for Harlem Clubs. Right here is where it all began." His voice dropped, and he looked into the distance as sadness enveloped him once more. "I was sitting at the base of that same tree when my sister came and told me that my dad had passed and, somehow, I always feel close to him when I'm here."

"I'm sorry that I can't know your father. He must have been an extraordinary man," she said with a wistfulness in her voice that surprised her. "I was born ten blocks from where I live now, and there was nothing idyllic about Riverside Drive, because I couldn't go out alone. And it was freezing cold and windy in winter." She wondered if it was a good time to discuss Allegory, Inc.

"Warren, my father will be able to leave the clinic in a few weeks and, with my end-of-year bonus, I'll be able to finish paying for the costs of his illness and to leave the club. This has been a difficult period, because my father used all of his financial resources to care for my mother during her long and expensive illness, and he tried to give her the best available care.

"Another reason why I want to leave Allegory is that my presence there has become divisive. I don't want another fight with Duff Hornsby."

"I understand what you're saying, but Hornsby is no longer president and, with one more infraction, he'll be expelled from the club. He thought he could break the rules with impunity because he's the wealthiest member of the club, but the board voted unanimously to censure him. Arthur Morgan is now club president, and I'm a board member."

"Congratulations."

"Thanks. I think. Let's walk a bit farther. I want to show you where I fished with my father." He pointed to a notch on a tree. "This was my height when I was six."

She loved him, and now she was learning what it was like to be a part of him, to know him intimately, beyond the physical and the sensual. Something inside of her wanted to express that to him. She took his right hand. "Did you ever kiss a girl here?"

With half a frown and half a squint, he said, "I've never brought a girl here or even considered it."

She stepped closer, reached up and pressed her lips to his. "This time with you means more to me that I know how to express, and I just had to somehow seal it for all time. A kiss seemed the proper way."

He looked around. "May as well do it right," he said with a smile playing around his mouth. His big right hand stroked her back while he gazed down at her, causing her to wonder what he saw. Without warning, he crushed her to his body and sent his tongue roaming in her mouth, seeking, sampling and reducing her to putty.

Expelling a long sigh, he grasped her hand and began retracing their steps. "This was certainly not the place for that," he said, referring to their passionate kiss.

When they returned to the house, it surprised her when Warren's sister opened the door. She hugged Warren and then looked at Jackie. "If he had brought you down here and taken you back to New York without my meeting you, I would have blasted him. I'm Dorothy. The family calls me Dot."

She looked at the tall and handsome woman and let the grin on her face have its way. "You two look enough alike to be twins," she said. "I'm happy to meet you, Dot. Don't be too hard on him. He at least told me that you existed."

"He told me about you, Jackie...after I guessed that there had to be a you, because he wore the signs like a blazer. Welcome. Next time you come, I want you to meet my three children, and my husband if he's not on a flight. He's a pilot."

"Dot likes to talk," he said to Jackie. "I smell food, and there's nothing so tantalizing as the odors that come from Mom's kitchen."

"That may be true, Jackie, but my brother will eat anything you put in front of him."

"I hope you don't mind if I don't touch that one," Jackie said, thinking that she liked Warren's mother and sister. But in the back of her mind lurked a fear that Warren would walk out of her life when he realized that she hadn't squared with him, for these people wore honesty the way a robin wears the red on his breast. She pasted a smile on her face and told herself to enjoy it while it lasted.

Warren didn't ask his mother how she felt about Jackie. Her opinion of the woman of his choice wouldn't figure in his decision, and his mother knew that. Nonetheless, her words as they were about to return to New York, "I sense that you've picked the right one, but we'll see," gave him a good feeling.

"I hope she'll come back to see me, with or without you," Jayne told him. "I enjoy talking with her, and I want us to be good friends."

"You're behaving as if I'm going to marry Jackie," he said. "I've never broached the subject to her."

"That's what she said. But you will, because she's in your blood. I knew it as soon as I saw the two of you together."

"Interesting," he said rather than confirming the validity of her remark. "I'll be glad to bring her with me on my next visit, provided she'll come. Thanks for being so gracious to her."

"Son, you know I don't act. However I behaved toward her was genuine."

"Thanks." He called up the stairs. "Jackie, what's holding you up there? We have to make a plane that leaves in an hour and a half." He listened to her footsteps as she dashed along the hall and raced down the stairs. Wasn't it time he rid himself of the nagging questions and reservations he had about her? Little things that caused him to hold back, that prevented him from embracing their relationship as fully and completely as he wished. When he asked, she'd said she had nothing to tell him. Perhaps she thought so; he didn't.

On Monday afternoon, as promised, he arrived at the clinic in Riverdale at a few minutes before four o'clock. "I'm here to see Clyde Parkton," he told the receptionist.

"He's waiting for you in the waiting room. Would you like tea or coffee? Clyde usually drinks tea in the afternoons."

"I'd love some coffee," he told her, looked around for Jackie's father and saw him in a far corner near a window. As he approached, the man stood and extended his hand

"Thanks for coming. I've been looking forward to seeing you. Have a seat. My daughter usually spends Sunday afternoon with me, but I didn't see her yesterday, and I assumed she was off somewhere with you. Was I right?"

He decided not to answer, leaned back in the chair and looked the man in the eye. "If you weren't right, you could be accused of tattling or even fomenting trouble."

Laughter rolled out of Clyde. "I see you keep your own counsel. That's a fine trait. Tell me something about your Harlem Clubs."

He decided to start at the beginning. "Clyde, I'm a computer engineer who began early and hit it big. When computer companies and chip makers began going under, I pulled out of the one in which I worked, took my shares and invested in a hotel, one that offered something different. Today, I own three of them, and I'm building a fourth. I built Harlem Clubs to give other African American kids a chance to do what I've done.

"After-school and weekend tutoring is the core of our program. In order for our pupils to remain in the program, they have to bring us their public school report cards and show that they're making progress. We offer music, drama, sports and chess, but these are available only to kids who attend the tutoring classes and are making measurable gains. A second infraction of rules brings permanent dismissal. I hire skilled teachers and pay them well. I have a director and department chairs. It's run like a school."

"I'm impressed. How long has it been operating?"

"Three years at full capacity."

"I've been thinking about what I'd like to do. I can stage plays, teach public speaking and chess, but if you'd like, I can also teach them certain classics. *Robin Hood of Sherwood Forest* and Shakespeare's *Macbeth* are infinitely more interesting than Harry Potter, and the Hatfields and McCoys make these street toughs look like wimps."

A waiter brought a tray of coffee, tea and chocolate chip cookies, and they settled into the business of getting to know each other. "Next fall, I'll be back at Columbia, but I'm only going to teach twice a week. If this illness has taught me anything, it's the value of life. What do you say I start with public speaking?"

"Great. There's nothing these children need more. Let me know when you want to start."

"My daughter is overly protective of me, so she'll raise a row, but…February first."

He thought that might be a bit early, but didn't say so. "Good. I'll furnish your transportation." He looked at his watch. "It's a quarter of six, and all we've done is talk. We'll play next Monday. I've enjoyed being with you."

Clyde stood, his smile warm and friendly. "It's really been my pleasure. See you next Monday."

A cocktail waitress who's father taught classics at an Ivy League school. How many more shocks would she give him? One day, he'd add it all up and get her reaction to it.

He had planned to go directly to the club, but changed his mind and went home. Jackie wouldn't be there.

He walked into his den, saw the red light blinking on his answering machine, checked his messages and called Jomo Adeedee, night manager of Holcomb Hotel in Nairobi.

"Holcomb speaking. What's up?"

"I'm sorry, sir, but we have a dozen guests sick here, and according to the doctor, they all have the same problem. I thought I should let you know."

"What kind of illness is it?"

"An intestinal disorder, like enteritis, but all have a very high fever. The doctor said they can have only tea with boiled water and dry toast, but one lady refused it. She wants to go to the hospital."

"If she insists on going, make it easy for her. I'll be there on the earliest flight I can get. Thanks." He hung up and telephoned Jackie.

"Hello." Something about her voice—so soft and feminine—either energized him or, when he was alone with her, could reduce him to putty.

"Hello, sweetheart. I'll be away for a few days, maybe longer. I have a problem at my Nairobi hotel, and I'm heading there as soon as I can get a flight. I can't talk long, but I wanted you to know where I'll be. I'll call you when I know what I'm up against. By the way, I spent an enjoyable two hours with your father, and I'm planning to visit him next Monday. If I haven't returned tell him why I won't keep the date."

"I hope you'll be able to clear up the problem quickly, because I'll miss you. Go with the angels."

"Thanks. I love you."

"And I love you."

He hung up, phoned his travel agent. "Audie, I need first-class passage to Nairobi on the first carrier going out. I prefer nonstop and first class, but I'll take whatever you can get."

Half an hour later she phoned him. "I got you first-class on Continental, nonstop. Check your e-mail for your electronic ticket, and if I were you, I'd step on it."

"Bet on that."

Jackie looked around the visiting lounge at the clinic until she saw her father sitting in a far corner concentrating on a newspaper. What a pleasure it was to see him there instead of in the bed he'd occupied for so long.

"How are you, Papa?" she said when she reached him. "You look wonderful. I've got good news. You'll be able to keep your address, although not your same apartment. Mr. Hall said the identical apartment above your old one is available, so I took that one, and by the time you're ready to leave here, I'll have your stuff out of storage, and Vanna and I will try to arrange everything exactly as you had it. Now all you have to do is get well."

"I'm already well. They're keeping me here for the money."

"No, Papa. Please be patient. You're recovering so well, and it would be a shame if you rushed out of here and had to come back."

He folded the newspaper and placed it in the magazine rack beside his chair. "When I get out of this money eater, I'm not coming back. A man in the room across the hall from mine told me he was shelling out five thousand a month for the room and extra for any medical care. His room doesn't have a view, and mine looks at the Hudson River. How on earth are you paying for this?"

Jacqueline had hoped that he wouldn't know what it cost her to keep him there but, knowing her father, she shouldn't have counted on it. Very little escaped him. "By honest means," she replied. "Now stop worrying."

But he persisted. "I hope Warren Holcomb isn't a part of the solution. I'd like to see you in a genuine relationship with him."

She had her father's genes, and they made her bristle at his words. "Papa, you didn't say that. I have not and would not take money from Warren or from any man who wasn't my husband. I pay my own way and no man can tell me what to do. I'm independent, and I intend to remain that way."

"Thank God for that. So why don't you want him to know that you have a Ph.D. and that you're senior editor of a good, popular magazine? If he finds out on his own, you'll be in a well of trouble."

"Some men can't handle that. Anyway, if I can get through the next three weeks, I'll straighten it all out, but Papa please don't tell him."

"I promised I wouldn't, and I keep my word, but if he asks me, I refuse to lie. I'll tell him that if he wants to know anything about you, he has to ask you. That man is highly intelligent, and I'll bet anything that he's suspicious. If he isn't, he needs a shot of common sense."

She prayed for time, because she knew well the truth of her father's words. On several occasions, Warren had suggested that he had questions about her and wanted them answered. Three more weeks, and she could tell him all that he wanted to know. She bade her father goodbye with a kiss on his forehead, waved at the receptionist, who'd become a fixture in her life, and went outside to face the bitter cold. She had hoped for the first time to spend New Year's Eve with a man she loved but, with Warren in Kenya, it wouldn't happen.

When she got home, she saw from the light on her answering machine that she'd missed a call, checked and heard Warren's deep and mellow voice. "I'll call back in an hour. I know it's your day off, but I'm hoping you'll be home."

She called her sister. "Do you think you'll be able to

come up in a couple of weeks to help me put Papa's furniture in his apartment?"

"Sure. Where's it located?"

"Same building, and it's identical to his former one, only one floor higher. He's anxious to leave the clinic, and I think that's a good thing."

"It sure will take an enormous financial burden off you. Can we do this in two days?"

"We have to."

"All right. I'll be up there Friday night after next."

That settled, she decided that dinner would be spaghetti and meat sauce plus a green salad. "Where is my head?" she asked herself and rushed to the phone. "Mrs. Holcomb, this is Jackie. I'm calling to thank you for your hospitality this past weekend. You and Dot were so gracious to me, and I wanted to thank you."

"My dear, you invite graciousness. I had wondered what you'd be like, and I was relieved and happy to learn what a good person you are. Please come to see me whenever you can."

"Thank you. I will."

After hanging up, she put a can of plum tomatoes in a saucepan along with fresh basil, oregano and spices and set the sauce to cooking. She sautéed the ground beef, seasoned it and added it to the thick sauce, washed lettuce and arugula and tore the leaves for her salad. She remembered to stir the meat sauce as it was about to burn.

"What's wrong with me? Why am I so inattentive?" She washed her hands, which she should have done after handling the meat and before she touched the lettuce. "When is he going to call? It's been more than an hour." She looked at her watch and saw that she'd been home less than forty-five minutes. Maybe she was getting mush-brained. She'd talked to him just yesterday, so why was she going crazy waiting for one hour to pass? If he wasn't all right, he'd have said so.

Exhausted from the mental and emotional workout she'd given herself, she sat down to eat her dinner. The phone rang and she bounded from the table sending razor-sharp pain through her leg when her knee struck the corner of the table. She hobbled to the phone.

"Hello."

"Hi. What's wrong?"

"Nothing."

"I said, what's wrong?"

"Well, in my rush to get to the phone, I hit my knee against the corner of the table."

"Ouch. How is it now?"

"Getting better. Are you all right?"

"Yeah, but I've got a problem here, and I hardly know where to start." He told her about the illness of his hotel guests.

"Get the hotel's menu for that day and ask for the recipes. Find out which of the sick guests ate in the hotel, what they ate, and what time they ate it. And check the kitchen to find out if mayonnaise or custard was put on the tables, because those items are associated with salmonella. And check the use of eggs. Did the dessert contain raw eggs? If possible, get someone who doesn't work there to check the kitchen. The cooks might not resist the temptation to cover up mistakes or sloppiness. And if I were you, I'd hire a registered nurse to check those people and take care of them."

"I've written all this down. Can you think of anything else?"

"Well, yes. Seafood could be the culprit if it wasn't well refrigerated before cooking and served as soon as it was cooked. Let me know how it goes. I'm sorry I can't be there to help you."

"You've helped a lot. I didn't know where to start. If I had this problem at one of my other hotels, I'd manage, but over here, getting information from a guy about a member of his tribe is as easy as pulling hens' teeth, and they don't have any. Besides, I don't know who's in which tribe. I can follow your suggestions without lining up the staff and grilling them. I'll be in touch, sweetheart."

He hung up, read over his notes and, with his arms for a pillow, rested his head on the desk. Who *was* Jackie Parks? She had sounded like a crime detective, one who knew her profession well. He got up, walked to the window and looked across the way at the Sheraton Hotel, his most serious competitor. She had so many facets, so many sides, but how could he complain? He liked everything he'd seen or learned about her. One thing was certain: She had a special reason for working at Allegory, and as soon as he got back to New York, he was going to make certain that she got a respectable uniform. He was sick and tired of seeing her walk around there with that skirt almost to her behind and every man there seeing, and probably thinking, what he thought when he looked at it. He put on a T-shirt, jeans and a pair of sneakers and headed for the kitchen.

With Saturday's menu and recipes in hand, the next morning he interviewed each sick guest, having decided not to leave the task to any of the locals. By noon, he had an indication as to the cause of the problem, but he wasn't sure. After tabulating and analyzing the results, he sat down with the nurse he'd hired to get her opinion. Ice cream was the one item that all the guests consumed.

"Find out whether it was made with a cooked custard."

"And?"

"If it was, that's probably not the source."

However, he wasn't convinced and headed for the kitchen. "Let me see the machine you use to make ice cream," he asked the head chef. He'd barely begun to examine the machine when he saw what caused the problem. The rotary blades had not been properly cleaned. He asked the chef, "When will you make ice cream again?"

The man displayed white teeth in a friendly smile. "In a few minutes. Want to stay and watch?"

He did indeed and said nothing while a sous-chef poured a custard mixture into the machine. "That machine wasn't clean," he told the man, "and that's why we have a dozen hotel guests ill with salmonella. Pour it out." He showed the man how to wash the old-fashioned ice cream machine that the chef preferred to a modern one and how to examine it for cleanliness. "Another such outbreak and I'll have to replace you."

"Yes, sir. I'm sorry, sir. Does this mean you will let me stay?"

Warren nodded. "This time, yes. But not if it happens again."

"Thank you, sir. You can count on me."

He went to the accountant. "No charges to any of the guests who are sick, and take care of their doctor bills. Keep a record of it, and send copies to me."

"Yes, sir. It's a pleasure to work for you, sir."

Next, he called Jomo Adeedee to his office and told him what he had found. "You have to supervise that kitchen more strictly. That should never happen in a first-class hotel. Those people won't come here again, and they'll advise their friends and acquaintances not to come. I pay you a very good salary, and I expect you to earn it. If anything else goes awry in this hotel, I will have to replace you. And remember, I have means of finding out what goes on in each of my hotels. That's all."

"Yes, sir." Adeedee backed out of the room, a habit that many Kenyans developed during British rule.

Back in his room, Warren called the airline and reserved a seat on a flight leaving Nairobi for New York the next morning. It was time for lunch, but he didn't feel like eating. He got a can of beer out of the minibar in his room, opened it and drank half. If this hotel was in the States, he'd face a spate of lawsuits. Every six months, he lectured the kitchen staff about cleanliness, sanitation and neatness and, although he told them the consequences of not following his rules, they had needed a shock, and they'd got one with twelve sick guests.

He wanted to find a gift for Jackie, something very nice, and not only because she'd helped him solve the problem, but because he loved her. Something distinctly Kenyan. She gave him professional advice—he was certain of that—and by following it, he discovered what gave his guests salmonella. She had a detective's instincts, a sociologist's perspective on social behavior—as he discovered when he overheard her lecture to a girl at Harlem Clubs—and she possessed refined manners and elegant taste. Yet, she worked as a cocktail waitress and was sufficiently skilled in judo to throw a six-foot-three-inch-tall man to the floor. He didn't like the way he was beginning to feel.

He left the hotel, strolled along Uhuru Avenue, turned into City Hall Way and headed for the marketplace. Here was the Kenya of the common man, where traders prepared their wares and women displayed for sale colorful baskets, woven mats, wood carvings of animals and humans, ornaments, hides and practically everything that the average family used. After hours of exploring the vast arena of goods, he had found nothing that he wanted to give Jackie. At the airport the following morning he saw a beautiful Kenyan doll with row upon row of beads around her neck, wearing a colorful cloth and straw skirt, and with her breasts bare in the manner of the Massai virgins. It seemed to suit Jackie, so he bought it.

Later, sitting in the same seat in which he flew into Kenya, he ruminated about Jackie and his feelings for her.

I don't have reservations about her qualities as a woman and a person, but I'm increasingly concerned that she may be someone other than who she purports to be. But, hell, why doesn't this plane move faster? It seems like years since I last touched her, smiled at her, held her and found my place inside of her.

He squirmed in his seat, moving his head from side to side against the soft leather that supported it.

"Are you comfortable, sir? Would you like another pillow?" the stewardess asked him.

"Thank you, but I'm, uh…fine. Just a bit tired." She hovered for a second or so giving the impression that she didn't believe him, then smiled and walked on.

In truth, he wasn't all right. He needed Jackie in his arms and in his bed, needed the love that she so generously lavished. Minutes after the plane landed at JFK International Airport in New York, he called her. Thank God for cell phones.

"The plane landed a minute ago," he said to her after their greetings. "I want to see you. I…need to see you."

"Then I'll be expecting you within the hour. Are you hungry?"

One of the things he liked most about her was the absence of coyness, the honesty with which she related to him. "Hungry? Not for food, but I may be later."

"Okay. You can have a kiss when you get here."

"Sweetheart, I could use a few dozen of 'em."

The warmth and ease of her laughter intensified his need of her. "I'll be here when you get here," she said, as if she realized he needed to know that she welcomed him.

Hurriedly, Jackie showered and slipped on a burnt-orange silk jumpsuit. She combed out her hair, buffed her face with a towel and fastened gold hoops to her ears, all the time trying to calm herself and slow down her racing heart. Warren's behavior seemed to her very uncharacteristic, but he said he needed her, and she wanted to be there for him, as he was for her. Her mother had always said that what had glued her parents' relationship so firmly was her father's need of her mother.

She called Ben. "I have an emergency. If I get there at all tonight, it will be very late. I hope this doesn't cause a problem."

"Take the night off. I hope your dad's all right."

"He's doing fine. Thanks, Ben. I appreciate this."

Half an hour later, she opened the door, took one look at him and spread her arms. "Darling. Are you tired?" she asked him. "Where's your suitcase?"

He squeezed her to his body. "It's in the trunk of my car. I didn't want to compromise you by walking into this building carrying an overnight bag." She closed the door behind him and walked with him to her living room. "Besides," he went on, "you're all I want and need."

Why was he so down? She wondered. She had never seen him without the demeanor that proclaimed he had accomplished much and was proud of it. He had always seemed to vibrate with masculine energy and strength, a man who wore an aura of power.

Testing with as much gentleness as possible, she asked him, "How did it go in Nairobi?"

He sat leaning forward with his legs wide apart and his forearms resting on his thighs. "Splendid, thanks to you. I did as you said, and figuring out the source of the problem proved easy. They had all eaten papaya ice cream, and it appears that the ice cream machine hadn't been properly cleaned before reuse. Ergo, salmonella."

Feeling the pain that emanated from him, she sat beside him and eased her right arm around his broad shoulders. "You solved it, and that's wonderful. Tell me why you are so...so depressed?"

"Jackie, some of those people probably saved for years in order to go on a safari or just to see Africa, and instead of the vacation of a lifetime, they spent it in a hotel, sick as the devil, with high fevers, miserable and with strange doctors who don't knock themselves out giving patients good care. I can't give that vacation back to them and for some it was a first and possibly only time abroad.

"Nothing of this sort has previously happened in my hotels or in any venture for which I've been responsible. I covered their hotel and medical bills, and I'm agonizing over whether I should have paid their airfare to Kenya. It seems such an awful shame."

"I think you did all that was necessary. There's no point in beating yourself up about it. You can't be simultaneously in three hotels on two different continents. You can only hire the best, the most reliable help you can get. Excuse me a minute."

She went to the kitchen, poured two tall glasses of club soda over ice cubes and took them back to the living room. "Have some. I could shell you some pecans."

He enjoyed a long sip of the drink, put the glass on the table before him and looked hard at her. "You'd shell pecans for me. Do you know what you're doing to me?"

She shook her head. "I know I want you to feel better, to feel good. If that's what I'm doing to you, I'm glad."

His stare became a simmering blaze and slowly grew into a storm. She'd never seen such turbulence in his eyes. She couldn't shake her gaze from his, for he swept her up in the tide of his consuming passion.

"You want to make me feel good?" he asked in a voice hoarse with desire. It was back in him, then, the harsh masculinity, the roughness that belied his class and his status. His male aura enveloped her, dragged her to him the way quicksand sucks in whatever touches it. "Do you?" It was as much a command as a question.

Her body swayed toward him and her eyes closed. "Yes. Yes." She dragged the words out of herself as her arms opened to him. He caught her to him.

"Everything I own is worth peanuts, compared to what you mean to me," he said, and then he gave her what she'd waited days for, the feel of his mouth covering hers and of his tongue probing into her. Heat sent hot blood racing through her veins. More, she wanted and needed more, and her groans told him so. She put his right hand on her left breast, and he dipped his hand into the bodice of her jumpsuit, freed her aching breast and covered it with his warm moist mouth. She thought she would die from the pleasure of it, and when that feeling of a hot swell attacked the bottom of her feet and started up her thighs, tremors shook her.

"I want you in me. Now. Right now," she moaned. She spread her legs to welcome him, but he picked her up and carried her to her bed. Minutes later, he had her clothes off her, stripped himself and wrapped her body tightly to his own.

"Make me feel good," he said. "Take me in. I'm almost out of my mind wanting you. He pulled her right nipple into his mouth and when she felt the tip of his penis at the entrance to her vagina, she raised her knees, took him into her hands, led him home.

"Oh…" she cried when he buried himself to the hilt inside of her.

"Are you all right?"

"Yes. Oh, yes," she told him, and within minutes he fired her until she screamed his name in ecstasy. "Warren. You're…I love you."

"Did you finish it? Did you? Did you? I can't… Oh, woman. I love you." He trembled violently and went limp in her arms.

After a long while, he asked her, "Did you get straightened out? That's the first time in my life that I couldn't wait as long as I wanted to. But I needed this with you so badly."

"I did, too."

He looked down into her face and smiled for the first time since he'd entered her apartment. "I suppose you did, because it usually takes you longer than that."

"Want to borrow a toothbrush?"

He stared down at her, a man whose antenna was on alert. "Why?"

"Don't you brush your teeth before you go to bed?"

"Wait a minute. You mean I'm sleeping *here?*"

She stroked his left cheek with her right hand, feeling as if she could devour him with love. "How else will I get some more of what I want?"

His face was open, relating all that she wanted to know about his feelings for her. "But I can't stay tonight," he said. "The thing I wanted to hear you say, the invitation I hoped for, and I can't accept it tonight. What made you change you mind?"

"I didn't. But you were so down that I couldn't help it. I don't want you to get back in that mood."

His face creased into a smile. "You are one sweet woman. I can't stay, but you can have what you want."

Alone in bed later, her mind replayed the evening. That second time would be forever etched in her memory. The ride was short, but oh, how ecstatic! And at the end, enthralled in passion, he'd told her, "I'm yours."

Chapter 10

Two weeks later, Jacqueline went with the woman who did her house cleaning to her father's apartment and spent the Saturday morning cleaning the kitchen, the windows and floors, for her father was scheduled to move in the following weekend. That night, Vanna arrived to help arrange the furniture and to ensure a warm atmosphere for their father's homecoming.

"Sorry I couldn't meet you," Jacqueline told Vanna when she got home after leaving Allegory that night. "This all happened so fast." She still hadn't told her sister that she worked as a waitress at a men's club.

"Not to worry. As you can see, I didn't need you," Vanna said with a suggestive laugh as she hugged her younger sister.

Jacqueline's gaze roamed the living room until it

landed on Allen Lewis. "Well, hello, Allen. It's wonderful to see you. You're a secret that Vanna's been keeping to herself."

"You've got one that you're guarding like the keeper of the British crown jewels," Vanna shot back. "Where is he?"

Jacqueline's breath returned when she realized that her sister referred to Warren and not to her job as waitress at Allegory, Inc. She looked at her watch and winked at Vanna. "Home by now. If I'd known you needed privacy, I'd have gone with him."

"You can always get a taxi. I'm told they run all night here in the Big Apple," Vanna said. Jacqueline's lower lip dropped. "Just teasing."

"I'll be over at your father's apartment around ten," Allen said. "I hope the storage company brings the furniture as scheduled. It'll take us most of the day to put the place in order."

Jacqueline looked hard at him, judging his motive. "You're going to help us get—"

"I'll be there until the last glass has been washed and the last book is on the shelves. Vanna didn't need to come up here. I would gladly have done it, but she argued that it was her responsibility."

"Hmm. I see. Well, your help is definitely welcome."

Jacqueline answered her doorman's buzz at nine the next morning. "A gentleman to see you, ma'am."

"Who is he?"

"A Mr. Holcomb, ma'am."

"Thanks. Please ask him to come up. Why hadn't she known that Warren would help them? He hadn't mentioned it, and she had decided that he had a conflicting engagement. He walked in with three cups of coffee.

"You're a darling," she said, and kissed his cheek. "I'll cook us some breakfast."

"Of course I'm a darling. Where's Vanna?"

"She'll be out in a minute. Allen met her at the airport, brought her here, and he'll be helping us today. I was surprised."

"Why? She's his woman."

"How'd you know that?"

"Easily. Allen spends every weekend in Florida."

"Vanna didn't tell me that, and you didn't, either," she said aware of her censoring tone.

He sipped the remainder of his coffee and crushed the paper cup into his fist. "I don't tell everything I know, especially concerning other people's affairs, and I hate tattlers. Besides, you don't tell Vanna everything that goes on between you and me, I hope."

Feeling chastised, she opened her mouth to answer him, but was saved the necessity when Vanna greeted them as she walked into the kitchen. "Hi, you two. Warren, I didn't realize you were going to help us today."

With a look that might have been designed to tame a tiger, he said, "Your man is here to see that you don't lift anything heavy, isn't he? What makes you think I'd let Jackie do this without my help?"

"Well 'scuse me. Honey, you just said one great big mouthful, and I am definitely not going *there*."

"Good," he said, displaying a sense of humor about it.

"Breakfast will be ready in a minute, Van. While you're waiting, here's some coffee, courtesy of the finest example of the human male ever created."

Vanna took the coffee, thanked Warren and scowled in Jacqueline's direction. "Are you and I going to have a fight about that? I know the worst example because I married him, but I refuse to sit here and listen to your misguided view on which man is the best specimen."

She looked at Warren and saw that he was about to explode with laughter. "Aren't you going to defend me?" he asked her. "A man wants a woman who'll go to the wall for him." He glanced at Vanna. "Doesn't he?"

Vanna sipped her coffee and spoke directly to Warren. "That's what I always thought, and it's what I've pledged to do. But you can't tell about these modern women."

"True," Warren replied. "By the way, how are your children?"

"Great. They're mad at me right now, I suppose, because they live for the weekend when they'll see Allen. My littlest one—she's two, you know—she'll crawl up in his lap the minute he sits down, and she'll fight anybody who tries to get her to move. Best thing is my son. He was so stubborn that I could hardly manage him, but he'll do anything Allen tells him to do, and he's much more obedient to me, too. When Allen leaves, all three of them set up a howl that you can hear for blocks around."

"He's a good father figure?"

She nodded. "He combines love and discipline,

and…well, he's made new children out of them, even my six-year-old daughter adores him."

"I like what I'm hearing," Warren told her. "Allen's been without a family of any kind for so long, and it looks as if God's begun to shower him with love. Take care of what's precious, Vanna."

"Believe me, I will."

"Breakfast is ready. I hope you two don't mind eating it in my company."

"We're big-hearted," Warren said, "and we might want second helpings, so we wouldn't dare exclude you. Right, Vanna?"

"Well…if you insist. By the way, Warren, what do you think of White Plains as a place to raise children? How're the schools?"

"Very good, the schools have a higher than average rating. Sweetheart, what did you put in these grits?"

Vanna laughed. "Southerners say 'these grits,' and I've gotten in the habit of saying it, too. What's in 'em, Jac?"

"Grits, water, low-sodium chicken stock and butter. You like it?"

"Absolutely," Warren said. "I hope you cooked a lot, because I want some more."

"I can always make some more in five or six minutes. Honey, I'll cook grits for you any and every day."

He stopped eating and put down his fork. "Don't say things like that in jest. If you want the job of cooking my breakfast every day for the rest of your life, you've never even hinted that to me." Vanna got up, taking her plate with her, went into the kitchen and closed the door.

"Warren, I have feelings that I've never expressed to you. I'm trying to straighten out my life. Getting Papa settled into his apartment is an important part of the changes I have to make. So please bear with me for another couple of weeks, maybe less."

"This sound serious, and I'm not surprised, because I often get the feeling that I have only a part of you. When we're most intimate, after we make love, I ought to feel that nothing separates us, but I *don't* feel that. Tell me this—will we love each other a month from now?"

She knew that a person of his intelligence had to be suspicious of her, but she hadn't thought the suspicion was sufficiently strong to worry him. "I'll love you, Warren, probably to the end of my days, and since I've done nothing of which I'm ashamed or that should lower me in your esteem, I'm hoping you'll still love me."

"So do I. May I please have some more grits?"

From that, she knew he'd dropped the topic, and that he would return to a discussion of it when she told him she'd straightened out her life. "We'll visit this discussion again, won't we?" she asked.

"Yes, we will when you tell me you're ready, but I decided some time ago that you shouldn't take too long."

"Excuse me while I get the grits." She headed for the kitchen, glad that it was at least out in the open.

"How'd that go?" Vanna asked from her perch on a high stool near the window.

"Better than I'd hoped."

"You never indicated to him that you wanted to marry him?"

She turned on the jet beneath the pot of grits and began to stir. "No, and I've had my reasons."

"Did you know that he wants to marry you?"

"He's said a lot of things that point that way. Now, let's drop it. What will be will be."

Vanna lifted her right shoulder in a shrug. "Honey, if I were you, nothing on this earth would make me take that man lightly."

"I don't, and how could I? I'm crazy about him."

"Really? Hell, he doesn't even know who you are. You've made a colossal blunder in this."

"Yes, I know, and let's drop it."

"I'm sorry, sis," Vanna said, "but I want you to be happy, and if he takes a walk, you definitely will not be."

"I know."

She took the grits and a three-inch piece of sage sausage to Warren and placed it before him. "This is really good," he said. "Somehow, I never associated you with cooking."

"Why not?"

"Just didn't. You're too sophisticated for the kitchen."

"Is that so? Well, pal, I can make any kind of soufflé, parfait, or plain old pie that you can eat."

He raised both hands, palms out. "All right. Don't get testy, and don't call me 'pal.' I was just telling you what I thought." After appearing to muse over something, he stopped eating and looked her in the eye. "When are you planning to invite me to dinner?"

He wasn't going to push her into a corner. "One day when it's convenient for both of us."

Thank God, he had a sense of humor. A grin took shape around his lips and slowly dissolved into a broad smile. Then, he laid his head back and laughed aloud. "Get you in a jam and you come out wearing boxing gloves. I'll get a calendar and mark my free days."

"Surely, you jest. Didn't Queen Elizabeth I of England use that method to let her suitors know which one she wanted to see on a given night?"

"Damned if I know. I majored in math and science."

His look said, what did you major in? And she could almost see his effort to refrain from asking her that question. *I must be the world's best actress,* she said to herself in reference to her having ignored the unasked question. Her charade had become too heavy a burden, one that she would be happy to shed.

"Let's go," Vanna called to them. "Allen called me on my cell phone, and he said the storage company is unloading the dining room furniture. They're going to unload it by room."

"Where're we going? I forgot," Warren said after they got into his car.

Vanna reminded him. "Riverside at Ninety-second."

The four of them worked together smoothly, but by noon, Jacqueline began to tire of the helpless-little-woman role. She moved a small box of books and Warren rushed to her to relieve her of the task. She put the books down and looked straight at him. "Honey, one of my wrought-iron skillets is heavier than this."

He stared right back at her. "I'm here, so I'm the one who's going to lift these heavy things. Not you." Evidently thinking that he might have annoyed her, he added, "Besides, if you pick up anything that's too heavy for you, you could rip something critical, and then you wouldn't be able to have my children. I want to be a father."

"Then you'd better let me handle it, or more than parenthood will be at stake. Are you sure you're dealing with a full deck this morning?"

He shoved the box of books out of his way and took the few steps that separated them. "Actually, I'm not. You've been dropping bombs all morning. Let's have it."

"I don't know what you mean."

"Oh, yes, you do. You're not your usually peaceful self, and I want to know why. I make a joke, and you come back with a smart-ass remark." She imagined that her eyes widened. Her bottom lip may even have dropped, but he didn't back down, although his voice softened. "Jackie, we love each other. If you're concerned about something, or if you're upset, share it with me. My shoulders are broad enough to carry your load and mine. And baby, I want to." He grasped her shoulders and pulled her to his body. "If I ever love you fully and completely and if you reciprocate, the angels will sing."

With his arms tight around her, he ran his tongue along the seam of her lips. "Open up to me."

She took him in and, for a minute, as his tongue savored every centimeter of her mouth, frissons of heat claimed her, marbles battled for space in her belly and she forgot about her charade and the pain that failure to level with him caused her. "You're precious to me," she said, with a voice that trembled when he released her.

"And you are to me. Don't let anything drive a wedge between us, Jackie. I need you."

If he only knew how much she needed him!

"Will you look at this?" Ben said to Warren and shoved a newspaper across the bar at him when he walked into the club Monday evening.

"Well I'll be damned. When did this happen?"

Ben cleared his throat. "Looks like it happened last night after they left here. What do you think it means for the club? Won't we all be implicated?"

"Not unless the prosecutor is a few bricks short of a full load. I wondered what Hornsby and Mac had in common, and now I know. Mac tried to ingratiate himself with me, but he's not the type I want around me. I invited him for drinks once, but after that I gave him a cold shoulder," Warren said.

"Humph! I never did feel comfortable around him."

Warren leaned forward with both elbows on the bar, his gaze perusing the *Times* story. "It's strange, Ben. Local law officials didn't break this case, the FBI did. Mac has a record for pimping. This is his third arrest. I wonder how Hornsby knew him."

Ben mixed a vodka and tonic and slid it to Warren. "That's not what bothers me. Suppose somebody decides that Hornsby was supplying our members with Asian sex slaves. Until last week, Hornsby was president of this club."

Laughter poured out of Warren, but not because Ben's words amused him. Rather, his mind had reeled at the thought of staid, older club members trying to handle a planeload of young Asian women. He said as much to Ben.

"Yeah," Ben said, with his usual poker face. "But think of the fun the rest of us would have."

Warren lifted his right shoulder in a quick shrug. "I'm not going to worry too much about our club members being implicated in a prostitution ring. This is too distinguished a group," he said, in a more serious tone. "What bothers me is the possibility that getting those women into the States was planned here with the use of our telephones and our computers."

Obviously shaken, Ben ran his hand over his tight curls and moved his head slowly from side to side. "Something tells me this story doesn't even scratch the surface. Imagine Hornsby operating a sex ring right under our noses. Well, at least he won't be back here."

Warren took a few sips of the vodka and tonic, mostly because Ben had given it to him as a brotherly gesture, put the glass down and registered for the Lincoln lounge. Alone.

He hadn't asked for service in a private room since his relationship with Jackie had blossomed to the point where it would be obvious to anyone who observed them together. But the dangerous notion flitting around in his head had to be exorcised, and quickly. He buzzed the bar.

"Ben, would you please ask Jackie to bring me some coffee and a bottle of club soda?"

Surprise at his request was still mirrored on her face

when she entered the private lounge. "Hi. You… uh…you wanted to see me?"

"I always want to see…Wait a minute. You're wearing slacks!"

Her right eye narrowed slightly. She put the tray on the serving table and looked at him with the expression of a fighter waiting for his adversary to come out of his corner. "You don't approve?"

"I not only approve, I'm overjoyed. Who gave you permission to make the change?"

When she poked out her chin, he expected fireworks, but she merely pursed her lips and said, "Me. I got tired of walking around here looking like an ad for a skin game. I got to thinking that it's my body, and if I'm sick of wearing that ridiculous skirt, why do I? I'm prepared to wear any color slacks that the club specifies."

He slapped his right fist into his left palm. "Right On! You look stunning."

"Thank you." She poured a cup of coffee and added about two tablespoons of milk. "Would you like a glass of club soda?"

"No, thank you, sweetheart, but I'll take the coffee, and I'll meet you at the usual place and time." He stood and put his arms around her. "Incidentally, Hornsby and Mac have been indicted for trafficking in Asian sex slaves."

Both of her eyebrows shot up. "I wondered why they huddled in the billiards room almost every night. I also wondered why Mac, who doesn't belong to Allegory, Inc., seemed to have free access to the place."

Warren's antenna came alive. "Well, members are entitled to have guests here."

She stepped back, her face clouded as if a thought worried her. He had long since come to expect anything from her except the gracious acquiescence of the average cocktail waitress whose livelihood depended on tips and, as usual, she didn't disappoint him.

"Guests? Nobody is going to make me believe that multimillionaire Duff Hornsby would have Mac for a friend or as a guest. The upper class does not dine with the lower class. Hornsby is a self-aggrandizing snob. Furthermore, he has a low regard for women, and I suspect that applies especially to non-white ones. He didn't fool me for one second."

A weight seemed to drop on him, and he lowered his lashes to prevent her seeing his reaction. The strength of her statement bothered him, but he tried to push his thoughts aside. The phone light blinked and, for once, he was grateful for the interruption.

"Excuse me a minute."

"Of course," she said. "I'd better get back to my station."

"Right. See you at the usual place." He lifted the receiver. "Yes, Ben. What is it?"

"Don't let Jackie stay with you too long, friend. She's got a couple of other calls."

"Thanks. I appreciate it. She just left. What's the buzz? Do you hear anything about Hornsby and Mac?"

"Only shock. This place must be full of dumb guys. I never trusted Mac. See you later."

Warren pushed aside the cold coffee. Untouched. Jackie's cool dissection of Hornsby and of his relationship with Mac had the semblance of a professional summarizing a case study. He nearly sprang out of his seat. Was she a plant, a mole placed in the club to report on its activities? Wouldn't that account for the fact that she neither acted nor spoke like a cocktail waitress, that she treated every person in that club as her equal and gave quarter to no one?

He remembered telling her, "You and your job don't match." From the first time he was in her apartment, she had been a paradox to him, and the more he got to know her, the more inconsistencies he saw in her. The strange thing was that he didn't see anything about her that he didn't like. But if she were a mole in the club, he didn't want her in his life. If it were true, she had abused his trust. Besides, although he despised what Hornsby had done, he hated tattlers and informers. He'd waited forty years to fall in love with a woman he wanted to marry, and now this.

He wanted to be sure of his ground, however, so he met her on 64th Street after she left work, as usual, drove her home, and walked with her to the front door of the building in which she lived. She gazed up at him, not suspecting his mood, and he thought his heart would break. He wanted her in his arms and to have his place inside of her. He took her hand and walked rapidly to the bank of elevators.

"I'm not coming up tonight." When a frown covered her face, he drew her into his arms. "I love you.

Remember that." Without waiting for her reaction, he kissed her quickly on the mouth. "See you tomorrow," he said and left her.

Inside her apartment, Jackie went about preparing for bed, but couldn't focus. How was she supposed to handle Warren's behavior? She slipped on her gown and realized that she hadn't showered, and when she turned on the shower and the water hit her hair, she knew she'd forgotten her shower cap. She got out, got the hair dryer and dried her hair. She'd been home more than an hour when she finally got into bed. Something wasn't right, or why would Warren have told her to remember that he loved her? She fought the covers for hours before falling asleep.

"Say, did you see this?" an assistant editor at *African American Woman* magazine asked her the next morning as they rode the elevator up to their offices.

"What?" Her thoughts remained on Warren and his unusual behavior the previous night.

The woman handed her the paper. "Thank God it's not the brothers this time. Why the heck are these Asian women so popular?"

"Beats me. I haven't given that any thought, but it certainly is an interesting question. Have a productive day."

She unlocked her desk, removed a short story and began rereading it. The story had a great premise, but the events didn't unfold in a logical sequence. She decided to give the writer another chance, and wrote out specific instructions for improving the short story.

That done, her thoughts returned to Warren. Surely

he wasn't involved with Hornsby in any way. She lifted the receiver to telephone Clayton Hall, her friend and former classmate who was now a police detective in Washington, D.C., thought better of it and replaced the receiver in its cradle. Had Clayton investigated Mac because she had inquired about him and accidentally connected him to Hornsby?

"I can't worry about it," she told herself, when she realized that Allegory could be in for very bad publicity. "I'll cross that river when I get to it."

Jacqueline didn't have to wait long to get to that river. One week after notice of the arrest appeared in the papers—a week during which Warren's behavior toward her had been lukewarm at best—she received at the club a court summons to appear as a witness against Duff Hornsby and Mac.

She showed the court papers to Ben. "Why do you think they want to question me? I don't have anything good to say about Hornsby."

"The District Attorney will question every club member and all the staff who had contact with them until he gets what he wants, and then the defense will do the same. All you have to do, Jackie, is tell the truth."

He could say that. The truth would expose her to her father, her sister, her bosses at the magazine and worst of all, to Warren.

"Thanks," she said, praying that he was right, but she had a chilling feeling that she was about to face the music. Vanna would arrive Friday evening to help her settle their father into his apartment, although during the past week he hadn't looked as if he needed help. And in spite of the distance that Warren maintained between the two of them, he'd played chess with her father on Mondays. He also drove her home from the club each night and walked with her to the apartment elevator.

"Is Warren in tonight?" she asked Ben at about eleven o'clock. "I haven't seen him."

Ben's eyebrows shot up. "Yeah. He's been here all evening. Hasn't signed out yet. You want to speak with him?"

She shook her head. "Not really. Thanks."

When she finished work at midnight, she left the club by the 64th Street exit, rushed to the corner of Fifth Avenue, hailed a taxi and went home. If Warren didn't take her home at night because he cared for her and wanted to see her safely home, she'd take care of her transportation. However, the telephone rang minutes after she walked into her apartment.

"Hello," she said, making her voice as officious as possible.

"This is Warren. Why didn't you meet me?"

She inhaled deeply and blew it out slowly. "I know it's February, Warren, but the interior of your car has been freezing cold lately. I decided to protect my feelings."

"Do you realize how you upset me? I worried that something bad had happened to you, and my first thought was that Hornsby had gotten revenge. I'm surprised that you would leave me parked there waiting for you when you'd gone home. You could at least have told me you didn't want a ride."

"Yes, I should have told you. I know I inconvenienced you, and it was inexcusable. But I'm hurt, and at least you didn't have to drive up here when you'd rather not have."

"Who told you I'd rather not drive you home? Since when are you privy to what's going on inside my head? If I hadn't wanted to see you safely home, I would have let you know it. You've got some explaining to do, Jackie, and it has to cover more than leaving me to wait indefinitely for you."

"Whatever you say, Warren. Surely you won't blame me for avoiding another instance in which you deliberately withheld your affection from me. Sleep well."

"You do the same. Good night."

She was not going to cry, dammit, and she wasn't going to miss him, either. Oh, hell! She did miss him, and she needed him more than he would ever guess. She poked out her chin. *I got along without you for thirty-three years, and I'll get along without you now,* she sang, as she stripped off her clothes and headed for the shower.

Warren hung up and stared at the telephone. This was not the end of it. He wanted an explanation for the inconsistencies he saw in her, and he intended to find out whether she was the one who put a finger on Mac and Hornsby. After that, he'd see. He knew how to get to her, and he would. She was his woman, and as long as she was in him, he didn't intend for any other man to have her.

* * *

Friday morning, the day before she and Vanna were to bring their father to his apartment and get him settled, Jacqueline visited him in the clinic.

"You didn't come to tell me I can't go home tomorrow," he said before he greeted her.

"No Papa, I didn't. Now that you're well, there are a couple of things I have to tell you." When his face became ashen, she held up her hand. "Your health is fine. It's not that. I asked you not to tell Warren about my degrees and my job at the magazine. I also asked him not to tell you that, in the evenings from six until midnight, I work as a cocktail waitress at Allegory, Inc., a Manhattan gentlemen's club." His lower lip dropped, but she didn't stop. "Warren is a member of that club, and that's how I met him."

"You? A cocktail waitress in a men's club? Why?"

She took a deep breath. "I wanted you to have the best, Papa. I'm glad I got that job, because I would otherwise never have met Warren."

"I've been in that club, and I know it's respectable, but you, a cocktail waitress. That's some stretch. When did you sleep?"

"Mostly on weekends."

"Well, I'll be home tomorrow, and you can quit that job."

"My contract stipulates that I give notice, so—"

He interrupted her. "So give it. The times I was there, the waitress looked as if she'd dressed for a porn show. What do you wear?"

Thank God she didn't have to lie. "Black slacks and a colorful tank top."

"Humph. I appreciate all you've done for me, but I want you to leave that job. What's going on with you and Warren?"

"I'm not sure, Papa. He's attentive, but seems a little cool. I haven't figured it out."

"Then ask him what the problem is, and he'll tell you. Never try to second guess a man. I'll say one thing—when he finds out the difference between who you are and what he thinks you are, he'll be furious at you for misleading him."

"I haven't lied to him, Papa."

"No? You can lie without opening your mouth. You'd better be glad that he loves you, and when you talk to him, don't leave anything out. Dumbest thing I ever heard of. What time you coming tomorrow?"

"About eleven. Is that okay?"

"Fine." He stood, put an arm around her and kissed her cheek. "I wouldn't like to see you and Warren break up. He's one of the finest men I know."

"I don't want it to happen, either, Papa. I'd be devastated."

"I know."

At the club that night, she avoided Warren. "Ben, please don't send me to Warren with anything. He's been cool lately, and I'm not handling that so well."

"So I've noticed. Warren is a man who bides his time, so don't do anything you'll have to apologize for."

"Thanks. You're a true friend." His smile surprised

her, for she saw it rarely. "Uh, Ben, I'm going to put in my letter of resignation on Monday. In a sense, I've enjoyed working here, but I have to move on."

His gaze pierced her with a knowing look. "Make sure you don't surprise Warren. If you do, you will regret it."

Chapter 11

Vanna was asleep when Jacqueline got home from the club, and she couldn't have been happier, drained as she was from the conversation with her father, from Ben's grudging acknowledgment of her problem with Warren, and his advice, and from the absence of the support that she needed from Warren. After sleeping fitfully most of the night, she got up early the next morning and began cooking breakfast for Vanna and herself.

"Every time I come here, you get home late. What are you doing out alone till midnight?" Vanna asked her.

"Wait'll I finish cooking breakfast." A few minutes later, she sat down at the table with a cup of coffee, told her older sister what she'd told her father and added, "At the end of this month, I'll pay off the surgeon and the last of Papa's bills at the clinic. I'll also leave Allegory, Inc."

With her eyes stretched to the limit of their width and her lower lip drooping, Vanna looked as if a bolt of lightning had just barely missed her. "What kind of tale did you tell Warren?"

"I didn't. He assumed that Allegory was my only job. If he'd known that I was a reporter and editor of a magazine, he would probably have taken steps to get me fired. He took an oath of allegiance to that club, and he is unswervingly loyal to it. I didn't dare test his loyalty so long as I needed that job."

"What a mess! I'm sorry I couldn't have been of more help. Imagine your having to work two demanding jobs in order to pay for Papa's medical care! How are things between you and Warren?"

"I really don't know. He's been cool lately, and I can't trace it to anything that makes sense." She told Vanna about Hornsby and Mac and their indictment. "But that wouldn't cause a rift between Warren and me. I don't understand it."

Having recovered from the shock of Jacqueline's work at Allegory, Vanna resumed eating her breakfast. "If you weren't afraid of his answer, you'd ask him. I'd better finish eating and get dressed."

Minutes before they were to leave the apartment for the trip to Riverdale, the phone rang. "Hello," Jackie said.

"This is Warren." As if she had to be told who owned the voice that sent fiery ripples up and down her spine.

"I'm driving up to Riverdale to get Clyde, and I'd like to take you along."

"You…you're what?" She sputtered. "He didn't tell me you were bringing him home. Yes, of course, I'd like to go. Vanna, too."

"I'll be at your place in twenty or twenty-five minutes."

She turned to Vanna, who stood nearby. "Warren's coming over—"

"So I heard. Looks like you two aren't communicating. Don't let that go on too long. Relationships either go forward or backward. They never stand still."

Didn't she know it? To her surprise, when she opened the door, Warren kissed her on the mouth, rimming her lips with the tip of his tongue. She wanted to sock him, and she wanted to love him. She stared into his dark, bewitching eyes and forced a smile.

"We're ready."

Allen awaited them at her father's apartment, and she watched while he wrapped Vanna in his arms and embroiled her sister in the hottest kiss she had ever witnessed. She closed her eyes to make certain she didn't look at Warren.

"Open your eyes," he said, and she realized that he was standing within inches of her. She looked at him through a prism as it were, for he seemed to sway to her like a sapling in the wind, and she thought she would faint. He took her hand and walked with her to the foyer.

"Are you dizzy?"

"I don't know. These last few days have been too

much. I'll have to go to court as a prosecution witness against Hornsby and Mac. And you... *I need you!*" Exasperated, she pounded his chest with her fists. "I need you. You hear me?"

"It hasn't been easy for me, either. I'm going to see my mother this afternoon, and I won't be back till Sunday night late. We'll talk the first of the week." He went to her father's bedroom with a large package that she hadn't noticed and spent about ten minutes there talking with her father before returning to the living room.

"He wants to rest a bit. I don't think I've ever seen anyone as happy as he is right now," Warren said to Jacqueline. "He's practically shining with it. I'll call you Sunday night."

"Give my love to your mother and your sister," she told him a second before he wrapped her tightly in his arms and, with lips parted, asked for entrance to the haven of her mouth. Unable to do otherwise, she opened up to him and excitement flowed through her when once more he was inside of her. His hands, warm and strong, stroked her back and then squeezed her to him. Oh, how she wanted to be free with him, to do with him as she wished. He released her when she moaned in frustration. She stared up at him.

"We've got three chaperones, sweetheart, and I have to get to the airport. I'll call you Sunday night."

She closed the door behind him, turned and saw that Vanna and Allen approached. "I see you figured out how to communicate," Vanna said.

"You're a good enough teacher," Jacqueline shot back.

Allen leaned down and kissed Jacqueline's cheek. "Maybe Warren's temperament will improve now. I was getting sick of him up at Harlem Clubs. Not one thing pleased him, and what's worse, he had no idea that he was being a pain in the rear. I'll see *you* later," he said to Vanna.

Warren walked into court that Friday morning and took an aisle seat ten rows back. As best he could tell, the prosecution had an airtight case. Hornsby and Mac had been caught in the act of getting the women through customs, taking them to a hotel, registering them and paying one week's lodging in advance. Seeing Jackie dressed like a fashion model hadn't surprised him, and when she took the witness stand on the fifth day, raised her hand and swore to tell the truth, he didn't expect to hear anything he didn't know.

"What is your name?" the bailiff asked.

"Jacqueline Ann Parkton."

"Are you employed as a cocktail waitress at Allegory, Incorporated?"

"Yes, I am."

Warren thought that response brought a buzz in the back of the court room, but he was still reeling from the knowledge that he was looking not at Jackie Parks but at Jacqueline Ann Parkton. And why hadn't he realized that anyway? Hadn't she told him that her father's name was Clyde Parkton? He lifted both shoulders in a slight shrug.

"Have you ever seen Duff Hornsby and Gage McDonald together in the club?" the prosecuting attorney asked her.

"Numerous times, sir."

"Were you ever suspicious of their behavior?"

"No, sir."

"What did you think of their friendship?"

"I thought it strange that a wealthy man of high status would choose McDonald for an associate. Not that there was anything wrong with it. It just didn't make sense to me."

"Thank you, Dr. Parkton. I may call you again later."

For a minute, Warren thought he would suffocate. Dr. Parkton. She had a Ph.D., and that was the paradox he'd found in her. Her language, taste, refinement, and her outlook on life. And what the hell was she doing working as a cocktail waitress? Was she a spy? Dr. Jacqueline Ann Parkton had a hell of a lot of explaining to do, and if she held anything back, he was out of there.

Tall and graceful, she left the courtroom, the only woman there who wore a hat. *If I could get my hands on her right now, I'd shake her till that hat fell off. I can't say she misled me, because I didn't ask her the questions that preyed on my mind.* He shook his head. *Maybe I didn't want to know. I guess I wanted that woman who seemed so perfect for me.*

A look at his watch told him it was nearly three o'clock and Valentine's Day. He walked out into the cold afternoon sunlight, shaken. He'd never felt so lonely in all his life. What else was he going to discover about the woman he loved? What he knew was all good, but he should have learned it in different circumstances. He got into the Town Car and headed up town.

* * *

She didn't see him in the courtroom, but she knew he was there, because he wouldn't miss her testimony. She sat in the ante room wondering what his reaction and that of her bosses at the magazine would be. She'd told them she had to be in court as a witness, but hadn't said why.

"A letter for you ma'am," a messenger said.

She thought, hoped that it was a note from Warren, but when she saw the return address of the defense attorney, something akin to icicles flashed through her. Now she wouldn't be left with one single shred of privacy. As a criminologist and consultant to lawyers, she knew what to expect.

At five o'clock, witnesses were excused, and she drifted down the white stone steps, looking from side to side with each step she took. He was nowhere to be seen. At the bottom, she got into a waiting taxi and went home.

The telephone rang, and she rushed to answer it, but the voice she heard was that of her sister, Vanna.

"How'd it go, sis?"

"The prosecutor is satisfied, but I don't think Warren is. I had to answer identity questions, so he knows who I am, although not what I do. I guess I can forget about him, because the defense attorney has served notice that he's also calling me to the witness stand."

"Let me know when, and I'll try to be there for you. Those lawyers can shred a person into little pieces."

"Tell me about it. I haven't heard anything from the magazine folks yet, but I wouldn't be surprised if they swung the hatchet. Well, I did what I had to do, and I will survive."

"Why don't you call Warren?"

"I refuse to beg for his attention, Vanna. I'm the one who needs support, not Warren."

"Listen, Jac, that guy loves you."

"I know he does, but he has solid grounds for backing away from me right now. You know, I should have gone to work tonight. I could have gotten there on time. It was a mistake not to go. We'll talk over the weekend. I think I'll go see Papa. Maybe he'd like to eat dinner with me."

"Come in. Come in," her father said when he answered the door, "I was just on my way out to dinner."

She stared at him. "Out to dinner! By yourself?"

"Young lady, I'm sixty-four years old, and I don't need to be wet-nursed. Warren and I are having dinner at DeSoto's."

"Oh! Uh…have a nice evening. I'll be over tomorrow."

"Don't you want to join us?"

What she wanted was to get away from there as quickly as possibly. Time enough to face Warren. "I'd rather not intrude. Warren and I have some things to straighten out, and I don't think this is the time."

His eyes censored her. "I don't suppose it is. Better wait till he gets over the shock of knowing who you are."

She didn't need that; she was miserable enough as it was. "I'd better go, Papa. This is not easy for me. I'll come over tomorrow afternoon." She reached up to kiss his cheek and stopped when her gaze captured Warren's

face. He stood there as an adversary, staring at her, his
pain as obvious as a shaft of light in the darkness. But
the power of his presence, and of his aura to heat her
blood had not diminished, and she looked at him with
hungry eyes.

"Hi," she said. The silence lasted so long that she
thought he would refuse to greet her.

"Hello, Dr. Parkton," he said at last. "How are you?"

"I've been better, thanks. See you tomorrow, Papa."

He hadn't wanted to be alone, and he hadn't wanted
the company of Dr. Jacqueline Ann Parkton. He
wanted Jackie Parks, the woman he knew and loved.
Half angry and totally discombobulated, he sought the
company of Jackie's father, the one friend who
wouldn't ask him a single personal question. Allen
would take one look at him and ask if he had a problem
with Jackie.

However, as soon as a surprised Clyde Parkton
opened the door, he heard himself pouring out the pain
he felt and Jacqueline Parkton's role in it.

"You'll probably feel a lot better about it," Clyde
told him, "when you know the entire story. Let's go
someplace and get a decent meal."

It didn't seem like the man to be casual about something so important. Warren looked straight at him and
asked, "Do you know the whole story?"

"Yep. She came to the clinic last Friday and told me
everything. Up to then, I had no idea she worked at
Allegory as a cocktail waitress."

Warren sat down, crossed his knees and leaned back in the chair. "Not long ago, at a moment when she should have confided in me, I asked her if she had anything to tell me, and she fudged her response with a promise to the effect that everything would be cleared up in a couple of weeks. I didn't know what to make of it, but I didn't press her. Clyde, I love Jackie, but today in that courthouse, I wanted to shake her."

Clyde went into the kitchen and returned with a drink of bourbon and branch water for each of them. "It won't be the last time. Women can exasperate you. Even in a good, happy marriage, from time to time, your wife will have you gritting your teeth."

"I suppose there's more to come."

"Yep, and she should be the one to tell you what that is."

The doorbell rang, Clyde opened the door and Warren's heart flipped over at the sound of her lilting voice. It didn't surprise him that she declined to join them for dinner, and he found no pleasure in his not-so-subtle jab at her in calling her Dr. Parkton. Strangely, being with Clyde gave him a feeling that life would return to normal, the sense of order that he'd always got from his father.

"I hope you will be able to forgive Jacqueline for not leveling with you," Clyde said after dinner, as they were about to part. "I think you will appreciate her reasons, so please keep an open mind."

He suspected that caring for her father during his long illness was at the crux of it, but did that prevent her from telling *him,* the man she said she loved? "I'll see you Monday as usual."

"Yes. I'm eager for us to try out that alabaster chess set you gave me for a homecoming. I really like it."

"It was my pleasure, Clyde. Good night."

He walked to his car with feet of lead and an even heavier heart. *Lord, I need her, and I know she needs me, but what can I offer her when my feelings for her are in such disarray?*

At the end of the following week, Jacqueline received notice that the defense would call her at the next court session. When the day arrived, she took the stand and looked around the room. Warren sat in an aisle seat midway across the room. She took the oath, drew in a long breath and waited.

"Dr. Parkton," the defense attorney began, "you enjoy exchanging the business suit you wear at *African American Woman* magazine for the sexy, revealing and man-mesmerizing getup you wear at Allegory, Inc. don't you?" His feral smile bared his teeth. "That skimpy little uniform had forty-seven men drooling over you every night, didn't it?"

"Objection," the D.A. said.

"Sustained."

"No to everything you said," she spat out.

"Come now, Jackie. A beautiful woman like you, surrounded by rich men, and you want this court to believe you haven't profited from your…er…considerable assets?"

"How dare you!" she said, rising from her chair.

"Answer the question," the judge said.

"You're apparently more aware of my assets than the men at that club were." Titters among the audience caused the attorney's face to redden, and she knew she'd made him mad.

"Answer the question," he said.

"I do not trade with my body, but your client, Hornsby, propositioned me, even put his hands on me, and I threw him to the floor."

"You want this court to believe you threw a 185 pound man?"

It was her turn to triumph. "Would you like a demonstration?"

"That won't be necessary," he said as titters floated throughout the courtroom. "You're excused...for now."

With the session at an end, she walked outside into blowing, grainy snow that hit her face like a blast of cold needles.

"That was awful." She looked up to see Ben in step with her. "Don't worry. We will support you. The defense has eight of us on the list to testify, and no matter what question he asks us, we're going to answer that he maligned your character willfully and maliciously, that among us your character is beyond reproach. And we will back up your story about Hornsby."

"Thank you, Ben. I feel violated."

"He'll get more than he asked for."

Yes, she thought, but where was Warren? It was his support that she needed.

* * *

At that moment, Warren sat in his car a block from the courthouse, using his cell phone to contact every club member scheduled to appear in court. "He tried to ruin her, and she deserves our support," he told each of them. "He indicted her and he indicted Allegory. She has always behaved properly, always abided by the club rules. Hornsby is the person who broke them. It's time we come to her defense."

Warren walked into the club around eight o'clock that evening, worried and exhausted. "That guy besmirched her character," he said to Ben, "in order to make a swine like Hornsby seem innocent. I left. I couldn't stand it."

"I know, and she was plenty upset."

"Sure, she was. I was so furious at that lawyer's insinuations, his cheap shots, that I wanted to plaster him. She can't help being distressed. Jackie's dignity is the first thing you notice about her."

Ben rested his forearms on the counter and leaned forward. "Don't worry, friend. We'll see her through this."

"Thanks." Ben wasn't naive, so the man had to know how he felt about Jackie. He didn't pretend. "It's important to me. Is the Lincoln room free?"

"Sure thing. Here's the key."

As soon as he locked the door of the Lincoln room, he used his cell phone to dial Jackie on hers. "Can you come to the Lincoln room?" he asked her. "I don't want this conversation monitored."

"Yes, I can. Do you want me to bring something?"

"I suppose you have to in order to avoid suspicion. Coffee will do."

Within minutes, she opened the door, put the coffee on the serving table and faced him. She didn't speak, and he didn't expect her to; it was his call.

"I was there today," he began, "and I left because I couldn't bear to listen to that lawyer impugn your character. I wasn't deserting you, and I won't. I've phoned each of the Allegory members who'll be called as witnesses, and each has agreed to drive home the message that you are a woman of impeccable character and that you have done nothing at the club to deserve his ridiculous accusations and insinuations.

"Jackie, you and I have a lot to deal with, and I am not going to shove it under a rug and go on as usual. But when this is over, I hope we can air it all out and determine whether we have anything going for us. What do you say?"

As if it were his problem and not hers as well, she laid back her shoulders and looked him in the eye, shrouded in dignity and pride. Her posture said she didn't crawl and refused to grovel, and he loved that about her.

"For over a decade, I avoided intimate entanglements. I didn't choose to love you, but I loved you in spite of the reasons why I thought it unwise. Living a dual life has been difficult for me, and now that there's no reason for it, I've given Ben my resignation. When we talk, I hope you will keep an open mind."

"Do you envisage a future for us?"

"I...hope for one."

He leaned back and looked toward the ceiling, because he didn't want her to know that, at that moment, he was overcome by a gut-wrenching desire of take her into his arms, protect her and love her. Wrapping himself in as much self-control as he could muster, he managed a smile. "All right. You may have more harrowing experiences before this trial is over. Defense attorneys like to destroy the credibility of a witness, and you're the most logical one for them to pick on. I'll be with you in spirit. Would you risk a lift home?"

Her smile set his heart to fluttering. "I think I can stand it."

Chapter 12

Jacqueline didn't let herself believe that Warren's support meant that she would have a future with him. After assuring her that he stood with her and would challenge the defense attorney's attempts to depict her as an unreliable witness of easy virtue, he drove her home from Allegory, walked with her to the door of building and told her good-night.

She understood that it was his way of telling her that no matter how deeply he felt about her, nothing of importance would happen between them until he knew all that was of relevance to know about her and was satisfied with what he'd learned. She conceded him that right, but she had only done her best to care for her father, and she was not going to give her blood for it.

As she walked into the witnesses' room the next day, tentacles of anxiety streaked through her. At the end of the day, she would know how much damage her good name had sustained during the trial, for the eight witnesses present all held membership in Allegory, Inc.

She spoke to the group, and each of them smiled and responded with, "Good morning." She didn't look directly at Warren, nor he at her.

The attorney strode toward the front of the court and announced, "The defense calls Arthur Morgan." Morgan took the oath, crossed his knees and leaned back in the chair as if it were he who presided over the case.

"As club president, have you ever witnessed an ungentlemanly act on Duff Hornsby's part?"

"I saw him flat on his back after Dr. Parkton floored him because he propositioned her and pawed her. Her behavior—"

"Just answer my question."

"Her behavior at the club has been impeccable. You maligned her good character."

His face red with anger, the defense attorney whirled around and faced the judge. "Your Honor, the witness is being disrespectful"

"He's your witness. You chose him," the judge replied.

Jacqueline relaxed, and her anxiety ebbed as successive Allegory members took opportunities to refute the attorney's statements debasing her.

But it was Ben who must have curled the attorney's

toes when he testified as club manager and evening bartender when she was on duty.

"I know what goes on there. And I will consider
myself a good father if one of my daughters grows up to
be as fine a woman as Jacqueline Parkton. Hornsby and
Mac may have planned their crimes at Allegory against
club rules, but they executed them someplace else.
Neither of them ever brought a woman to Allegory."

She had long ago come to regard Ben as the big
brother she never had, and his words to the court deepened
her affection for him. After that day's session, she
welcomed the opportunity to complete the layout for the
next issue of the magazine. The next morning when she
entered the building that housed *African American Woman*
magazine, Jeremy met her with his usual warm smile, took
her briefcase and walked with her to the elevator.

"You did us proud, ma'am," he said. "Nobody can cut
you down. Who you are is written all over you."

She hoped Jeremy's reaction to the revelation that she
was a nighttime cocktail waitress was shared by others
of her colleagues. "Thank you, Jeremy," she said. "Your
confidence means a lot to me."

However, the first thing her gaze caught when she sat
down at her desk was a memo from the magazine's publisher. "May I see you as soon as you arrive? L.Z."

"Here it comes," she told herself. "Well, he won't see
me cry or hear me beg."

He began as she entered his office. "I want a reason
why you shouldn't be relieved of your duties. The
magazine can use the publicity, but not this kind."

He was matter-of-fact and unfeeling, as if she hadn't taken his low-grade magazine and raised it to a quality instrument of national prominence. She cut straight to the chase. "I needed to pay for my father's long-term care at a residential clinic in Riverdale and for his surgery. I took an evening job that, along with my salary here, enabled me to do that."

He tapped a red pen on his desk in a slow and rhythmic movement. "That's all?"

"Yes. That's all."

"You're suspended without pay until the trial is over, and I suggest you start looking for another job."

Without a word, she strode out of his office and returned to her own, where she set about cleaning out her desk. An hour later, her secretary walked into her office.

"I'm leaving, Dr. Parkton. Everybody except the editors and bigwigs are on strike. If L.Z. fires you, he won't have a magazine. You've always been there for us, so we're putting it on the line for you."

News traveled rapidly in that organization. "Don't," she said, horrified. "I appreciate what all of you are doing for me, but I don't want you to lose your jobs."

"It's a done deal, ma'am. The building's almost empty, and we're not coming back to work again till you get your job back. Period."

She stood, hoping in that way to emphasize her words of appreciation, but her secretary rushed over and put her arms around Jacqueline. "You've been our angel, and every one of us loves you. God bless."

Seconds later, Jacqueline still stood at her desk.

Alone. Had she heard correctly? She locked her desk, remembered that she wouldn't return to the office, unlocked it, put the key in the top drawer and walked out.

"Why are you at home this time of day?" Vanna asked Jacqueline when she answered the phone later that day. "Are you sick?"

"No, I'm not sick." She explained what had happened at the magazine offices.

"You mean to tell me that jerk sacked you after you made the magazine what it is? That's against the law," Vanna yelled.

"He's the publisher, so he can do what he likes. I'm sure he intends to, but right now he doesn't have a magazine, because all of his employees except three assistants and two junior editors are striking in protest. I need rest, anyhow. Day after tomorrow, the trial resumes. I'm sick of it. They're supposed to be trying Hornsby and Mac, but from the way the defense lawyer treats the witnesses, you'd think we're on trial."

"I know. They try to destroy the witnesses' credibility."

They spoke for a short while, but Jacqueline couldn't focus on the conversation. She wanted to call Warren. However, she didn't want to go to him as a defeated woman, but with her status and dignity intact. "I'll deal with it," she told herself. "I won't let this get the better of me." Her closet needed reorganizing, and she got to work on it.

Two days later, as she left the courthouse, she felt a hand grasp her arm and turned to see Edmond Lassiter. She hadn't known that he was in the courtroom.

"Come with me, Jacqueline," he said.

She stared at him. "Where did you come from?"

"I read about what that awful lawyer tried to do to you, and I've been here every day since. I want to take you away from these horrible lawyers. I could have pulverized that man for maligning your good character."

Her presence of mind returned, and she stopped walking. "Mr. Lassiter, I appreciate your good intentions, but I'm fine, and I can't go with you."

"Please." He slipped an arm around her waist. "I want to take care of you." He resisted her attempt to ease out of his embrace.

"Mr. Lassiter, there's no reason for this. Please release me."

"*What* is the meaning of this?" She glanced back to see the owner of that familiar voice. "She asked you to release her. *Move* your arm," Warren said in a voice that signaled no tolerance for nonsense.

"Who's this man?" Lassiter asked her.

She didn't want to hurt him, but she also didn't want to destroy any chance she might have of mending her relationship with Warren. She spoke gently. "Mr. Lassiter, this is Warren Holcomb."

"And?"

She looked into Warren's dark and somber eyes, saw the demand in them, and knew it was a moment for truth. "He's...my significant other."

Lassiter's eyes seemed to double in size. "I didn't know," he said, shaking his head as if denying it. "I'm so sorry, so terribly sorry. I meant no offense."

She glanced at Warren who seemed to her taller and more broad-shouldered than usual. "No offence taken," he said.

"What's that guy to you?" Warren asked Jacqueline as she stood beside him watching Edmond Lassiter drag himself down the stone steps, his shoulders hunched and his head bowed.

When she said, "He's someone who misplaced his affection. I warned him, but the warning had no effect, and it's a pity, because he's a nice man." The sadness in her voice distressed him. He didn't want her to sympathize with the man, but he admired her compassionate nature and didn't voice his feeling about her concern for Edmond Lassiter.

"I have to go to Harlem Clubs for a meeting that it wouldn't be wise to postpone, but I can drive you home, unless you'd like to go there with me."

She seemed dejected, down…there was no other way to describe it, a mood foreign from what he thought of as her demeanor. "I'd love to go with you," she said, "but this has been a difficult day. I'd…rather go on home."

He looked at her for a long minute, seeing the pain and the unhappiness mirrored on her face, and an ache crept into his heart. "I'm so sorry. Will you be all right?" She nodded. "I *have* to keep that appointment, but I'll be in touch with you later."

The urge to hold her and love her nearly overwhelmed him as he sat in the car with his thigh touching hers. He parked at her address, cut the motor and turned

to her. "Leaving you right now is one of the most difficult things I've had to do in a long, long while, because
I sense that you need me. But I can't call off this
meeting. It's a matter of the future of Harlem Clubs."

"It's all right, Warren. I'll…deal with it."

As soon as he could, Warren brought the board
meeting to a close. With the corporate pledges he had
received, he could open a branch of Harlem Clubs in the
Bronx where one was badly needed. The meeting had
been as successful and as satisfying as any he'd
convened, but he couldn't yet rejoice in it; his thoughts
resided with Jackie and what could possibly have de-
moralized her. He didn't telephone her, because he
didn't want superficial contact with her; he needed to
see her, to touch her, to hold her and to find his home
inside of her.

He found a parking space near the building. "Dr.
Parkton, please."

"Who should I say is calling?" the doorman asked him.

"Warren Holcomb." He hadn't seen that doorman
before, so he tipped the man, took the elevator to the
twenty-first floor and rang Jacqueline's bell. He recognized in himself a peculiar emptiness that he hadn't
been able to identify. It had been with him since he saw
Edmond Lassiter's arm around Jacqueline. It wasn't
jealousy; he'd never been jealous of anyone. Yet, he felt
impelled to stake a claim.

He cautioned himself as he waited for what seemed
like years for her to open the door. He looked at the gold

watch on his left wrist, saw that only a minute had elapsed, and wondered at his impatience to see her. The sound of the door chain heightened his anxiety.

"Hi," she said, as if his visit weren't extemporaneous. "This is a nice surprise."

He found that he couldn't speak, that the sight of her in old jeans, a sloppy T-shirt that emphasized the youthful prominence of her breasts and her completely disheveled hair excited him and created a kind of wildness in his aroused libido. Without makeup, her natural beauty brought to his mind the purity of early-morning sunrise.

He stared down at her, reminding himself that she needed him. Suddenly, she sucked in her breath, and knowing that she had seen what he felt, he opened his arms and wrapped her to his body. In his arms at last, her softness and yielding sweetness nearly unraveled him, and he shoved aside his resolve to keep a distance between them until she told him everything. Her lips, ripe and glistening, beckoned from inches away and, God help him, he had to taste them.

"Oh Jackie." He heard the sound of his capitulation as he crushed her lips with his hungry mouth. And when she parted them for his tongue, he knew that his self-control would be as smoke in a wind storm, and that in spite of himself, he would get hard as soon as she began sucking on it. He plunged into her, relishing again every crevice, every sweet centimeter of her mouth.

Shudders shot through him when she gripped his shoulders and sucked his tongue deeper into her mouth.

Then, as if she needed more, she grabbed his buttocks and pressed herself to him. He didn't think he could stand it, and when she fumbled for his hand, found it and rubbed it across her breast, he trembled in anticipation, his blood raced to his groin, and he lost it, yanking the T-shirt over her head and letting it hit the floor.

He reached for her bra, but she had already unhooked it and opened it for the pleasure of his eyes and his lips. He swallowed the liquid that accumulated on his tongue, bent his head and sucked her nipple into his mouth. Her cry of pleasure filled the room, and he hardened to full readiness. When she pressed herself to his bulging sex and trembled in anticipation, his nerve ends seemed to catch fire. He stopped suckling her.

"Will you make love with me? Do you want me? Do you—"

She interrupted him. "Yes. Oh, Warren, you don't know how I need you."

He picked her up, carried her to her bed, placed her on it and peeled off her jeans and bikini panties. He got out of his clothes as fast as he could, and at last he held her skin to skin and breast to chest. He took a deep breath, steadied himself and kissed her eyes and throat. "You're everything to me," he whispered. "You and you alone." But she let him know that she was in a hurry when she led him directly to her breast.

"I won't be denied. I've waited for this," he told himself and let his tongue kiss, nip and lick its way down her body. Her hips began to sway, to undulate and to beg, exciting and thrilling him.

"Warren," she moaned. "Honey, I'm going mad."

But her plea only made the route to her treasure more exhilarating, and—taking his time—he parted her folds and thrust his tongue into her, kissing, sucking and licking. He had to show her how much he loved and cherished her.

"I want you in me. I want to burst wide open," she moaned.

"I've been without you so long," he said, kissing his way up her body. "Tell me you love me."

"I do. I love you so much. Stop teasing me."

"I'm not teasing, sweetheart. I love you, and I want every bit of you."

The feel of her fingers gripping his penis almost sent him over the edge. She spread her legs, raised her body to his and...

She was hot and tight as he plunged into her, praying for the strength to contain himself. And she gave herself to him, swinging into his rhythm and returning every gesture, every loving movement. Within minutes, he felt her tense and begin pulsating and tightening around him. Then, as she gripped him, screams tore out of her, screams that were music to his ears. He let himself go, and the bottom fell out of him, shattering him into pieces as he spilled the essence of himself. Helplessly enervated, he collapsed in her arms.

After a few minutes, he tried to lift his body with the help of his elbows, but he didn't have the strength. He already knew that no other woman had suited him as she did, but after tonight, he didn't think he could live without her.

For nearly half an hour, they didn't speak, but held each other as if it would be the last time. After a while, he couldn't bear it any longer. He needed complete intimacy, being as one with her, and he didn't have it. He separated them, took her hand in his and began to pour out his feelings.

"Jackie, I don't feel at this moment what I *should* feel. I need to feel as one with you, to know that nothing separates us, that I'm yours and you're mine. I don't. And after what I just experienced with you, I ought to be happy, but I'm not. I can't bridge this gulf between us. *Talk to me!*"

So it was D-Day. She imagined how he felt, because that sense of separateness troubled her. She reached for his hand, and he let her hold it. "My mother's long illness made my father bankrupt, and I took the job at Allegory to help him and kept it when he, too, became ill, and his care became my responsibility.

"I'm the senior-most editor at *African American Woman* magazine, or at least I was. Because I'm a criminologist—" she said and his gasp barely reached her, but she heard it nonetheless "—I am also a consultant to law enforcement agencies, and a paid lecturer on criminal behavior, speaking at colleges, women's groups and community organizations. The lectures helped pay for my father's surgery. Vanna couldn't help because she gets no child support from her ex-husband,

and she has a hefty mortgage and a low-paying teacher's salary."

His fingers slipped away from hers, and something akin to icicles circled around her heart. But she forced herself to continue speaking. "At first, I didn't tell you about my day job, because I knew of your loyalty to Allegory, and I feared that you would think me a mole and—considering the oath you took to Allegory—your integrity would win over whatever feeling you had for me. Later—"

He interrupted her. "Did you report Hornsby and Mac to the authorities knowing that would implicate every member of the club?" He moved and sat on the edge of the bed.

"No, I did not report them, although the first time I saw Mac, I sensed he was a criminal, and when I checked, I discovered that he had been indicted twice for promoting prostitution but hadn't been convicted."

"And you didn't tell me?" He was standing then.

"If I had told you, you would have had me fired and done what you're doing now. I couldn't risk losing the income that enabled me to take care of my father."

"And after we made love? After we confessed love for each other?"

She didn't look his way, but she heard the soft rustle of his clothing and knew that her worse fear was about to materialize. "I was more scared then than I had ever been, afraid of losing the job and of losing you."

"I love you, Jacqueline." It was the first time he had

called her that. "But this is more than I can handle right now."

She blinked back the tears. "Don't drag it out, Warren. If you're going to leave me, please go."

"I'm sorry about this," he said, and she heard the sadness in his voice.

She didn't glance in his direction, but she knew from the fading sound of his words that he was leaving her. "Will you get up and lock the door?"

In pain and frustration, she pounded the mattress with her fist. "Damn the door. Just leave, please. I wish you hadn't come."

He walked back to the bed. "What happened today that upset you?"

"Compared to this, nothing much. The publisher fired me, because the trial revealed me as a sexy cocktail waitress, and that's not good for the magazine's image."

His whistle split the air. "Good Lord. I'm so sorry." He sat on the edge of the bed and stroked her shoulder, but she moved beyond his easy reach.

"I don't want your pity. I want you to leave. Goodbye," she said, turning over and burying her face in the pillow. She didn't know how long he stood there or when he left, because it didn't matter.

She awakened the next morning to the light that poured through the unclosed blinds and sat, nude, in the disheveled bed that reeked of sex and male musk. After blowing out a long breath, she willed herself to get up and face the day. A check of the front door proved that it had remained unlocked throughout the night.

Coffee had never smelled or tasted so good, and she was on her third cup when the telephone rang.

"Hi, Dr. Parkton," her secretary said. "Old L.Z. sent us all letters by courier asking us to come back to work. We all told him we'll do that as soon as you're back at your desk. Would you believe even the two junior editors walked out? He'll give in soon." She thanked the woman and set about gathering the makings of a gourmet meal for herself, Vanna and Allen, if he agreed to join them. Around noon, she telephoned her father.

"You didn't tell me a thing," he said. "I had to learn from the newspapers that you'd been fired, and that all but three of the magazine's employees were striking in protest. How's Warren taking this?"

"Last night, I told him everything, and he walked."

"I imagine so. Play your cards right and he'll soon be back. He loves you, but from his perspective, you were wrong."

"*His* perspective? What do *you* think?"

"I agree with him. He'll be over Monday to play chess, and I'm sure he'll have something to say about it."

After hanging up, she phoned Ben. "I don't have a job. The publisher thinks the notoriety surrounding me is bad for the magazine. I'm too washed out to come to work tonight, Ben. Besides, Warren and I have split, and I don't want to see him."

"Why'd he walk?"

She told him. "My father thinks he was justified, and I guess he was. I'll call tomorrow."

"All right, Jackie. If you need help, I'm here."

She thanked him, went into the living room, flipped on the television and sat down to watch the five o'clock local news. The reporter began the lead story, and Jacqueline jumped out of the chair. The publisher of *African American Woman* magazine had capitulated to the demands of his employees. Jeremy spoke for the group.

"Dr. Parkton fought our battles when we couldn't do so ourselves, and every one of us loves her for the angel that she is. She made the magazine what it is today, and she deserved better than she got from the publisher. Dr. Parkton, we won the war, and your office is there for you."

She couldn't believe it, although she knew it was true. An hour later, Vanna arrived with Allen. "Girl, Allen told me the good news," Vanna said when she walked in. "That never would have happened to me 'cause, unlike you, I don't pay much attention to people's problems. But I'm going to start."

"Can you stay for dinner?" Jacqueline asked Allen, singing the words. "I've pulled out all the stops."

His perfect white teeth glistened in a smile. "You bet, provided I can take Vanna home with me the minute I swallow the last mouthful."

"Hmm. Can't make it plainer than that. Sure. I have to be in court tomorrow, so early to bed won't hurt me."

After a meal featuring cream of mushroom soup,

filet mignon, lemon-roast potatoes, steamed leeks, spinach, green salad, crème brûlé and espresso coffee, Vanna followed Jacqueline into the kitchen.

"Allen wants to buy a house in Westchester, move us up here and get married, though not in that order."

She hugged her sister, glad that she could smile and mean it. "This is wonderful. I'd been expecting it. After June?"

"Right. After school closes. Where is Warren tonight?"

"I told him everything last night, and it was too much for him," Jackie said.

Vanna's lower lip dropped and stayed there for a minute. Then her eyebrows lifted. "He'll be back. We'll talk about that tomorrow."

The following morning, she sat in court with Vanna beside her, squeezing and opening her fist as if she were giving herself stress relief. Finally, the jury filed in and the foreman handed their verdict to the judge.

"Guilty on each count," the foreman said as the judge read them to the court.

"Thank God," Jacqueline said aloud. "Let's go, Vanna." She glanced across the room to where Warren sat with more than a dozen members of Allegory, Inc. "Let's get out of here."

"Now let me tell you something," Vanna said when they were back in Jacqueline's apartment. "Men are stubborn, and especially when it comes to correcting their stupidities. You write Warren a sweet little note as if your relationship was as rosy as it has ever been, thanking him for supporting you and going to bat for you after that lawyer attacked you. What the heck! It won't hurt to send him a couple dozen red roses."

It was noon, Saturday, over a week since she'd last seen Warren, and Jacqueline's bravura in respect to their breakup was rapidly deserting her. She missed him. Everywhere she turned, something reminded her of his smile, his walk, his wink, his sweetness. She walked from one end of her living room to the other and back several times, wondering what was the best strategy. Lacking an acceptable alternative, she got a sheet of her personalized stationery, wrote the note Vanna suggested and added, "In case you're interested, yellow roses and calla lilies are my favorite flowers. Love, Jacqueline." She put the note in an envelope, got her raincoat from the hall closet and walked over to Broadway to the florist shop that she patronized.

"I'd like two dozen long-stem red roses, and please deliver them to this address with this note."

The florist, a man, looked first at the envelope and then at her. "Yes ma'am. I sure hope he knows how lucky he is." She paid the hefty charge, thanked the man and went home, less certain of the wisdom of what she'd done.

Warren left Harlem Clubs late that Saturday afternoon and headed home. He hadn't been to Allegory since the trial ended; if he saw Jacqueline, he would want her and wouldn't have the right even to touch her. He also didn't want to go home.

On an impulse, he telephoned Clyde. "I'm at loose ends, friend," he said. "How about a game of chess?"

"Can't think of anything I'd rather do," Clyde said.

"Your mind's not on this game," Clyde told him after they'd played a while. "A three-year-old wouldn't have done that."

"Yeah. I'm sorry. Let's quit for now." He ran his hand over his tight curls. "Clyde, I was foolish. I hurt her."

"That's true, and I probably would have done the same as you. Pride is as poisonous as some snakes, but it takes a while to see that."

"Tell me about it."

"It won't keep you warm on a cold night, either."

"I know, but I guess I had to go through this. Thanks for the company. I'll see you Monday."

Clyde stood and clasped Warren's hand. "I hope the two of you can mend your differences. You're a fine man, and I'm proud to know you."

"Thanks. I… You don't know how much I appreciate that. Does it mean I have your blessings?"

"You've had my blessings from the day you came to the clinic and fought for Jacqueline's interest. Get to work on it."

"Thank you, sir."

He drove home slowly, aware that his lack of concentration made him a poor driver. He parked in the garage and entered through the kitchen as he usually did, and when he went to the foyer to turn on the lights that flanked his front door, he saw the note that someone had pushed beneath the door. Flowers? Who would send him flowers?

He rationalized that he had to get his dinner at a take-out shop, so he would stop by the florist, not that he believed the note was anything more than a joke. He got a meal of crab-fried rice, dim sum and satay from the Thai restaurant on Montague Street, walked a block farther and entered the florist shop.

"Yes, indeed, Mr. Holcomb. Have a seat while I make the arrangement. They're lovely, our very best," the florist told him, beaming, "and here's the note. Enjoy!"

He didn't recognize the handwriting, so he turned the envelope over, and read "Jacqueline Ann Parkton, Ph.D." He tore the note open and, standing in the middle of the florist shop, read and reread it. "Love, Jacqueline." He stared at those two words until they seemed to increase in size and cover the entire page. She wanted a reunion. His heart thumped so wildly and so loudly that he feared he might be having an attack.

"Are you all right, sir?" the cashier asked him.

"Uh, fine. I'm fine." He walked to the door, took out his cell phone and called her. "I wanted to do something about us, but I'd messed up so badly that I didn't know how to mend things. I want to see you. Right now. May I come up to your place?"

"If you're here in twenty-five minutes."

"I'll be there," he said, his Thai dinner forgotten. He rushed to the florist, who bent over a bag of potting soil, and tapped him on the shoulder. "I'd like a dozen calla lilies and a dozen yellow roses," he told the man. "Wrap them as if you were about to propose."

"Yes, sir!" the florist said.

With flowers in hand, he raced home, put his own roses in a bowl of water, got into his car, and headed for West End Avenue. The doorman was dealing with another visitor, so he didn't wait to be announced. And as if fate were against him, two lovers—one in the elevator and the other standing in front of it—forced him to wait while they prolonged their goodbye. At last, the door closed and, with six minutes left, he relaxed against the wall of the elevator. He didn't run to the door of her apartment, but he didn't think he had ever walked so fast.

His shaking fingers pressed the doorbell, and his breathing slowed to a halt as the knob turned and the door opened. She looked first at her watch, then at his face, and finally at the large bunch of flowers he held, and her own face creased into a grin that worked its way into a welcoming smile. Then, she laughed and opened her arms, and like a refugee from a howling storm, he sprang into them. Home at last.

"I'm sorry," he whispered, locking her tightly to his body. "I walked away from you when you needed me."

"I'm the one who was wrong. You gave me more than one chance to tell you everything, but I didn't trust your love for me."

He held her at arm's length and looked hard at her. "I never even imagined that I loved a woman until I loved you, and make no mistake, I love you all the way to my gut, down deep where I live. You're everything to me. Do you believe that?"

She could barely speak, but she managed to say, "I believe you."

"I've waited a long time for you, Jacqueline. I know you love me, but are you willing to—"

Her gaze took in the open door, and she interrupted him. "Here. Let me take these flowers. Come with me. We're standing in the open door broadcasting our business." She reached behind him and closed the door, took the flowers in one hand, held his with her other one, and headed for the kitchen.

"I made you some supper. It isn't much, but when Papa called a little while ago, he said you just left him, so I know you're hungry." After putting the flowers in vases, she had a feeling of happiness so acute that a giddiness swept over her, and she grabbed his arm for support.

"I'm fine," she said when his arm went around her to steady her. Her lips brushed his cheek, and she moved away from him, hoping to collect her wits so that she could feed him. "Have a seat right there while I do this," she told him, pointing to the kitchen table. She spooned rice into their plates, covered it with generous portions of shrimp diable, and filled their salad bowls with a mixture of lettuce and arugula. As she worked, her hands shook, and she felt his gaze on her, but she resisted looking at him. She didn't remember ever having been so nervous.

"If I didn't love you, and if I wasn't sure you loved me," she said as she pulled up her chair, I wouldn't feed you in the kitchen." She bowed her head and said the grace. "Dear Lord, we humbly thank you for this food and especially for giving us each other. Amen."

His eyes widened when he tasted the shrimp. "Hmm. This is good stuff. Now, as I was saying, will you build a life with me? I want a family, and I know that can be a problem, because you're a professional woman and you're entitled to pursue your profession."

Her nervousness evaporated like steam in a furnace, and she placed her fork on the side of her plate. "If you are proposing, you are not supposed to be sitting in that chair."

He finished chewing a shrimp. "I thought most men were in bed when they proposed."

"I wouldn't expect a proposal from 'most men,'" she told him and stared when his eyelids half-covered his dreamy eyes, and the dimple in his left cheek winked at her until his face bloomed into a grin.

"I'll be a good husband to you, and I'll take good care of you and our children."

"You are not going to get out of it."

"I don't want to get out of it. I just want to finish this fantastic shrimp dish. It's been days since I ate a decent meal, 'cause I've been too miserable to eat. I'm starving."

She got up, gave him a second helping and poured two glasses of wine. "I almost forgot the wine. You've got me in a stupor."

His grin made her want to savor his mouth. "Really?" he said. Once he'd finished eating, and drained his glass, he got up and walked around to her chair. "Come with me. I'll clean up later."

In the living room, he motioned for her to sit down, then knelt before her. "I love you. Will you be my wife and the mother of my children? I'll do everything within my power to make you happy every day for as long as we both live."

She didn't think she could contain the joy that she felt, and as her heart raced like a crazed thoroughbred, she slid to her knees and wrapped her arms around him. At last she had her place inside of him where she alone belonged. "Yes. Yes. And I will love and care for you every day for as long as I live. I'm the luckiest woman on earth."

"And I'm the luckiest man."